THE MAN WHO SWORE
HE'D NEVER GO HOME AGAIN

THE MAN
WHO SWORE
HE'D NEVER
GO HOME AGAIN

A STEWART HOAG MYSTERY

DAVID HANDLER

THE MYSTERIOUS PRESS
NEW YORK

THE MAN WHO SWORE HE'D NEVER GO HOME AGAIN

Mysterious Press
An Imprint of Penzler Publishers
58 Warren Street
New York, N.Y. 10007

First Mysterious Press edition

Interior design by Maria Fernandez

Library of Congress Control Number: 2024918838

ISBN: 978-1-61316-613-0
eBook ISBN: 978-1-61316-614-7

10 9 8 7 6 5 4 3 2 1

Printed in the United States of America
Distributed by W. W. Norton & Company

For Milton Supman (Soupy Sales) 1926–2009

THE MAN WHO SWORE
HE'D NEVER GO HOME AGAIN

CHAPTER ONE

I t was a crisp, clear October night and I was strolling down Commerce Street in Greenwich Village for dinner at the Blue Mill with a college chum of mine, Ezra Spooner, who'd become a tax attorney. *My* tax attorney, believe it or not. Ezra had warned me that he had serious, grown-up business to discuss with me about opening something called an *individual retirement account*, which was not a subject I'd thought would be high on my priority list at the age of 28. Or, like, ever. But my life had undergone a radical financial upsurge in recent months.

This was thirteen years ago—1982, if you're keeping track at home—and to be honest I wasn't so much strolling down Commerce Street as I was walking on air. When my first novel, *Our Family Enterprise,* had been published in June, the *New York Times Book Review* had hailed me as "the first major new literary voice of the 1980s." It had been sitting atop every major bestseller list for sixteen straight weeks. Paramount had purchased the film rights for a jaw-dropping six figures. I'd signed a huge contract for my next book. And I'd become a major celebrity. My face had been plastered on the cover of *Time* magazine. I'd made smooth, witty appearances on *Good Morning America* and *The Tonight Show.* Undertaken a 25-city promotional tour. I'd even been flown to London, where I'd not only given television and print interviews but also purchased a fabulous new wardrobe at Strickland and Sons, Savile Row, which had prompted *Gentleman's Quarterly* to give me an eight-page photo spread gushing that I embodied "the looks and style of a Hollywood leading man from the golden age of the Thirties."

There was no getting around it. My life was every aspiring writer's wildest fantasy come true.

And I was just getting warmed up.

The Blue Mill was my favorite restaurant in New York City. It had opened in the early 1940s, and whenever I walked in the door, its vintage décor gave me an inkling of what life in the Village must have been like in those days. The menus were handwritten on individual chalkboards parked beside each wooden booth. The waiters were career professionals who knew their regular customers such as me by name. No less than three of them beamed at me when Ezra and I walked in, shook my hand and admired my new barley tweed suit, which I wore with a navy blue shirt and yellow knit tie. I was freshly shaven and gave off the faint, elegant scent of the Floris No. 89 talc powder that I'd discovered in London.

As Ezra and I were being led to our booth he paused to say hello to another of his clients, a top-drawer actor's agent who was finishing up dinner with a woman in a cream-colored cashmere turtleneck sweater who happened to be the hottest, classiest young actress in New York, Merilee Nash. Merilee was six feet tall and utterly gorgeous, with long, shimmering golden hair combed back from a high forehead and mesmerizing green eyes.

I couldn't stop staring into those green eyes.

Merilee couldn't stop staring right back into my blue ones. "You're Stewart Hoag," she said in a husky voice.

"Yes, I know."

"I loved your novel."

"Thank you. Not that my opinion counts for much, but you're not too terrible at the acting thing. Might want to consider doing it for a living."

"I'll do that," Merilee said, her eyes remaining locked on mine. "The liver, bacon, and onions are exceptional tonight, but promise me you'll order extra mashed potatoes to sop up every tasty bit."

"I promise."

"Do you keep your promises?"

"Always."

Merilee and her dinner companion stopped by to say goodnight to us not long after Ezra and I had started in on our martinis. She wore a snug-fitting buckskin jacket over her turtleneck, even snugger-fitting faded jeans that did her mile-long legs absolutely no harm, and suede cowboy boots.

"It was a thrill to meet you," she said to me. "I'm going straight home to write about you in my diary."

"Do you really keep a diary?" I asked, getting lost in her green eyes again.

"No," she confessed.

"So you just lied to me."

"Yes."

"Not exactly the ideal way to start a relationship, is it?"

She lowered her gaze so that she was looking at me through her eyelashes. I instantly felt myself shiver all over. "Is that what we're doing?"

"I'm a writer, remember? I live in a fantasy world."

"I envy you." As she started away from our booth, she deftly slipped a piece of paper into my lap. I dared to dream it was her phone number.

And it was.

After dinner, Ezra asked me if I wanted to share a taxi uptown. I said I felt like walking a bit. As soon as we parted company I called her from a pay phone two doors down from the Cherry Lane Theatre, which was staging Sam Shepard's *True West* starring John Malkovich and Gary Sinise.

The phone conversation was brief.

"Good tip on the extra mashed potatoes."

"Where are you?"

"A pay phone on Commerce Street."

"Oh, thank God. I'm a five-minute walk away on Charlton Street." She gave me her street address. "Hurry, will you?"

It turned out that Merilee Nash lived in one of the precious, landmark Federal-style Charlton Street townhouses that had never been broken up into apartments. She was standing there waiting for me in the doorway at the top of the front steps, still wearing her cream-colored cashmere turtleneck and tight jeans.

"Did you buy this place when you struck gold in the Woody Allen movie?" I asked her. She'd won an Oscar for Best Supporting Actress.

"No, I grew up here. It's my parents' house. My father imports and exports minerals."

"I suppose someone has to."

"They're away for the year in Buenos Aires, so I'm house-sitting, as it were."

"So you're a city kid?"

"Yeppers. Went to Brearley before they sent me off to Miss Porter's School in Farmington to become a properly bred young lady. My mother went there. My grandmother went there. It's a family tradition."

"And *are* you a properly bred young lady?"

"Oh, heavens no. But I excel at fooling people."

When I climbed the front steps and walked in the door, Merilee and I found ourselves staring at each other again. And staring.

"I'm so glad you're tall," she said. "That means I can wear heels."

She waited until I closed the door before she impulsively kissed me. Passionately. I kissed her back. Passionately.

"Your perfume . . ." I gasped in between kisses. "It's intoxicating."

"It's not perfume. It's avocado oil soap." She broke away, gazing at me. "If we're not in bed naked within two minutes, I'm going to consider this evening a complete failure."

And that was how it all began between us, in case you've ever wondered. Not everyone's definition of a traditional courtship, but looking back across the ups and downs of my past thirteen years with the great Merilee Nash, I can say with all honesty that absolutely nothing between us could possibly be described as traditional.

After three or four hours of truly remarkable wild monkey sex, she announced that we absolutely had to take a bubble bath, padded naked into the bathroom, and started filling the mammoth claw-footed tub.

"Your presence is requested in the master bathroom, young sir," she called to me when it was full.

I joined her in the steaming hot tub, sighing contentedly. She turned off the hot and cold taps and settled herself at the other end of the tub with a contented sigh of her own, grinning at me as she rested her ankles on my shoulders. I kissed her toes one by one by one. She had ten. Still does. I kiss her toes whenever we take a bubble bath together. Some rituals are worth preserving.

"I don't normally do this sort of thing," she said, turning serious. "In fact, I've *never* done this sort of thing."

"I know."

"You do? How?"

"Because word travels fast in our circles. You'd have a reputation, and you don't. You said you were house-sitting here. Where do you live when your folks aren't in Buenos Aires?"

"Wherever my work takes me. Short-term rentals in the Hollywood Hills if I'm shooting a movie out there. Bozeman, Montana, if I'm on location. Chicago, if I'm doing experimental one-act plays with the Steppenwolf Company. A friend's spare bedroom if I'm in a play here. I'm a vagabond. Back when I worked the old Keith-Orpheum circuit I lived out of a trunk. I'd do two shows a night and sleep on the midnight train to Ashtabula or whatever second-rate town our next stop was. I could pack that trunk so fast that they used to call me Ten-Minute Merilee."

"Was this before or after you went straight from Yale Drama School to playing Juliet in the New York Shakespeare Company's production of *Romeo and Juliet* in Central Park?"

She gave me a saucy smile. "And where do you live when you're not ravaging innocent young actresses?"

"The same cheap fifth-floor walk-up on West Ninety-Third Street where I've lived ever since I moved here from Cambridge six years ago. I spent three of those years writing my novel. Another year finding a publisher and rewriting it. And I've been on tour promoting it for months."

"Our water's getting lukewarm. I could add more hot water, *or* we could dry each other off and get back into bed."

"I like your second idea better."

After we'd toweled each other dry I held her in my arms and kissed her softly, then not so softly, which led to us diving into bed for another round of wild monkey sex. We slept for a while after that, happily exhausted.

When I awakened, she was delivering two mugs of steaming hot coffee, dressed in a red flannel nightshirt and heavy wool socks. The house was cold. There was a fireplace in the bedroom but no firewood. We snuggled together in the nice warm bed, gulping our coffee, which was good and strong, the way I like it.

"It's Stafford, by the way," I said.

"What is?"

"My middle name."

"Mine's Gilbert. Old family name. So tell me, Stewart Stafford Hoag, how much do you love your apartment?"

"It's freezing in the winter, boiling in the summer, and the skylights leak whenever it rains. There's not much to love, aside from the fact that the rent's two hundred and twenty-five bucks a month. Actually, I've been thinking about making a major upgrade. I can afford to now."

"How long would it take you to move in here instead?"

"An hour. I don't need much besides my clothes, my typewriter, my pin that certifies me as a charter member of the Soupy Sales Society, and my Ramones albums. They're on vinyl. Do you have a turntable?"

"Father does, yes. But there are two things about me that I should warn you about."

"Okay . . ."

"I've always wanted a vintage British ragtop. I must have one."

"No problem. I know a British writer whose cousin was a Formula One race car mechanic over there until he moved here to service and sell British sports cars to rich Wall Streeters. His garage is in Scarsdale. I can take the Metro North up there tomorrow and drive back in something you'll be crazy about."

She blinked at me. "You could actually do that?"

"If I say I can do something, I can do it."

"There's a secure twenty-four-hour garage around the corner where I can keep it. I'll pay the first month's rent later today."

"You said there are two things. What's the other?"

"I've always, I mean *always*, wanted a basset hound. A classmate of mine at Miss Porter's, Annie Richards, breeds them on her family's farm outside of Rhinebeck. My puppy, Princess Flavia, is thirteen weeks old now and—"

"I take it Annie is a fan of Sir Anthony Hope's *The Prisoner of Zenda*."

"Good guess."

11

"I never guess."

"I'll be able to pick her up in my new ragtop. I've already made an appointment with a vet in SoHo so she can get her rabies and distemper shots, tags, license, and so on. Would you mind living with a basset hound puppy?"

Living with a yappy, slobbering, non-housebroken puppy wasn't exactly my idea of heaven, but I was so besotted by this gorgeous, gifted woman that there was absolutely no way I was saying no. "I don't see that as a deal-breaker."

"Good. And, just to set your mind at ease, I'm not sold on the name Princess Flavia. It seems a bit precious. We can decide on a new one."

"So there's a 'we'?"

"Darling, there's been a 'we' since we first set eyes on each other. I don't have to tell you that, do I?"

I smiled at her. "No, you don't."

I put the clothes that I'd been wearing last evening back on and caught a cab uptown to start packing. After I'd put an old navy-blue turtleneck sweater on over a Sex Pistols T-shirt, torn jeans, and my Chuck Taylor All Stars black high-tops, I phoned my agent, Alberta Pryce, better known as the Silver Fox, to tell her I was moving in with someone.

"Well, this is exciting news, dear boy. I didn't know you've been seeing someone."

"I haven't been."

"How long have you known her?"

"Since last night."

"Kind of sudden, isn't it?"

"Doesn't seem like it to us."

"What's this lucky young woman's name?"

"Merilee."

"Merilee . . . Merilee . . . Oh, God, don't tell me you and *Merilee Nash* have collided like two taxicabs and fallen instantly in love."

"Okay, I won't."

"Hoagy?"

"Yes, Alberta?"

"I'm unbelievably happy for you."

Then I got busy. I had two large suitcases and two garment bags. I'd amassed a hell of a lot more of a wardrobe than I'd realized, but I could leave my spring and summer wardrobe behind for now. I'd continue paying rent for the time being. After all, I had my huge collection of books and childhood memorabilia here. My suits, blazers, slacks, trench coat, and shearling coat filled the garment bags. I filled the two suitcases with dress shirts, sweaters, jeans, and some of my shoes. But there was still a lot left that I would need. Clearly, this was going to take two trips.

I put on my 1933 Werber A-2 flight jacket and horsed the suitcases and garment bags down the five flights of stairs. Caught a cab on West End and directed him to my new home on Charlton Street.

I unlocked the door with my very own key and heard Merilee making noises upstairs.

"Honey, I'm home!" I called out, as I made my way up the narrow stairs with my garment bags.

"I'm up here," she called back. "In my old room."

I huffed and puffed and went up one more flight from the master bedroom, where I found Merilee busy making closet space and clearing out drawers. She was wearing an old flannel shirt and jeans and had her waist-length golden hair tied up in a bun.

"These old houses have such small closets that I thought we'd put your things in here, since this will be your office." She helped me hang my garment bags in the closet. "You can keep your typewriter here. This will be *your* space. The master bedroom will be *our* space. Does that make sense?"

"Perfect sense." I went back downstairs and returned with my suitcases.

"I've called the phone company and they're going to install a second line for you. You can have your own phone in here and the kitchen phone will have both lines on it."

"I should warn you that the phone company isn't exactly known as a rapid response team. It may take them weeks."

"As soon as I gave the installation person my name, he assured me it would be done this afternoon."

I grinned at her. "Sometimes I forget who I'm talking to."

She threw herself into my arms and kissed me. "Did I tell you how much I missed you while you were gone?"

"No, you didn't."

"Well, I did."

"Prepare yourself, because I have to make another trip."

She tilted her head, inspecting me with her mesmerizing green eyes. "This is the first time I've seen you dressed in jeans and an old sweater. And I love your antique motorcycle jacket."

"Flight jacket, actually. I bought it in Provincetown the summer before my junior year at Harvard. And just in case you thought I was pulling your leg . . ."

I turned back the collar to show her the pin that identified me as a charter member of the Soupy Sales Society.

"I never thought you were pulling my leg. But you're welcome to any time you want, handsome."

Except for right now, because someone was pounding on the front door downstairs.

"Ah, that must be our firewood delivery," she said. "I haven't made a fire yet this season and was completely out."

She hurried downstairs to let the firewood men in while I dumped the contents of my suitcases on her bed so that I could make my second trip up to West Ninety-third Street. As I made my way downstairs, empty bags in hand, one husky, bearded young guy was depositing a stack of wood next to the fireplace in the master bedroom while the other was making a larger stack in the living room.

"Whatever's left can go down in the cellar," Merilee instructed him.

"Will do, Miss Nash," he assured her.

"Off I go," I called to her as I started for the front door.

"Wait a sec . . ." She joined me in the entry hall. "Do you want to go out for dinner tonight or just snuggle in front of the fire, eat bread and cheese, drink wine, and kiss ourselves silly? Which reminds me, what's your favorite kind of wine? I hope it's red, because I can't stand white unless it's of the bubbly variety and even that has to be dry, dry, dry. . ." She peered at me. "You look poleaxed. Am I overwhelming you?"

"Nooo, I just didn't realize you were such a juggernaut."

"I'm not usually like this. But it's been ages and ages since I've been this madly in love. In fact, I'm not sure I ever have been."

I stroked her face. "That makes two of us, blondie. And it's Chianti Classico."

"Good answer."

I carried my empty bags out the door and caught a cab back to my place. On my return trip I threw open my dresser drawers and dumped my flannel shirts, T-shirts, socks, boxer shorts, ties, and cuff links into one of the suitcases and carefully nestled in a selection of a dozen albums that I can't live without. I stowed some more shoes in my Il Bisonte weekend bag along with my shaving kit. I fastened my solid steel 1958 Olympia portable into its carrying case. That left only what I needed from my desk, which I tucked into my battered soft leather briefcase along with *Waiting for Winter*, the collection of John O'Hara short stories and novellas that I read every few years just to remind myself what good writing is.

Then I stood there in the middle of my tiny living room, took a deep breath and allowed the insanity of what was happening to sink in. Merilee and I had known each other for less than twenty-four hours. Possibly the way we felt about each other right now would burn itself out in a matter of days, and I'd be dying to get far, far away from her, no matter how gorgeous, gifted, sharp-witted, and sweet she was. And she'd be dying to let me go. After all, a normal woman doesn't ordinarily invite a man who is practically a total stranger to move in with her. And that total stranger doesn't ordinarily say yes.

But, as you've probably figured out by now, neither one of us was normal.

◆

The phone company truck was pulling away just as my cab arrived. Merilee was playing with the buttons on the new kitchen phone when I came staggering in the front door with my second load of earthly possessions, huffing and puffing.

"Darling, your desk phone is all set up," she informed me gaily. "You have a new number of your own. It's also accessible on this phone, as is mine. Here, let me help you with those." She grabbed my Il Bisonte bag and my briefcase and started up the stairs ahead of me. She'd cleared her things from the desk, all except for a gooseneck lamp and a vase with asters.

"Are the asters too girlie-girlie for you?" she asked me bashfully.

"Not at all. I love them."

I removed the Olympia from its case and parked it on the desk.

"So that's your typewriter," she observed with reverence in her voice.

"Indeed. I bought it secondhand from Mr. Adelman at Osner's on Amsterdam Avenue. Name any famous New York writer who still believes in vintage type-writers and I guarantee you he or she gets them serviced at Osner's."

"I love it," she said, running her hand over it.

"That," I said, "makes two of us."

I stowed my desk calendar, address book, check-book, and passport in the top drawer, which she'd thoughtfully emptied. She'd also removed my suits, blazers, slacks, and coats from their garment bags and hung them so that they draped perfectly. The shoe rack on the closet floor was half filled. I filled it with the other shoes I'd brought.

"Do you want the master bath to yourself, or shall we share it?" I asked.

"I want to share it, if that's okay with you."

"More than okay. My shaving things may interest you. They were my grandfather's."

"Ooh, let's see. . ." She followed me down to the master bath, fascinated by Grandfather's straight razor and its strop, which went over a hook on the back of the door, his silver soap dish and my boar bristle shaving brush. She twisted the cap on my white tin of Floris No. 89 talc powder and took a whiff.

"You, sir, are an old-fashioned gentleman," she said admiringly.

"Some traditions are worth preserving. I also inherited Grandfather's amazing set of gold cufflinks. My dress shirts all have French cuffs so that I can wear them. Are you sure I won't be crowding you in here?"

"Are you kidding? I'm loving this. I have a fresh toothbrush for you."

"Great, thanks. I didn't bring mine. Or any shampoo."

"Not to worry, I must have eight different kinds." She opened a cupboard to reveal an entire hair care store. "I also have four different kinds of soap, though I'd appreciate it if you didn't use my avocado oil soap."

"Wouldn't dream of it."

She narrowed her eyes at me. "You look tired, darling."

"It's nearly five o'clock, I've been doing a lot of schlepping, I still haven't finished unpacking, and I got very little sleep last night."

"I should warn you that you may not get very much tonight, either."

"Which I am eagerly looking forward to."

"Why don't we relax for a while? Do you possess skills as a fire builder?"

"I'm an ace, provided I have proper kindling. Does your father have a hatchet in the cellar?"

"He does, but you won't need it tonight. The delivery men were nice enough to provide us with a supply of kindling."

"Then all I need is a couple of pages of newspaper and I'm all set."

"Would you like to build us a fire in the living room fireplace so we can curl up on the sofa and smooch like a pair of horny teenagers?"

"Am I going to get to second base?"

"Don't press your luck, writer boy. Yesterday's *Times* is on the coffee table in there. If you'll build the fire, I'll open the Chianti so it can breathe. I also stopped at an Italian deli and got us a few nibblies in case we get hungry."

"Sounds perfect. Let me just grab a few albums from my suitcase."

She was opening the cork on the wine when I joined her in the kitchen. On the counter there was a loaf of crusty bread, marinated artichoke hearts, sausage, provolone, olives, and peppers. It all smelled so good my stomach started to growl.

The living room wasn't large or fancy. A comfortably worn sofa and easy chair were parked before the fireplace, where a stack of firewood was piled in an old copper washtub next to the hearth. The kindling was on top. I put my albums on a shelf by the turntable next to Shostakovich's Symphony no. 5 in D Minor. Her parents were into classical music. I didn't know what Merilee was into. I didn't know what her favorite *anything* was, although Chianti Classico was certainly a good start.

Before I built the fire, I made sure the chimney flue was open. In the city it's easy to tell. You can hear the sound of the traffic outside. I wadded up some newspaper and stuck it under the cast-iron grate. Then I positioned a half dozen pieces of kindling on the grate in a crosshatch pattern, set two logs lengthwise on the kindling, and angled a third atop them. I lit the newspapers with a kitchen match that I found in a box on the mantel, and used a bellows to get the kindling crackling. Soon the seasoned maple and applewood logs were starting to crackle, too, and I had a perfect roaring fire.

I put Alberta Hunter's *Amtrak Blues* on the turntable and flicked on the amp just as Merilee came in carrying a tray laden with food and set it on the coffee table. She returned to the kitchen and came back with the wine and two glasses. She wore her flannel shirt and jeans, and she was barefoot.

"This music is nice," she said as she filled our glasses and handed me one. "Mellow and romantic, yet naughty. Who is she?"

"Alberta Hunter. She's in her eighties. Recorded this at the Cookery two years ago."

"It's perfect. And you weren't bragging about your fire-building skills."

"I never brag."

We clinked glasses and sampled the wine.

Her eyes searched mine carefully. "Good?"

"Way better than good. I hope you got another bottle of this."

"I got a case."

"I *must* be tired. For a second there I forgot who I was talking to."

We snuggled together on the sofa, warmed by the fire, and kissed—a long, soft kiss, to reassure ourselves that what was going on between us was the real thing.

Then she sipped her wine, gazing into the fire, and said, "Imagine if I'd been sitting at a different table with Frank last night. Imagine if we hadn't gone to the Blue Mill at all."

"And Frank is . . . ?"

"A packager at my agency. That's the new thing. They bring a studio a finished screenplay, director, and stars who are all agency clients. That way they keep all of the commissions in the same building."

We fed each other cheese and bread and drank more wine.

"Do you have a project in the works?"

"Robert Altman is interested in talking to me about I-don't-know-what. And there's a rumor that David Mamet has finished a new play. But the short answer is no." She crinkled her nose at a pile of screenplays on the floor next to the coffee table. "I'm very choosy."

"You have to be. People expect you to be in quality films, not *Porky's*."

"Yet you'd be surprised at the dreck they send me. A play is always going to be my first choice. The stage is my home. But after I did that movie for Woody, and won my Oscar, you wouldn't believe the way people jumped. So I did the Sydney Pollack movie last year with Redford in Bozeman and that's made me a mainstream Hollywood star. It's a fine movie, and it was a good working experience, but I want to be an actress, not a movie star."

We'd made our way through the Alberta Hunter album. I put Erroll Garner on and set two more logs on the fire before I sat back down.

"And who's this?"

"The Elf, Erroll Garner."

"He has such a delicate touch."

"No one else sounded like him."

Her eyes searched mine. "May I ask you a personal question?"

"You can ask me anything."

"How long has it been since you've gone home to . . . you called it Glendon in your novel. What's your hometown's real name?"

"Oakmont."

"Oakmont? I've spent a huge chunk of my life in Connecticut and I've never heard of it."

"I'm not surprised. It's one of those old mill towns in the eastern part of the state that's closer to Rhode Island than to Miss Porter's School. I haven't been home since I graduated from high school eleven years ago. I had a major falling out with my father over the brass mill that my family owned and operated for five generations."

"So I gathered from your novel. How much of it is autobiographical?"

"Well, I didn't have an affair with my high school English teacher, if that's what you're wondering, but quite a bit having to do with the mill is barely fiction at all. It went belly-up my junior year at Harvard and Oakmont was left in a state of carcinogenic ruin. The mill poisoned the river and the groundwater, and sickened the mill hands and their families. And just for good measure, when it folded my father reneged on the health and pension benefits he'd promised the nonunion mill workers. Just fled for Vero Beach with my mother and left them there to get sick and die. We haven't spoken since."

"That's . . . horrible."

"He's a horrible guy."

"Would you rather do something besides talk about him?"

"Since you mention it, I'd rather unbutton your shirt."

"Okay, we could do that instead."

When I kissed her nipples, her breath caught. Soon we were making love on a blanket in front of the fire while the Elf serenaded us with "Stardust." We were more patient than we'd been the night before. There was no hurry. We were for keeps now.

◆

I'd phoned ahead so that Clive was waiting there for me at the Scarsdale train station, in the passenger seat of a mouthwatering little canary yellow Austin-Healey bug-eyed Sprite with its top down.

"This what you had in mind, mate?" he asked, grinning at me as we shook hands. His was a true mechanic's hand. Strong and knuckly, every crease permanently blackened with grease. He was small and wiry, with thinning wisps of gray hair.

"One of my all-time favorites," I said, grinning back at him.

"She's a sixty-one. I've just rebuilt her from the ground up. I've got a couple of other possibilities that might suit you as well. Hop in behind the wheel and drive her back to the garage."

"Gladly."

It was a beautiful autumn morning. The leaves were in peak color. The sky was a bright blue, the clouds puffy and white. I shoved the seat back as far as it would go and took off.

The Sprite was peppy, responsive, and so snug it felt like an extension of my own body. It was a joy to zip around the posh streets of Scarsdale, which only two years earlier had achieved major tabloid notoriety when a local cardiologist named Herman Tarnower, author of the best-selling *The Complete Scarsdale Medical Diet*, had been shot to death by his spurned lover, Jean Harris. Strange, scary things happen in fancy suburbs. That was why I planned to never, ever live in one. Ever.

Clive directed me to the outskirts of the business district, then down an alley behind a kitchen appliance warehouse to his garage, a converted warehouse where a mechanic was inspecting a Morgan that he had up on one of the risers. I steered the Sprite inside, shut off the engine, and sat there with my hands on the steering wheel.

"What do you think?" Clive asked me.

"It's an absolute dream to drive, but I have one major misgiving."

"Fire away."

"My lady friend and I are both six-footers and the leg room will be a challenge. Not to mention that we're picking up our new puppy tomorrow."

"What kind of pup?"

"A basset hound."

"I love those buggers. They were bred to hunt rabbits, you know."

"No, I didn't."

"They're superior scent hounds. Second only to bloodhounds."

"I didn't know that, either."

"They have short legs, but there's nothing small about their heads or their bodies. The three of you will definitely need something roomier. Have yourself a look around."

I got out and looked around. He had a couple of sedate Bentleys that were of no interest to me. Also an Austin Mini Cooper, which was a car I'd always liked. But Merilee had said she wanted a ragtop, so Merilee was going to get a ragtop.

I kept looking but didn't have far to go. Not as soon as I spotted *it*—the red 1958 Jaguar XK-150 roadster with 60-spoke wire wheels. The XK-150 had always been one of my dream cars. As beautiful a car as had ever been built. It had a burled walnut dashboard, biscuit-colored leather seats with enough space behind them for groceries and such. Not to mention a modest-sized boot, which is to say trunk. Clive had detailed it to perfection. It positively gleamed. As I stood there, staring at it, my heart began to race.

"She's the best car I've got," Clive said. "And she's got the size you need. I rebuilt the engine and transmission myself. Practically everything under the bonnet is new. So are the brakes and the tires. It comes with a ninety-day warranty. Anything goes wrong and I'll fix it for free. But take my word for it, nothing will go wrong. You're not the first to admire her. So far three middle-aged Wall Street toffs have taken her out and pissed all over themselves. But not one of them is willing to meet my price. Keep trying to dicker with me."

"Well, you won't have to dicker with me. Whatever price you quote is the price I'll pay. May we . . . ?"

"Let's go," he said, tossing me the keys.

I got in, nestling into the leather seat. Clive got in next to me. I started it up with a throaty roar. Drove it around the neighborhood until he directed me to a residential district that was hilly with curving streets. The steering was incredibly responsive. The gears shifted smoothly. When we hit a stretch of open road outside of town and I let it out to seventy, then eighty, then ninety, it hugged the road with ease. I took my hands off of the wheel and it steered a straight path on its own. Its alignment was perfect.

I was sold by the time we got back to the garage. When he quoted me the price I didn't blink, which required considerable effort on my part because I still wasn't used to having money. "I have my checkbook with me, but I suppose you'll want a bank check or something."

"Not necessary. My cousin Harry said you just wrote a huge bestseller and sold it to the movies."

"It's true, I did."

"So let's go in the office and get the paperwork done." I followed him into his tiny cluttered office. "Is your lady friend a writer as well?"

"Actress."

"Would I know her work?"

"Her name's Merilee Nash."

His eyes widened. "Are you telling me that Merilee Nash is going to be driving this car?"

"She most certainly is. I'm buying it for her as a present."

"Tell her from me that working on it was a labor of love."

"I will. How long will the title transfer and registration take?"

"Not long," he said. "We can drive over to the DMV as soon as we finish here and she'll be all yours by this afternoon."

"Excellent. This will make her very happy."

He squinted at me, tilting his head slightly. "You're one lucky bloke, aren't you?"

"Honestly? I didn't used to think so. But lately I've been coming around to the idea that I might be."

❖

It was late afternoon by the time the DMV had issued me temporary plates. The permanent ones would be mailed to the Charlton Street house. It was getting cold out, so after I drove Clive back to his garage we put the top up and he gave me directions for how to get to the Hutch. Then we shook hands and off I went.

I drove her at a steady sixty-five, not zipping in and out of lanes, just cruising along and enjoying the ride. I was reverse commuting but there were still plenty of cars on the road, though none as nice as the one I was driving.

When I pulled up in front of Merilee's house I tapped the horn, hopped out, pounded on her door, and hopped back in.

She turned on the porch light and opened the front door, gaping at me. "My god, Hoagy! What did you do?"

"You said you wanted a vintage ragtop. I got you a vintage ragtop."

"It's *gorgeous*. I thought you'd come back with a beat-up little MG or . . ."

"Not good enough for you." I tossed her the keys. "Take her for a spin."

"Okay, let me just get my license." I moved into the passenger seat while she darted inside, came back out, and settled herself into the driver's seat, savoring it. "My god, the leather even smells good."

"Want the seat moved closer?"

"No, it's perfect. Our legs are the exact same length, remember?"

"Yes, I believe we figured that out in front of the fire last night."

"This isn't really happening."

"Yes, it is. Let's ride, blondie."

She put it in gear, eased away from the curb, and drove it around the neighborhood, chortling with delight and drawing admiring looks from everyone who was strolling along. She was a good driver. Handled the manual shift with finesse. Worked her way over to Varick, made a left, and took that to Commerce Street so she could drive by the Blue Mill and honk as an homage.

"It handles like a dream," she said, grinning from ear to ear.

"Wait until you get it on the highway tomorrow."

"Smooth?"

"Not only smooth, but there is *plenty* under the hood. It'll go a hundred no problem, not that we'll ever drive it that fast."

"Speak for yourself, handsome."

She circled back to Charlton and pulled in at a garage around the corner on Hudson. It was a big four-story garage with two attendants.

"HELLO, ROCCO!" she called out to a young Italian guy with a twenty-inch neck. "I'm in need of my parking space, as you can see."

He gazed at the Jag with pure envy. "Whoa, you don't fool around, do you, Miss Nash?"

"I have Hoagy here to thank for it. It's his car, too. He'll have keys. It belongs to both of us."

"Sure, whatever you say. I found you a nice dry space on the second floor. Not a drip in sight, and it's wide enough that no one will slam their door into you. I'll take care of it like it's my own baby girl."

As I got out I scrutinized the monthly parking rates that were posted on the wall and realized that the Jag's parking space cost $176.42 more than my entire apartment. I was definitely moving up in the world.

Rocco got in and drove it carefully up the ramp to the second floor.

Merilee hugged me tight and kissed me, tears streaming down her face.

"Are you crying?"

"I can't help it. I'm just so happy!"

"Good. You deserve to be happy."

We strolled back to the Charlton Street house, arm in arm.

"I was thinking we could try out the fireplace in the master bedroom this evening," she said. "I have a bottle of Prosecco chilling."

"Just one?"

"Okay, two. We can snuggle under the covers and drink them. How does that sound?"

"Now it's my turn to say it."

"Say what, darling?"

"This isn't really happening."

"Build us a fire when we get home. I'll meet you under the covers and convince you that it is."

CHAPTER TWO

M erilee had a need for speed.

She hit eighty-five on the Taconic as we headed up the beautiful Hudson River Valley the next morning and stayed there, loving the way the Jag hugged the road. The sky was overcast. The river was slate gray when we caught sight of it at Ossining, where we passed Sing Sing, the maximum-security state prison that popularized the 1930s New York gangster movie expression "getting sent up the river." We were heading about a hundred miles up the river to Rhinebeck, a quaint hamlet generally considered to be a two-hour drive from the city. With Merilee's foot on the gas, we'd be there in less than ninety minutes.

It got chillier as we headed north and, being a ragtop, the Jag was not exactly toasty warm. It did have a heater but—as was the case with most British cars—it didn't provide what a typical American would say qualified as heat. Brits are accustomed to living in cold houses, working in cold offices, and driving around in cold cars. They think we're wimps.

I was wearing my shearling-lined ankle boots to keep my feet warm. Merilee had on a pair of heavy wool socks under her hiking shoes.

She was thoroughly prepared to pick up Princess Flavia. While I'd been in Scarsdale getting the Jag, she'd been picking up a collar, leash, and three different brands of puppy chow that the vet had recommended for Flavia to sink her puppy teeth into. Also a puppy carrier, which was presently tucked behind my seat. But Merilee had refused the vet's recommendation to get a crate for Flavia to sleep in at night as opposed to letting her have free run of the house.

"No dog of mine is going to live in a cage," she stated firmly.

"So is this a good time to have *the talk*?" I asked as we sped along.

Merilee stiffened. "You're not going to propose to me, are you?"

"No, I'm not. The thought never entered my mind."

"Good. You scared me there for a second."

"I could tell. You just inched over ninety. We're nearing Poughkeepsie. There'll be state troopers out patrolling, since it's a college town." Vassar, to be precise. "You might want to ease down to a more sedate seventy-five."

"Why hasn't the thought entered your mind?" she demanded, easing off on the gas a bit. "What's wrong with me?"

"Not a thing, aside from the fact that I've only known you for three days."

"Oh, that. Fair enough. Well, then what did you mean by *the talk*?"

"The puppy's name. We have to come up with a new one."

"Indeed. The name Princess Flavia makes me want to fwow up."

"Do you have one in mind?"

"Actually, I've had one in mind for as long as I can remember. It's from what is probably my favorite episode of *The Honeymooners.*"

I looked at her in shock. "Wait, you're a serious actress. Yale, Shakespeare in the Park. Are you telling me *you're* a fan of the original thirty-nine?"

"Hoagy, I've seen all thirty-nine episodes so many times I know them word for word."

"This can't be possible. You're the perfect woman."

"Flatterer. I take it you're a fan, too?"

"Way beyond that. I actually joined a club called RALPH and attended a Raccoon Lodge convention at a Ramada Inn in Paramus. It was awesome. At least two hundred of us showed up there wearing raccoon hats. And Joyce Randolph—who, as I don't have to tell you, played Ed Norton's wife, Trixie—made an appearance to sign autographs and have her picture taken with us." I shook my head in disbelief. "I'm amazed that you're a fan."

"You shouldn't be. I admire great performers, and Jackie Gleason, Art Carney, and Audrey Meadows were the greatest comic ensemble in television history. Gleason was larger than life, pure and simple. Carney was a genius at physicality and timing. Not to mention a truly gifted dramatic actor. He won a

Best Actor Oscar for *Harry and Tonto,* don't forget. And Audrey Meadows was the greatest deflator I've ever seen. She could take all of the air out of Gleason's balloon without so much as saying a word. All she had to do was cross her arms. She was like a silent movie version of Eve Arden."

"You mentioned that the dog's name comes from your favorite episode. You must be talking about episode six."

"Good guess."

"I never guess. It's the one when Norton starts sleepwalking every night in and out of their apartments and out onto the fire escape. Ralph takes him to the Sanitation Department doctor because Trixie's afraid he's going to fall off of the fire escape and kill himself. The doctor thinks Norton's suffering from a suppressed trauma and injects him with a truth serum. Wasn't TV fun in those days? We just totally bought the idea that there was a Sanitation Department doctor *and* that he was totally willing to give Norton a truth serum. Everything is so reality based now. It takes the fun out of—"

"You're babbling, darling."

"Sorry. Whenever I get started on the 'Mooners I can't stop. It turns out he's pining for his lost childhood dog. Starts calling for her in his sleep. 'Luluuu!' Is that the name that you had in mind?"

"Luluuuu!"

"You didn't answer my question."

"Luluuuu!"

"Okay, does that mean yes?"

"Luluuuu!"

"I'm going to take it as a yes."

"But only if you're okay with it, too."

"Actually, I was thinking more along the lines of Clytemnestra."

Her face dropped. "You don't actually mean that, do you?"

"Never forget that I am a living, breathing Charter Member of the Soupy Sales Society." I turned back the collar of my flight jacket so she could glance at my cherished pin.

"Forgive me, darling. It may take me a while to get used to your sense of humor."

"I'm an acquired taste. I'll admit that."

Annie Richards, Merilee's basset breeder friend from Miss Porter's School, lived on a 200-acre farm on the outskirts of Rhinebeck. She'd grown up there. Her father was a professor of anthropology at Vassar and her mom was a sculptor who took care of the chickens and also Annie's two little girls when the puppies needed Annie's full attention. Annie's husband, Tom, was a stonemason who built walls and paths and whatever else anyone wanted.

Merilee followed the directions she'd written down for me to read to her. We passed through Rhinebeck and soon found ourselves several miles deep into farm and apple orchard country. Annie's farm had been in the family a long time, according to Merilee, and her mother had been a Miss Porter's girl herself. Soon we were on a narrow dirt road called Mile Creek.

I studied the directions. "Okay, we're supposed to take this past a silo, make a right, and there should be a whirligig at the foot of the driveway."

"There it is," she said, spotting it excitedly.

She eased the Jag slowly along a rutted dirt driveway through an apple orchard that eventually opened out into a meadow. There was a huge vegetable garden that was mostly covered over now except for pumpkins and squashes. There was a rambling old white farmhouse, a barn with a chicken coop attached, and a cottage set a distance away where I imagined Annie, Tom, and the girls lived. The scent of old money wafted in the chilly morning air along with the chicken manure. Beyond the cottages there was a stone yard filled with pallets of fieldstone and cobblestone, a dump truck, and two beat-up pickup trucks. Two huge bearded guys were standing over the hood of one of the pickups, poring over a list. As we pulled up in front of the farmhouse a young, round-faced earth mother type came out to greet us wearing overalls, clogs, and a friendly, gap-toothed smile.

"That's Annie," Merilee exclaimed in delight.

A basset hound was ambling alongside her, barking its head off at us.

"If that's Princess Flavia, we're going to need a bigger carrier."

"That's not our puppy, silly man. It's her mommy." She parked the Jag, got out, and she and Annie hugged.

"It's so good to see you," Annie said warmly. "It's been *years*." She seemed like a relaxed, happy person. Comfy in her own skin.

"So good to see you, too. Say hello to Hoagy, better known as Stewart Hoag."

Annie's face lit up. "The author? I loved your book. Loved it."

I thanked her as the basset hound let out a low, demanding whoop.

"This is Priscilla, Princess Flavia's mother, and she does not like to be ignored," Annie explained.

So we patted her and made a fuss over her. And we met Annie's mom, Anthea, who was a gray-haired version of her daughter, right down to that relaxed, comfy manner that comes from having enough money to live exactly the way you want. Then we wandered over and met Annie's husband, Tom, and his assistant, Pat, who couldn't stop staring at Merilee.

After that we went into the farmhouse, which smelled like pumpkin bread because Annie was taking a loaf out of the oven to cool in the huge, old-fashioned kitchen. "Any interest?" she asked us.

"Plenty of interest," I said as Merilee nodded in agreement.

"I just made a fresh pot of coffee."

"This just gets better and better."

Priscilla stretched out on the kitchen floor not far from the big basket that had once held six pups and now just held Princess Flavia, soon to become Lulu, who was curled up fast asleep. At thirteen weeks Lulu was nine-tenths ears, paws, and large black nose. Annie woke her up, lifted her out of the basket, and passed her to Merilee, who cradled her in her arms and got her nose licked.

"You are *the* most adorable little dog I've ever seen," she cooed at her. "Yes, you are. Yes, you are."

"Merilee, if you're going to talk baby talk to her then we'll have to rethink this whole thing."

Annie laughed. "It happens with everyone, Hoagy. She'll get over it."

"Can I get that in writing?"

Merilee stuck her tongue out at me before she passed Lulu over. I got my nose licked, too. Also a long, quizzical gaze that she had not given Merilee. It was if she seemed to be trying to make up her mind about me. Or something.

The edges of the loaf had cooled enough that Annie could cut off a couple of slices. Then she poured the coffee. I put Lulu down on the floor and quickly discovered that she was not yet very nimble on her exceedingly short puppy legs. In fact, she had a hard time not tripping over her own ears. We sat at the table and sampled the tasty pumpkin bread, drank the strong, hot coffee, and watched Lulu rumble and stumble her way around the kitchen.

"She's extraordinarily smart," Annie told us. "In fact, sometimes I swear she understands every word I'm saying. She's very nearly housebroken, too, which is well ahead of schedule. The only trouble she gives me is that she's an incredibly finicky eater. Turns her nose up at all of the high-end brands of puppy chow. I've resorted to spoon-feeding her jars of Gerber's strained chicken. Our vet said there's absolutely nothing wrong with her. You'll just have to figure out what she wants to eat, and you will."

I finished my pumpkin bread and coffee, stretched out on the floor, and let her climb all over me before she plopped down on my tummy so I'd pet her some more. She began nibbling on my fingers. "She likes fingers," I reported to Merilee.

"She likes *you*, darling."

"What's not to like?"

"It's true," Annie said. "Would you mind leaving him here with me? Tom is starting to bore me."

Merilee snorted. "Not going to happen. He's mine. Has been for three whole days."

"*That's* how long you two have been together?"

"It happens that way when it's meant to be," I said.

She nodded thoughtfully. "Wise words. Who was it that said them?"

"I did, just now. Annie, our bedroom is on the second floor. How is she on going up and down steps?"

"About as klutzy as you can imagine. She's pretty good at going down. Uses a sideways roll maneuver.

Going up is like climbing Everest for her. But if she wants to get there, she will. She's very stubborn. She is a basset, after all. She won't be able to get up on the bed without a stool for quite a while. In fact, she may always need a stool. Bassets aren't great leapers."

Annie's two little girls came galloping in, all energy and noise.

"Is Princess Flavia going away?" one of them asked mournfully.

"Yes, she is, Cassidy," Annie replied.

"But we want to keep her," the other one said.

"You know we can't, Rebecca. But we'll be breeding another litter before long, okay?"

"Oh, okay." And just like that, went galloping away.

Merilee smiled at her old friend. "You seem so happy here."

"I am. I have everything I've ever wanted. I'm not exactly the picture-postcard Miss Porter's girl, but this is me. I'm sorry you two won't get a chance to meet my dad. He's very funny, and he'd enjoy both of you, but he teaches an afternoon class today, and you have a long drive back to the city." With a sigh she got to her feet and said, "I'll have to take Priscilla upstairs now and put her in the bedroom.

You're taking her last baby away. She's going to get very upset."

Merilee's face fell. "I'm getting sad now."

"No, don't. It's totally normal."

Meanwhile, Priscilla's last baby was studying me again from her perch on my tummy, her eyes locking onto mine as if she were attempting a Vulcan mind meld so that she could pull all of my memories from my brain and transfer them into hers. It seemed a bit strange to me as I lay on Annie's kitchen floor that morning back in 1982.

But in the years to come, I would realize it was just Lulu being Lulu.

◆

I piloted the Jag back to the city. Merilee rode shotgun with Lulu parked in her lap in her carrier. She whimpered for a few minutes as we drove away—Lulu, not Merilee—but I informed her that we didn't tolerate whimperers in our world and she immediately ceased and desisted.

"Not to worry, Lulu," Merilee assured her. "We are going to spoil you rotten. You'll see the best Broadway shows and eat in the finest restaurants. And you're going to love your new house more than you can imagine."

The stairs to the master bedroom did prove to be an issue, as Annie had warned. Going down was no trouble. Lulu would turn sideways and sort of barrel roll her way down. But going up was going to require a bit more growth and strength, so I took pity on her and carried her upstairs for the first few days. And gave her a stool so she could climb up and join us in bed, where she seemed very happy. She loved to curl up between us, her tail thumping. Loved it a bit too much whenever Merilee and I wanted to get busy, actually. She would start climbing around on us, which was most emphatically not acceptable. So I had to put her down on the floor, where she'd grumble sourly for a moment before falling silent, knowing that we'd allow her to return to the bed when we were ready to sleep.

It was Merilee who took her to the vet to get her rabies and distemper shots, tags, and license so that she was street legal.

"How is her weight?" I asked when they returned home.

"He said the average weight of a basset female her age is twenty to twenty-five pounds. She weighs eighteen, which is a bit light."

"I'll say. I know someone who has a Maine Coon cat that weighs more than that."

"But he's not concerned. She's perfectly healthy. We just have to find a food that she likes, that's all."

Translation: I spent a lot time on the oak-planked kitchen floor, spoon-feeding her Gerber's strained chicken.

Dog-walking duty quickly fell on me, too, because Merilee was almost never home. She had meetings with producers, directors, and playwrights. She had auditions. She had dance classes, yoga classes, weight-training classes. She was always somewhere. So I was the one who took Lulu for three walks a day on her leash—early morning, midday, and bedtime. She didn't care for the leash. Kept getting tangled up in it. Also walked sort of sideways, as if she were heading into a stiff headwind. But she was a very good girl about letting me know when she needed to go out and seldom had accidents.

I wasn't entirely housebound. I gave guest lectures to creative writing students at Columbia and NYU. Did an hour-long interview with National Public Radio and an interview at my publishing house with a reporter from *Paris Match* for the upcoming French publication of my novel.

And I met my agent, the Silver Fox, for drinks at her table in the lobby of the Algonquin Hotel, the fabled onetime home of the famed Algonquin Round Table wits such as Dorothy Parker, Robert Benchley, and Alexander Woollcott. It was still a dream come true for me to meet a famous literary agent for drinks there. *My* literary agent. The Silver Fox, whose formal name was Alberta Pryce, had sold my first two short stories to the *New Yorker* when I was twenty-four and had gone on to sell my novel for a small fortune when I completed it three years later. She was a legend in the publishing world. She was known as the Silver Fox not only because of her close-cropped head of silver hair but also because she routinely outfoxed the toughest publishers in the business. A small, trim, immaculately dressed woman, she had represented the likes of Daphne du Maurier, John Cheever, Irwin Shaw, and Norman Mailer. I was her latest discovery, although she detested that word. "Agents don't discover talent," was the way she put it. "Talent reveals itself to us."

She rang for our waiter and ordered a martini. I ordered a Macallan and positioned Lulu under the table in her carrier, where she was dozing contentedly.

"How are things between you and the divine Merilee? I take it the two of you are still together."

"Not only together but we got a puppy, as you can see."

"I'm incredibly happy for you, dear boy."

"Thank you, Alberta."

"Have you decided what you want to do next?"

"I'm doing it. Enjoying life with an incredible woman with whom I'm madly in love."

"Maybe that's your next book," she suggested, stubbing out her cigarette. "A madcap love story."

"Maybe it is. The only problem is that one of us would have to die of an incurable disease at the end. I'm not ready to die, and I certainly don't want to kill off Merilee. We're having too much fun."

"I understand, dear boy. Just don't bask in this state of bliss for too long. You're a major writer now. A certain responsibility comes with that, so do yourself a favor and remember something. The great ones, and I've had the honor of working with a number of them, always end up back at the typewriter before long because they still have more to say and absolutely no one in the world can stop them from saying it. That's who they are. That's who *you* are."

◆

I wasn't back at the typewriter being major the next day when the phone rang. I was sitting on the kitchen floor, spoon-feeding Lulu her Gerber's. Merilee was at dance class. I got up and answered it. The call was on my extension number.

"Is that you, Hoagy?" a young woman asked in a rather tentative voice.

"This is Hoagy. And you are . . . ?"

"You may not remember me, since it's been a lot of years, but it's Maggie. Maggie McKenna, from Oakmont."

"Maggie McKenna! As if I could ever forget my best childhood friend and first sweetie. How many hundreds of hours did we spend back-to-back on the floor of the Oakmont library together devouring books and Snickers bars? Hell, I spent my whole childhood there with you."

"I'm sorry to bother you, because I know how hectic your life must be, but your agent was nice enough to give me your number when I explained the circumstances."

"What circumstances? What's going on, Maggie?"

"Hoagy, I'm sorry to tell you that my mom has died. She'd been fighting leukemia for quite a few years. The torch had already been passed. I got my master's degree in library science and have been the director of Oakmont's library for two years, although Mom still insisted on coming to work when she felt up to it. There's an open-casket wake tomorrow evening starting at five o'clock at Huffman's Mortuary, and her funeral is Sunday at noon. Please don't feel any pressure to come. I know that when you left here, you swore you'd never come back here again. I—I just thought you'd want to know."

I sagged inwardly. Maggie's mom, Mary McKenna, had been a widow whose husband, a brass mill hand, had died of liver cancer when he was forty-two. Mary had taken a special interest in me. Not just because my father owned the mill, or because Maggie and I were best buddies, but because she'd sensed that I had a gift. Steered me toward authors like Kerouac and Vonnegut, whom she thought I'd like. Encouraged me to start writing stories myself back when I was a teenager. If it hadn't been for Mary McKenna, I'm certain I would never have become a writer.

"I'm so sorry she's gone, Maggie. That damned mill gave so many people fatal diseases. My father should be in jail, I swear."

"Actually, her leukemia had nothing to do with it at all, weirdly enough."

"Well, then, what . . . ?"

"She was murdered."

CHAPTER THREE

"**D**id you just say she was *murdered*?"

Maggie let out a sigh. "I did. Someone smashed the back of Mom's head in with that heavy cast-iron Mark Twain paperweight she always kept on her desk."

"But . . . who? *Why*?"

"We have no idea yet. I found her face down on her desk Saturday after closing time. She hadn't called me to come pick her up—she couldn't drive anymore—and it was getting late, so I got concerned. Drove over here and found her in a pool of blood. It was . . . horrible. I called our Connecticut State Police resident trooper, Pete Schlosski, and he—"

"Wait, you don't mean Peter the Beater, do you?"

"Yes, I do."

Pete Schlosski, better known as Peter the Beater by one and all at Oakmont High, had been something of a local legend due to his penchant for drifting off in class—a budding Rhodes Scholar he was not—and idly flogging his meat with one hand in his pants pocket. No one ever figured out whether he was playing with himself consciously or was half asleep. Everyone was aware of it, and the other boys, myself included, tormented him mercilessly in the hallways. Not one teacher had the nerve to speak to him about his peculiar behavior, but when Mrs. McKenna caught him playing with himself while he was seated in a comfy chair at the Oakmont Public Library, dozing his way through a history textbook, she tore up his library card and banned him from the premises for a year. It had upset him greatly, Maggie told me at the time, because the library was the one place in town where he could go and not be taunted.

"So he became a state trooper?"

"He did. Married Mary Ellen Coleman. Remember her?"

"Uh . . . no."

"They have two kids and he's a good resident trooper. People respect him. He's fair, evenhanded and no one calls him Peter the Beater anymore. He immediately passed Mom's case on to the Major Crime Squad and a homicide lieutenant is working on it. A forensics team has dusted the paperweight and her desk for fingerprints and examined the floor around her desk for shoe prints. They're incredibly thorough. The library has been closed all day to the public. It's reopening tomorrow morning. Mom's desk is cordoned off with yellow police tape."

"But they have no idea who . . . ?"

"If they do, they haven't said a word. I sure can't imagine why anyone would do such a thing. Mom was *loved* in Oakmont. Hey, listen, I won't keep you from your work any longer. But I just thought you'd want to know."

"You're not keeping me from anything. And I'm coming. I'll see you tomorrow before the wake."

Maggie let out a gasp of shock. "Seriously?"

"Absolutely."

"But you swore you'd never, ever come back here."

"I know I did, but I can't *not* come. Your mom was very special to me."

"And you were very special to her." Maggie's voice sounded strangely hollow.

"Besides, there's zero chance I'll run into my father. Or my mother, for that matter."

"Are they still living in Vero Beach?"

"As far as I know."

"Have you spoken to them since you left for Harvard?"

"That would be a no."

"You know how to carry a grudge better than anyone I've ever met."

"Everyone ought to be good at something. I'll see you tomorrow afternoon. You'll be at the library?"

"I'll be here. Don't be too shocked when you get to town."

"Meaning . . . ?"

"A lot has changed in eleven years. Just prepare yourself, okay?"

"Okay. Thanks for calling me, Maggie. And, again, I'm so sorry."

I hung up and sat back down on the floor with Lulu, feeling a deep, heavy sadness. Lulu curled up in my lap and gazed at me curiously. She was getting a vibe off of me that was new to her. She started to lick my face, but then stopped and nestled her head in my neck and shoulder instead. I stroked her.

We'd been sitting there like that for a good long while when Merilee came home and found us there. Lulu didn't stumble over to yip at her mommy happily. She just stayed right there with me on the floor.

Merilee peered at me, immediately concerned. "What's happened, darling?"

"Someone who was very important to me, Mrs. McKenna, the Oakmont town librarian, has died. Her daughter, Maggie, just phoned to let me know. There's a wake tomorrow, and her funeral is on Sunday. I'm going to go. I have to pay my respects, although the circumstances of her death are a bit bizarre."

"Bizarre as in . . . ?"

"She was murdered."

Merilee's lovely green eyes widened. *"Murdered?"*

"Someone beat her brains in with the Mark Twain paperweight that always sat on her desk."

"Who on earth would want to murder a small-town librarian?"

"Good question. She'd been fighting off leukemia for several years. Still showed up for work when she felt up to it, but she'd passed the torch to Maggie, who's the official library director now. Maggie was my best friend when I was a kid. Hell, we grew up together in that library. She was also my high school sweetheart."

Lulu remained in my lap with her head nestled on my shoulder.

"How long has Lulu been sitting there with you like that?"

"I don't know. Quite a while. She sensed right away that I was upset. I don't know how."

"Because she's grown attached to you, darling. When are you leaving?"

"In the morning. Do you mind if I take the Jag?"

"Not in the least, because I'll be coming with you." Lulu let out a squeal of protest. "What I meant to say is *we'll* be coming with you."

"Not necessary. It's a toxic town full of bitter people, and the name Hoag is a dirty word there."

"Nonetheless, we're coming with you. I have nothing planned for the next couple of days. Nothing definite, anyway."

My eyes searched hers. "Are you sure about this?"

"Positive. It matters to you, therefore it matters to me."

"You won't have a good time."

"I don't care about that. I care about *you*. Look, we've had nothing but giddy fun together since we met. But there are tough times in life, too. This is one of them, and I'm right here for you."

My chest felt tight. I hadn't thought it was possible, but I loved this woman even more than I'd realized. "I don't know what to say."

"Just say yes."

◆

We left after breakfast, Lulu riding in Merilee's lap in her carrier. The morning was bright and sunny. Both of us wore jeans, sweaters, and leather jackets. Her leather jacket was an Armani, but my vintage Werber flight jacket had infinitely more panache, and she would have "borrowed" it in a second if I'd let her. She'd already "borrowed" two of my favorite old flannel shirts. I was discovering there was a small downside to living with a beautiful six-foot-tall movie star—my cherished old clothes looked better on her than they did on me.

We were toting two small suitcases in the Jag's boot, which is to say trunk, and had a garment bag folded behind our seats. Merilee had made us brisket sandwiches from last night's dinner for the long drive because she hated highway fast food. That made two of us. She'd also filled a thermos with hot French press espresso.

"Have I told you how fetching you look today?"

"Why, no. Thank you, kind sir."

"I was talking to Lulu, although you don't look too shlumpy yourself, blondie. Okay, ow, you're not allowed to punch the driver."

"Would you mind telling me some more about brass?"

"If you wish."

"I wish."

"Okay. A whole lot of it was manufactured in Connecticut. There used to be four huge mills in the state. Now there's only one left, Century Brass in Waterbury. Brass is an alloy made mostly of copper and zinc. In order to machine it into things like faucets and hinges, they add lead in the manufacturing process.

"Lead, as we have come to learn from our experience with lead paint, is highly carcinogenic. When house painters repaint old houses these days and encounter lead paint, they have to wear special masks and gloves. But no one was aware of how awful the lead used in brass manufacturing was for a long time. Or so they claimed. I'm convinced that people like my father knew and simply refused to acknowledge it. The Hoag Brass mill poisoned the Oakmont River. Also the groundwater. The mill workers got cancer and leukemia from inhaling the dust in the mill. Their wives and children got it from the water they drank and bathed in. But my father wouldn't listen to the warnings from environmentalists. *Nervous Nellies,* he called them, as he gazed out his office window at the dead fish floating on the Oakmont River."

"That's horrible," Merilee said in dismay.

"It gets worse. The brass industry isn't the only one that has turned pockets of Connecticut into toxic brown zones. There used to be a huge water tower outside of Oakmont that wasn't a water tower. It was an *ink* tower. There was a paper mill there. Paper mills dumped ink into the rivers all over the state. Clothing manufacturers did the same thing with dye. And then one mill after another was abandoned after we started importing cheaper foreign goods that were free of environmental regulations. That's the American way. Makes you feel warm all over, doesn't it?"

It took us about an hour on I-95 to get to Darien, where we stopped at a gas station to stretch our legs.

Lulu walked around on her leash and took care of personal business. We did the same thing another hour later after we'd made it past New Haven, where we pulled in at a rest stop in Westbrook that had a scenic view of Long Island Sound. Sat at a picnic table and ate our brisket sandwiches and drank the still-hot espresso from the thermos. I spoon-fed Lulu some Gerber's and gave her a drink of water before I walked her for a few minutes. She was being a good sport about the long drive. Never whined. She was riding on Merilee Nash's lap, after all. A million dogs and fifty million men would have traded places with her in a second.

Then we got back into the Jag for the last leg of our journey. It was about a three-hour drive to Oakmont. A few miles after we crossed the Connecticut River at Old Lyme, we veered inland on I-395 from the lovely coastline to the unlovely industrial heart of the state. Before long we reached Norwich, or Narrich as the locals pronounce it, a manufacturing city that had been incredibly prosperous a hundred years ago but was now incredibly blighted. I got off of I-395 a few miles past there and onto a series of narrow roads that twisted their way for mile after mile past scrap metal yards, truck-parts warehouses, boarded-up factories, vacant retail spaces, moldering bungalows, and the occasional enclave of beautiful Victorian homes. Remnants. It was a hodgepodge of remnants.

Soon we arrived at Oakmont's neighboring city, Fulton, which was thriving thanks to the presence of a regional hospital. Fulton had a shiny new shopping center that sported an A&P supermarket, four fast food restaurants, a variety of shops, and a cineplex.

"I just saw a sign that said Oakmont is five more miles," Merilee reported. "We've almost made it to your old stomping grounds, darling."

And with that I realized that my jaw had started clenching.

"Look, look!" she exclaimed. "Is that the old water tower that's actually an ink tower?"

"Indeed it is. They still haven't torn it down."

The road made a sharp curve and I saw the sign for Oakmont. Downshifted and made a right turn that took us into woods and marsh on the outskirts of town. Soon we were crossing a bridge over the Oakmont River, which gave off a putrid smell that was equal parts dead fish, untreated sewage, and toxic chemicals. Around the next bend was the huge, abandoned redbrick brass mill that had been in the Hoag family since the 1880s and was now surrounded by barbed wire and KEEP OUT signs. Some sections of it were crumbling. Others were charred, as if bored kids had tried to set fire to it. Practically every window had been broken.

"Say hello to my family legacy," I said.

After we passed the cemetery and Huffman's Mortuary, we arrived at the village green. I had fond memories of Oakmont's village green from when I was ten years old. It had looked like something out of a Norman Rockwell painting. It had a well-tended lawn with a bandstand and park benches and a cleared area where mill hands used to pitch horseshoes on warm summer evenings.

That was then. The village green was now nothing more than a giant, weedy vacant lot strewn with fast food wrappers and beer cans. The bandstand and park benches were history.

In my youth the green had been surrounded by thriving, locally owned businesses. There was Super Drug, which had the best chocolate shakes and comic books to be found anywhere. Super Drug no longer existed. It had been torn to the ground. John the barber's shop, with its old-fashioned barber pole, had also been torn down. Bennie's family-owned grocery store was still standing but was vacant and boarded up, as were the village diner and the hardware store. All of the homey small-town businesses that once surrounded the green were gone—all except for Mallory's, the town saloon, with its Pabst Blue Ribbon neon sign.

If people needed to buy groceries or fill a prescription, I imagined they went to Fulton now. Not that there were very many people left. At least half of the small, squat mill workers' houses were either boarded up or had collapsed into ruins. Twenty thousand people had lived in Oakmont when I was a kid. Now it felt like a ghost town. Maggie had tried to warn me, but it was still a shock.

"Did I remember to warn you that since my name is Hoag, I'm not going to be the most popular person in town?"

"Yes, you did."

"Just wanted to make sure."

I slowed down as I neared the enormous hilltop mansion that had been my boyhood home.

"Is that the old homestead?"

"Yep. Had been in the family for four generations until my folks fled for Vero Beach."

It was barely recognizable now. Had been broken up into what appeared to be a dozen tired-looking rental apartments. The four-car garage at the foot of the driveway was still there. Our old caretaker, Rigby, had lived in an apartment over the garage. He died of lung cancer before I left town.

I eased my way past the old place. I didn't have to worry about traffic. The Jag was the only car on the road. Took a right onto Hope Street and discovered that the elementary school and day care center had been leveled. The Congregational church's windows were boarded up and its doors padlocked. Town Hall remained open, but it had fallen into disrepair and there were only three cars parked there.

The only building in town that appeared well cared for was the 1894 slate-roofed brick public library, which my great-grandfather had built because he believed it would be a vital helping hand for the children of the mill workers. So had my grandfather and father, though my father once confided in me that he mostly considered it a superb tax write-off.

"It's a lovely old library," Merilee said as I pulled into the parking lot and gazed at it, a wave of nostalgia washing over me.

She let Lulu out of her carrier, put her on her leash, and walked her over toward a grassy spot next to the pavement, tossing her long blond hair in the fetid breeze. "Do you think it always smells this horrible?" she asked, crinkling her nose.

"I don't think it does. I know it does. Got your pocketbook?"

"Yes, I do."

"Good. I'll the lock the car, but that's still no guarantee someone won't try to break into it."

I locked both of our doors before we started toward the library's entrance.

I crashed into more nostalgia when we walked inside. Chiefly, it was the smell that triggered it. The faint vanilla scent that old library books give off. There's no other smell like it, and it took me straight back to my childhood.

It was chilly inside, and looked exactly the same as it always had, aside from the glass case in the entry hall displaying the inscribed copy of *Our Family Enterprise* that I'd sent Mrs. McKenna as well as my *Time* magazine cover and copies of the many prominent newspaper reviews I'd received—not to mention Oakmont school yearbook photos of me dating all of the way back to the third grade, when I'd borne an astonishing resemblance to a ferret.

Yellow police tape still cordoned off the front desk. Evidently the forensics specialists were not done, although they'd allowed the library to reopen. There was a knitting circle of four elderly white-haired ladies warming themselves on the comfy armchairs by the fireplace. All four of them wore their hair in the style that was popular among non-chic white-haired ladies back in 1982, short and rounded so that it bore a rather eerie resemblance to a light bulb. There was a nickname for such ladies. They were known as Q-Tips.

Maggie was chatting with them. She wore a bulky dark blue cardigan sweater that might well have been knit for her by these very ladies. When she spotted me, she immediately burst into tears. I went to her and gave her a hug. She'd been a plumpish five-foot-five with curly red hair when I'd left town. She was a bit trimmer now. Her face had lost its baby fat and her jawline was sharper. But her red curls still tickled my chin.

"Damn, Hoagy, *I promised* myself I wouldn't cry. I'm so sorry."

"No need to be sorry," I said as I held her tight and let her have herself a good cry. The knitters grew teary-eyed themselves as they watched us there.

"It's just so good to see you. It's been *forever.*"

I handed her my linen handkerchief. "Yes, it has."

She dabbed at her eyes, sniffling. "I'm afraid it's cold in here. Fuel oil's gotten incredibly expensive and we have almost no money. I'm forced to set the thermostat at sixty-two and make do with a good fire." She glanced over my shoulder and noticed Merilee standing a respectful distance away holding Lulu on her leash.

"I brought a couple of guests. Hope you don't mind."

"Of course not," she assured me, as she gave Merilee a curious squint of recognition.

"The short one is Lulu."

"She's adorable. How old is . . . ?"

"Four months. Is it okay if we let her off her leash?"

"Of course. She won't pee on the rug, will she?"

"Wouldn't think of it."

Merilee unhooked her and Lulu went ambling off in the direction of the library's staff lounge.

"And the tall, blond one is Merilee. She won't pee on the rug either."

Maggie's curious squint of recognition had become a wide-eyed, awestruck gaze. "My God, you're *Merilee Nash*," she said in a hushed voice as the Q-Tips murmured excitedly among themselves.

"It's true, I am."

Maggie continued to gaze at us, stunned. "Are the two of you . . . ?"

"Yes, we are," I said.

"How long have you . . . ?"

"Nine days, going on ten," Merilee said. "I didn't want him to make the trip all by himself. I won't attend the wake this evening, because I'll be a distraction, but I'd like to attend the funeral and graveside ceremony, if I may. Your mother meant so much to Hoagy."

"Why, of course. We'd be honored. She was *so* proud of you," Maggie said to me. "My gosh, she practically erected a shrine to you."

"I was just looking at it. Did I really look like that in the third grade?"

"I swear, Hoagy, seeing you on the cover of *Time* magazine was the proudest moment of Mom's life."

"I understand that you're carrying on the family tradition here," Merilee said to her.

"Yes, I am."

"It's such a sweet old library."

"For me, it's home," Maggie said. "Although I'm afraid that Oakmont's a shell of what it was when we were growing up. So many families moved away that the schools had to close. A school bus takes the remaining kids to Fulton. And we have to attend

Fulton's Congregational church now. Ours is no more, as you may have noticed. There weren't enough parishioners left to keep it afloat."

A cat suddenly let out an outraged yowl and came streaking out of the librarians' lounge toward the Q-Tips over by the fire.

"Don't tell me you still have Frodo," I said in disbelief.

"No, he died ages ago. That's Leon. The patrons love him and he keeps the mice under control."

I swore I heard slurping noises coming from the direction of the staff lounge. Merilee heard them, too. Mystified, we tiptoed in there and discovered that Lulu was hungrily devouring the food in Leon's dish.

"Maggie, what do you feed Leon?" I called to her.

She followed us in there, directing her gaze at a stack of 9Lives canned mackerel.

"Is that canned mackerel for . . . cats?"

Maggie peered at me, mystified. "Well, yeah, Hoagy. Leon *is* a cat."

"But Lulu isn't."

"What does it matter, darling?" Merilee said gleefully. "She's found her cuisine of choice! Maggie, you can't believe how happy this makes us. Thank you so, so much."

"Um . . . you're welcome?"

As Lulu polished off the remains in Leon's bowl my gaze fell on the lounge's daybed, where Maggie and I had lost our virginity together when we were sixteen. "That daybed looks awfully familiar," I said, tugging on my ear.

Maggie immediately blushed. "Mom took naps on it when she felt well enough to come in."

"It's awfully good to see you again, Maggie. I'm not seeing a wedding ring on your finger. You're still single?"

She nodded. "I had a serious thing going with a dentist in Fulton named Victor up until two years ago. Real sweet guy. Marathon runner. But when push came to shove, I just couldn't see myself talking about impacted wisdom teeth over the dinner table for the rest of my life. Plus I had my hands full trying to manage Mom's leukemia treatments, run the library, keep the house clean, buy groceries, and so on. So I broke it off."

"What about your kid brother, Kevin? He must be, what, twenty-five? Hasn't he been able to pitch in?"

A look of utter misery crossed Maggie's face. "Kev's a no-good crack freebaser and small-time thief. Mom did *everything* she could to get him into a treatment program so he could get clean, learn a trade, and make a life for himself, in exchange for which Kev stole her television set. Also her gun from the nightstand in her bedroom. That's how he treated his mother, a leukemia patient. By breaking her heart."

"She owned a gun?"

Maggie nodded. "Dad's old Colt thirty-eight. Everyone in Oakmont has a gun. It's not a safe place." She looked at me curiously. "You live in New York City. You must own one, too."

"Nope."

"Why not?"

"Guns go off. Did she replace it after he took it?"

"Sure did. Another Colt thirty-eight. She also went the tough love route. Threw Kev out of the house, changed the locks on the doors, and called Pete Schlosski on him. Kev ended up serving ninety days in county lockup—for the second time. The first time was for breaking into cars in the A&P parking lot in Fulton. Kev's my brother, and I love him, but he's trash. So is Destiny, his so-called girlfriend. She's a poisonous little ninety-pound crackhead tramp. They freebase together. He's been staying with her on the convertible sofa in the back room of Mike Mallory's saloon ever since Mom threw him out. She works there as a barmaid. Also gives guys quickies on that very same couch to pay for crack."

"I remember Mike Mallory as being a decent family man."

"Those days are long gone. He helps himself to freebies from Destiny whenever he wants. That's why he keeps her around. He's also the town loan shark, and he fences stolen goods. Kevin borrows money from him to buy drugs and keeps digging a deeper and deeper hole for himself. Mike and Mom used to be good friends, but she was so furious with him for loaning Kev drug money that she chewed him out and told him she'd never speak to him again." Maggie sighed wearily. "Naturally, Kev never stops asking *me* for money. I won't give him any. Hell, half the time I don't even know who I'm talking to. One minute he's speedy, the next minute he's angry or in a deep funk. People who freebase crack are *scary*. Hey, have you found a place to stay while you're here?"

"Not yet."

"Remember Pat Dennis? Her late husband, Gene, owned Super Drug."

"Oh, sure. I used to swipe comic books from him. I was so crafty he never suspected a thing."

"Well, Pat's the manager of the apartment building that they converted your old house into. She lives in one of them rent free for her trouble, and she keeps Rigby's apartment over the garage available for people who've come home to visit family. Rents it out by the night, like a motel room, except it has a full kitchen and you can lock your car downstairs in the garage. I don't think anyone's staying there now. Shall I call her for you?"

"That would be great. Thank you."

"I'll be right back. I have to use the phone downstairs in the children's library because Mom's desk is still off-limits." And off she went.

"She still loves you, you know," Merilee said to me with total certainty.

"We were high school sweethearts ages ago. Don't be silly."

"I'm not being silly. I'm being a woman, and women know these things about each other. Trust me, she isn't over you. That's why she didn't marry her dentist."

At our feet, Lulu rolled over onto her back and started making all sorts of contented *argle-bargle* noises. She'd found her cuisine of choice at last. Canned mackerel for cats, which she still eats to this day.

I was just about to give her a belly rub when the library's front door opened and in walked a big, husky Connecticut State Trooper wearing a Smokey hat and full uniform, his black garrison belt creaking with every stride. The belt was equipped with a .357 Smith and Wesson revolver, radio, nightstick, and handcuffs. His uniform shirt was slate gray with royal blue epaulets piped in gold. His necktie was a royal blue knit with a gold tie clasp. His trousers were a dark blue with a royal blue stripe. His black oxfords were shiny. The trooper wore his uniform proudly, as if it validated him. Pete Schlosski was someone who needed validation. Aside from the uniform, he hadn't changed a bit. He'd never been a bright-looking guy, and he still wasn't. It was chiefly because of his eyes, which were just a bit too close together, and his jaw, which stuck out like a snow shovel.

"I had to come inside and find out who owned that vintage Jag with New York plates that's out in the parking lot," he said. "It's *you*, Hoagy. I should have known."

"Maggie phoned me with the sad news. I came to pay my respects."

"Hell of a thing, somebody beating poor Mrs. McKenna's brains in," he said heavily.

"Hell of a thing. Are the investigators closing in on who did it?"

"Not that I know of, but they've assigned the case to a crackerjack Major Crime Squad homicide lieutenant, Buck Mitry. He's super sharp. Black fellow. If anyone can figure out what happened to her, Mitry will."

"Well, it's good to know that they're taking the investigation seriously."

"You bet they are. Mary McKenna was a respected member of this community, or what's left of it."

"How are you, Pete? Or should I call you Trooper Schlosski?"

"Anything but Peter the Beater," he said, reddening. "You guys used to torment me endlessly."

"That was high school, Pete. No one gets out unscathed."

"I don't know how I survived, but I did. And now I have a good job, a beautiful wife, and two lovely little girls."

"Glad to hear it. Truly."

He was staring at Merilee now. And staring. "I would swear that you're Merilee Nash, the movie star."

"I don't think of myself as a star. Just a working actress."

"And whatever you do," I said to him, "don't get her started on her old days on the Keith-Orpheum circuit. Merilee, say hello to Pete Schlosski, whom I've known since we were, what, ten years old?"

"Nice to know you, Pete," she said. "The long-eared one is Lulu."

"Gosh, she's a cutie." He bent down and picked her up, scrunching her ears and getting his nose licked for his trouble. He made a face. "Say, her breath is kind of . . ."

"She has unusual eating habits, as it turns out," I said. "I understand from Maggie that Mrs. McKenna kicked Kevin out of the house."

"High time she did, too," he said gruffly. "He's served county time twice. The next time he goes down, and I guarantee you he will, he'll end up in a state penitentiary for a year or more. He was a source of real pain to her. He and that girlfriend of his, Destiny."

"Maggie said he's living with Destiny in Mike Mallory's back room. She's a barmaid there."

"Barmaid is a polite word for it. Mallory's used to be a nice, clean family place where you could take a date for a beer. Not anymore. A real low class of swamp Yankees hang out there now. I have to break up fights pretty much every Saturday night. And Mike's a sleazy loan shark who's mixed up with a couple of drug dealers named Sly and Shade. They work out of Willimantic, have gang ties, and are not to be fooled with. Sly fancies himself an up-and-comer. Sharp dresser, a real talker. Shade's his muscle. A dum-dum."

"And how is Mike mixed up with them?"

"He keeps loaning Kevin money—money that Kevin can't afford to pay back unless he resorts to crime—so he can keep on buying crack from them. How does that sound to you?"

"Like Mike's hands aren't completely clean."

"Exactly."

Maggie came upstairs from the children's library and said, "You're all set, Hoagy. Pat Dennis said Rigby's old apartment is available through Saturday, and the garage is empty so you can lock your car in there, too. She's ready for you any time. You'll find her in apartment A, first on the left."

"That garage has a good padlock on it," Pete said to me. "Make sure you use it or that Jag will be gone in the morning."

"Do you have any news from Lieutenant Mitry?" Maggie asked Pete.

"Afraid not, Mags. Just catching up with our hometown celebrity. And, boy, wait until Mary Ellen hears I met *Merilee Nash*. You coming to the wake this evening, Miss Nash?"

"I think not. I don't want to be a distraction. But I'll definitely be at her funeral on Sunday."

"What time is the wake?" I asked Maggie.

"It starts at five o'clock. Will probably last two hours or so."

I glanced at Grandfather's Benrus. "It's nearly three. We'd better scoot. I'll see you there."

Maggie's eyes moistened. "Hoagy, it means so much to me that you're here. When I phoned you in New York, I honestly didn't think you'd come."

I gave her a hug. "What can I tell you? You were wrong."

Merilee put Lulu back onto her leash and we headed outside to the Jag. Pete had parked his weathered tan Ford Crown Vic next to it.

"How are you holding up so far?" Merilee asked me.

"Honestly? I'm even more depressed than I thought I'd be, and we've only been here an hour. I sincerely hope things don't get any worse."

That was my sincere hope, all right.

But, zowie, was I dreaming.

CHAPTER FOUR

I t would have felt distinctly weird to pull into the driveway of my childhood hilltop home no matter what, but it was absolutely surreal now that it was a barely recognizable apartment complex. The elaborate rose garden and emerald green lawn that Rigby used to tend had been paved over to make parking spaces for the tenants. About half of the spaces were filled, none with cars that were remotely new or flashy.

The only thing that looked at all the same was Rigby's two-story domain at the foot of the driveway. He'd parked his '52 Plymouth pickup in the garage, where he'd also stored his power mower, gardening and household repair tools. He'd lived in a one-bedroom apartment upstairs.

Maggie had said that Pat Dennis was in apartment A, first on the left. I drove up the hill to her door, parked outside, and we got out. Merilee kept Lulu on her leash.

The door to unit A opened almost at once and a slat-thin, slightly bent Q-Tip came out to greet us wearing a wool coat and a sour expression on her lined face.

"Well, if it isn't Stewart Hoag," she said with a complete absence of warmth. "I remember you from back when you were a little stinker who used to steal comic books from my Gene's Super Drug."

"Wait, he *knew* I swiped them? I thought I was so skilled and crafty that he never noticed."

"Believe me, he noticed."

"Why didn't he grab me by the scruff of the neck and make me pay for them?"

"Because your daddy owned the building. Gene was afraid if he so much as laid a finger on your precious head that that your daddy would double his rent. My Gene was a gentle soul, and your daddy was a holy terror of a man. Like father, like son, no doubt,"

Pat said as she glared at me, the Jag, and Merilee with beady-eyed disapproval. "Seems like you've done plenty okay for yourself. You're a best-selling writer now, and I suppose this is your famous movie star."

"Hi, I'm Merilee," she said, making an effort to be cordial. Which was entirely wasted.

"Guest apartment's twenty-five dollars a night," Pat said brusquely. "If you make any long-distance calls, you'll have to pay for them yourselves. You're welcome to stay here until Mary McKenna's put in the ground on Sunday, but your pup better not pee or chew on anything or you'll have to replace it."

"She won't," said Merilee assured her.

"It's furnished and has linens. Nothing fancy, but it's clean. You're welcome to use the kitchen, but there's nothing in the fridge except for a few condiments. The A&P in Fulton is pretty decent. If I were you, I'd keep that fancy sports car locked in the garage, day and night. I'll give you the key."

"Thank you," I said. "We'll do that."

Pat glared at Merilee again. "Miss Nash, I enjoy your movies. They're not dirty or violent. And you seem well-bred. I can't imagine how you ended up with Monty Hoag's miscreant son."

"It surprised both of us."

"How long ago did Mr. Dennis pass away?" I asked.

Pat's face darkened. "Not long after your daddy shut down the mill. Business at Super Drug dropped sharply, what with so many people moving away. And those who stayed could no longer afford their medications because he took away their health benefits. When Gene fell behind on his rent, your daddy evicted him. Gene always kept a loaded handgun in a locked drawer behind the druggist's counter. Most druggists do. They dispense narcotics. That makes them a target. The day after your daddy evicted him, Gene closed up early, unlocked the drawer, put that handgun in his jacket pocket, and went for a long walk in the woods. It took a trooper with a trained police dog two days to find his body. He'd stuck that pistol in his mouth and shot himself." She stood there in stricken silence for a moment. "It wasn't just the cancer and leukemia patients who were Monty's victims. My Gene was, too."

"I'm sorry, Mrs. Dennis."

"Don't be. I don't want your pity. I've read that novel of yours. Everyone in town has. I just have one question. Did you really have an affair with Lillian Allen, our high school English teacher?"

"No, ma'am. There's a reason why they call it fiction. Besides, I didn't use her real name."

"Didn't matter. Everyone knew who you meant. She was the only pretty young teacher in the English department. Well, I'm glad to hear that. I always thought she was a fine young woman. Couldn't imagine her engaging in such perverted behavior."

"Has she moved away?"

"When they closed the high school, she got herself a job at a school in Portland, Maine." She glanced at her wristwatch. "I imagine you'll want to get settled in. Mary's wake will be starting before long." She handed me the apartment key and reached inside her front door for the key to the garage padlock. "You don't need me to show you the way. And walking down this hill is hard on my arthritic hip. But I *will* need a twenty-five-dollar cash deposit."

I pulled out my wallet and handed her a twenty and a five.

"I'll slip the receipt under your door later when I head out to Mary's wake."

"Thank you," Merilee said as the old woman went back in her unit and closed the door on us.

"Nice warm reception," I said to Merilee as we strolled down the driveway toward our temporary digs.

"My lord, she practically accused you of putting that pistol in her husband's mouth and pulling the trigger."

"My last name is Hoag, so she holds me responsible."

"I'm beginning to grasp the full weight of why you swore you'd never come back here."

"In which case I'm glad you came. It's one thing to tell people something and another for them to experience it for themselves."

I unlocked the apartment and the padlock to the garage door. After I'd raised the garage door, I walked back to the Jag and eased it down the driveway into the garage. There was nothing in there except for a ladder and a few paint cans. Nothing like when it had been Rigby's domain. After I'd grabbed our bags, I padlocked the garage shut and joined Merilee and Lulu in the apartment.

It didn't smell musty in there. Pat kept it clean. The harvest gold shag carpet was freshly vacuumed. The blue-and-gold linoleum kitchen floor was spotless, as was the white tile kitchen counter. It was an eat-in kitchen that had a yellow Formica table with chrome legs and four matching yellow vinyl chairs. It still looked like 1960 in there. The stove was electric, as was the heat. There was no dining area. Just a small living room with an easy chair and sofa covered in brown mohair, a coffee table, and an eighteen-inch Sylvania television set. The bedroom was small and the mattress on the queen-sized bed wasn't exactly firm, but we'd make do. No bathtub in the bathroom, just a stall shower. There was a linen cupboard with fresh sheets, pillowcases, and towels.

Lulu searched the entire place, ears and nose to the ground, snuffling and snorting before she finally climbed up onto the sofa and curled up there.

Merilee went to work unzipping the garment bag and hanging my gray flannel Strickland and Sons suit and her black Ralph Lauren dress in the bedroom closet. Then she stowed the small number of shirts, sweaters, and so on that we'd brought in the dresser. Her cosmetics bag and my shaving kit went in the bathroom. I put Lulu's bowls in the kitchen, filled one with water, and set it on the floor next to her empty food bowl. She jumped down from the sofa and lapped up some water before she stuck her large black nose in the food bowl, found nothing, and let out a snuffle of extreme dissatisfaction.

"Not to worry, girl. You and Mommy will soon be off on a grand adventure to Fulton, where they're sure to have 9Lives mackerel for cats and special dogs."

Merilee joined us in the kitchen. "It's not the Four Seasons, but it'll be fine for a couple of nights. Although I would like to register a complaint, sir."

"Okay . . ."

"You haven't kissed me in more than three hours."

"You're right."

I took her in my arms and I kissed her softly.

"Thank you, darling. Just for that I'll show you the presents I brought." She unzipped the tote bag that had held our sandwiches and coffee thermos and pulled out not one but two bottles of Chianti Classico, a corkscrew, a two-cup French press coffee maker, and a Ziploc bag of coarse-ground espresso.

"Merilee, you're a genius."

"Do we have time for a glass of wine before you have to leave for the wake?"

"We'll make time. Besides, I need the fortification. Open-casket wakes give me the creeps. Everyone standing around a corpse that resembles wax fruit, raving about how *lifelike* the person looks." I opened one of the bottles with the corkscrew, found two juice glasses in the kitchen cupboard, and poured us generous jolts. We clinked glasses and I said, "To Mrs. McKenna."

"Indeed." After we'd each taken long, grateful sips Merilee said, "Next time we'll have to bring proper wineglasses."

"Trust me, there will be no next time."

She opened the refrigerator and put the bag of espresso in there, pausing to poke around. "Hmm . . . we have some mayonnaise, French's mustard, ketchup, and, for some reason, a jar of anchovies."

"Why on earth would there be a jar of anchovies in here?" I reached inside for a closer look. "My God, they're totally encrusted in salt. This jar must date back to Rigby's days." I opened it, not without diffi-culty, and peered in at its contents. "No mold. They're still good. Want one?"

"That's very kind of you, darling, but no thanks."

But somebody else did. Lulu started climbing up my leg, yipping and yapping.

"Lulu, 9Lives mackerel is one thing, but you don't actually want to eat an anchovy. Trust me, they're incredibly fishy."

The yipping and yapping only got louder.

"Okay, you asked for it, but you'll be sorry." I extracted one, rinsed off the caked salt, and held it out to her. Almost lost two fingers to her puppy teeth as she gobbled it down, her tail thumping happily.

"Have you ever heard of a dog eating anchovies?" I asked Merilee in wonderment.

"Never. The former Princess Flavia certainly has an adventuresome palate."

"Only if you consider *adventuresome* another word for *weird*. I guess I'd better get dressed while I finish my wine. If you'll be kind enough to drop me at the funeral home on your way to the Fulton A&P, I'd appreciate it."

"My pleasure. I can pick you up on my way back if you you'd like."

"Thanks, but I'll bum a ride to Mallory's, which is where people traditionally gather for a cold one after a wake. It's only a two-block walk from here. Pete Schlosski will give me a lift if no one else will."

"He seems like a nice guy. Did you boys really call him Peter the Beater?"

"Yes, we did. And it wasn't just the boys."

"God, kids are mean."

"Of course they are. They're people."

◆

I dressed in my gray flannel suit with a white shirt, sober tie, and Grandfather's monogrammed gold cuff links. We had the same initials. His name was Stevenson Stafford Hoag. I was given the same middle name in his honor. I didn't bother with my trench coat. It wasn't that chilly out. I rode shotgun with Lulu in my lap in her carrier. We'd agreed it wouldn't be wise to leave her alone in the apartment while Merilee was away because she might get frightened and do something heinous like start chewing on the sofa. After Merilee had pulled the Jag out of the garage, and then padlocked it shut, she put the keys in her shoulder bag and steered us back in the direction of the town green.

"I'll be damned . . ." I mused aloud.

"About what, darling?"

"I never had an inkling that Gene Dennis knew I was swiping his comic books. And to think he didn't complain about it to my father because he was afraid to."

"Was your dad that much of an ogre?"

"Times ten. Everyone in town was terrified of him."

"Including you?"

"Me? No, I just hated him." Mallory's was already doing a brisk business. Otherwise, the former town green was deserted and utterly dark. Soon we passed the ruins of the mill and crossed the bridge over the Oakmont River. "Just keep going on this road and we'll hit Huffman's Mortuary in a mile or so. After you drop me off, stay on it until it dead-ends. Make a left and you'll hit Fulton in five miles."

"I remember. It so happens I have an excellent sense of direction, sir."

Soon we saw a whole lot of lights up ahead and more than a dozen cars parked in the mortuary's parking lot.

"Why don't you drop me right here? I'll walk the rest of the way. I don't want to show off by pulling up in a fancy ride."

"As you wish." She pulled over to the curb. I passed Lulu over to her and got out while she deposited Lulu back on the passenger seat. "Shall I rustle us up a couple of omelets for dinner when you get home? It would just take me a couple of minutes."

"Sounds good."

"Unless, that is, you come staggering in at one A.M. reeking of beer and cigarettes."

"Not part of my plan, believe me. I'm afraid the supermarket bread won't be up to our Little Italy standards, but if you poke around you may find some crusty Portuguese rolls. There used to be a big Portuguese population around these parts, working the mills and fishing the waters off of Stonington. And there used to be a huge mushroom farm not far from here in Franklin that sold to the local markets. If they're still around, you'll find an amazing selection of mushrooms."

"All we need is an onion and we'll be in business."

"And don't forget Lulu's canned mackerel."

"Believe me, darling, I won't."

I blew her a kiss and shut the door. Walked the rest of the way to the mortuary and started up the path as she went speeding off with a throaty roar, turning the heads of the four young swamp Yankees who were standing out on the front steps pulling on cigarettes and passing around a pint bottle of Old Overholt rye. They hadn't dressed up for Mary McKenna's wake, unless you consider buffalo check wool shirts, jeans, and work boots dressed up. They gazed at me in chilly silence as I strode past them in my bespoke tailored gray flannel suit.

Inside, it was brightly lit. There were floral arrangements, a table with paper plates of cookies, a coffee urn, and a stack of Styrofoam cups. At least two dozen people were milling around, drinking coffee and talking in hushed tones.

Maggie spotted me right away and came bustling over to me. She was wearing a dark purple velvet dress, tights, and wool clogs. She took my hands in hers, which were warm and moist, and kissed me on the cheek.

"You can't imagine how glad I am that you came," she said, getting teary-eyed. *"She'd* be glad. Come see her. I'll take you over to her. She looks so beautiful."

I suppressed my overwhelming dread and said, "Sure, okay."

As Maggie led me over to the open casket, I wondered if she could sense my dread from how tightly I was clutching her hand. If she did, she gave no indication of it as we stood there, hand in hand, gazing down at the brightly colored replica of the woman in a pink dress who had once meant so much to me.

The mortician at Huffman's had done quite a job of reconstructing the back of her head. There was no way to tell that someone had taken her Mark Twain paperweight to it. It had been eleven years since I'd last seen Mary McKenna. She'd been an attractive, energetic woman of forty-two when I'd left town.

She'd died at age fifty-three, and had been battling leukemia. She looked considerably older and quite frail.

Maggie said, "Doesn't she look beautiful?"

"Beautiful," I said, my own eyes moistening as Maggie and I continued to hold hands. "I wish I'd had a chance to tell her how much she meant to me."

"She knew, sweetie. She knew."

We moved along so that others could view her. Maggie led me over toward the coffee urn, where her kid brother, Kevin, stood slurping coffee and sniffling. He wore a buffalo check wool shirt, jeans, and hiking boots, which seemed to be the official uniform of Oakmont's young and useless. He had a wispy moustache and stringy hair that looked as if he hadn't washed it in that calendar year. He wasn't much taller than Maggie, maybe five foot seven, and ultra-edgy. His hands were trembling. He'd been fourteen when I left town. I remembered him as being a lazy, stupid weasel. The years hadn't changed him much, except that now he was a drugged-out lazy, stupid weasel.

"You remember Hoagy, don't you Kev?" Maggie said to him.

99

"Duh." He glowered at me, sniffling. "Your dad bailed on Oakmont and you bailed on Maggie. Makes you kinda hard to forget."

"Hoagy did not bail on me," she said to him crossly. "He was fortunate enough to get into Harvard, then moved to New York City and became a fine writer."

He rolled his eyes. "I know. It's all I ever hear about."

"I'm sorry for your loss, Kevin," I said politely.

"What loss? Oh, you mean Mom? She wouldn't have anything to do with me, so I'm not exactly sobbing my guts out, you know?"

"Now is not the time to talk about this," Maggie said to him quietly.

"Fuck that shit." He pulled a Marlboro from his wool shirt pocket and lit it with a disposable lighter.

"There's no smoking in here," she pointed out.

"Fine, then I'm gone. I promised Destiny I'd meet up with her at Mallory's anyway. First round is on the house tonight as a tribute or whatever, so she'll be super busy slinging drinks." He started for the door, leaving Maggie shaking her head in despair.

As Kevin was leaving, Pat Dennis, our landlady, was coming in, accompanied by two of the Q-Tips from the library's knitting circle.

"Are you and Miss Nash getting settled in?" she asked me.

"Just fine. She's grocery shopping in Fulton. I'll be heading back soon for dinner."

"She seems like a gracious person."

"That she is."

"Much too good for the likes of you."

"Shame on you, Pat Dennis," an outraged Maggie spoke up in my defense. "I'll have you know that the *New York Times* considers Hoagy the first major new literary voice of the eighties."

"I'm just riding him a little, Maggie. I'm old. I'm allowed to."

"You're not allowed to be nasty."

"Hoagy knows I didn't mean anything, don't you?"

"Since you're my landlady, and I don't want to sleep in the street tonight, I'm going to say yes."

But Maggie was still peeved. She took my hand again and led me away from Pat. As we worked our way around the room, I noticed that most of the people in the mortuary were looking at me with a distinct absence of human kindness. It was a true thrill to get back to where I didn't belong.

"I'm totally basking in the warm reception I'm getting," I said.

DAVID HANDLER

"They can't help themselves, Hoagy. They still hate your father for the way he shafted everyone when he closed the mill. And no one ever got along with him when it was still running. He always acted like an entitled prick."

"Still does, as far as I know. Your mom managed to get along with him well enough."

"Because she wouldn't take any guff from him. Also, the library had meant a lot to his father and grandfather, so he felt obligated to carry on the tradition. Whenever Mom needed money for books or building maintenance, he gave her whatever she asked for. The library was a legacy of sorts. It's a shame you and your dad still don't speak, though I certainly understand why. Are you in touch with your mom?"

"Not at all."

"She must miss you."

"I wouldn't know. Mother was the queen of denial. She smiled. She played bridge. She drank sherry all day. I imagine that's exactly what she's still doing in Vero Beach."

I was now aware of a hulking presence next to me and realized it was Pete Schlosski in full uniform and Smokey hat. He tipped his hat at Maggie and said, "Your mom looks so lifelike."

"They do a wonderful job here."

"Hoagy, I wonder if you remember my wife, Mary Ellen? She was one class behind us in high school."

Mrs. Peter the Beater was a small woman with black, frizzy hair. On the chubby side. I didn't remember her.

"Sure, I recognized you right away."

She lit up, delighted. "We took Spanish together one semester."

"And now you and Pete have two little girls. Nice to see you again, Mary Ellen. Wish it could be a happier occasion."

"Doesn't Mrs. McKenna look beautiful?" Pete said to her.

"Incredibly lifelike," Mary Ellen agreed as I realized I was going to totally lose my mind if I didn't get out of there.

"I'd better cruise on over to Mallory's, hon," Pete said to her. "Make sure things don't get out of hand."

"Do you mind giving me a lift?" I asked him.

"I don't mind at all."

"I'll stick around and coffee-klatsch for a little while," Mary Ellen said. "I can get a ride home from one of my girlfriends. Take care of yourself, hon."

He grinned at her. "Don't I always?"

I gave Maggie a hug and promised her I'd stop by the library in the morning. Her eyes moistened again when she gazed up at me.

As we headed out. I couldn't help noticing that the trooper's uniform gave Pete an air of confidence and authority that he'd sorely lacked in years past. The same four swamp Yankees were still sitting outside smoking cigarettes and passing around the pint of Old Overholt.

"Are you chowderheads just going to sit out here and drink, or go in and pay your respects?" he asked them roughly.

They mumbled various unintelligible things before they stubbed out their smokes, drained the bottle, and moseyed in.

"Sometimes I swear there's hardly anybody left here anymore except for losers," Pete said to me as we strode toward his Crown Victoria cruiser. "The four of them rent a two-bedroom house a few doors down Elm Street from me. Owner hasn't been able to unload it. Two of them, the Pardo brothers, are high school stoner buddies of Kevin McKenna. They still hang out together. I see him going in and out of there all of the time."

"How do they make a living?"

"Fill out roofing crews, tree cutting crews, and such when someone needs an extra unskilled hand. Haul stuff to the dump for elderly folks. Mostly they just drink, smoke dope, and watch cartoons."

We got in his cruiser and he started it up, sitting up straight, his shoulders square. The man loved his car almost as much as his uniform. As he drove past the ruins of my family's mill he said, "The old hometown isn't much, is it? I wish I'd had the brains to go away to a good school like you did and move to New York City. But I didn't. Besides, New York scares the crap out of me. So many people, so much crime. I belong here with Mary Ellen. I was surprised you remembered her."

"Recognized her the second I saw her. She had a cute little bod in high school."

"Still does," he said, winking at me.

He pulled up in front of Mallory's and parked. Quite a few cars were parked on both sides of the street. Nothing brings people out like free beer.

Inside, about two dozen swamp Yankees were drinking Pabst on tap, smoking cigarettes, and talking in the general direction of each other in raised voices. All men, no women. Mallory's had four booths, six tables, and an old hardwood bar with ten stools.

Mike Mallory was busy filling mugs from the beer tap. I remembered him as a balding, chubby guy. He was now totally bald and outright fat. Kevin was in urgent conversation with him as he worked the tap. Mike shook his head repeatedly, his jowls jiggling.

As Pete and I drew closer to the bar I could hear him. "Kev, I can't help you until you kick in some dough."

"Yeah, but—"

"There's no 'Yeah, but.' I don't know how many times I have to tell you." Mike looked up, grinning at us. "First one's on the house," he said over the din of raised voices.

"Not while I'm on duty, thanks," Pete said.

"How about you, fancy Dan? I haven't seen anyone wearing a suit in here in I don't know how long. Hey, wait, I know you. You're Monty Hoag's kid, Stewart. Cleared out the day you graduated from high school, am I right?"

"You are, Mike. I came home for Mary McKenna's funeral. My friends call me Hoagy, by the way. You can call me Stewart."

He let out a huge laugh as he drew a mug and handed it to me. I thanked him and took a gulp, gazing around the saloon.

A few of the guys looked familiar from high school. They returned my gaze coldly. Not one of them came over and said hello. They still clung to their hostility.

"I hear you wrote yourself a best-selling book just-like-that," Mike said to me with a snap of his fingers as Kevin continued to linger near him, his eyes avoiding mine.

"It wasn't just-like-that," I responded with a snap of my own fingers. "It took me three years to write it and another year to sell it. But I was lucky enough to get a good publisher who pushed it hard and it's sold better than I could have hoped for."

"Good for you. It's nice to see someone from this shithole make something of themselves."

I circulated a bit, mug in hand. A sexy little chihuahua of a girl in her early twenties zeroed right in on me. She had dark brown eyes that seemed too big for her narrow face and long, straight black hair that she parted down the middle. Squeaky clean she was not. *Dirty* was more the word that came to mind. Her hair looked greasy and her complexion was grainy. She wore a skintight yellow knit dress with absolutely nothing on underneath it. Her nipples were right there to look at, as was the curve of her ass. She wore a pair of white boots. No stockings. And she reeked of patchouli, which hadn't been my favorite scent back when every head shop smelled of it and still wasn't.

After she got done looking me up and down in a most inviting way, she flashed a smile at me and said, "Hiya, good-looking. I'm Destiny."

CHAPTER FIVE

"Nice to meet you, Destiny. I'm Hoagy. You're Kevin's girlfriend, right?"

"Sorta," she said, edging me over closer to the wall. "You are one classy-looking dude. You don't live here, or I'd sure as shit know you."

"I used to live here. In fact, Kev's sister, Maggie, and I were high school classmates. I live in New York City now. Came back for their mom's funeral. It's a shame you had to work tonight and miss her wake. I'm sure Kev would have appreciated you being there with him."

Destiny let out a harsh, jagged laugh. "Shows how little you know. He and the old lady hated each other. And she was incredibly nasty to me. Called me a slut. Told me to stay away from him. The bitch wanted him to go into drug treatment but wouldn't find a place for him unless he broke up with me."

"You don't sound too upset that she's dead."

Destiny shrugged her narrow shoulders. "She thought I was a bad influence on him. Do I look like a bad influence to you?" she asked, flirting with me now.

"No, you look like a real nice girl to me. You're awfully pretty, too."

Her big brown eyes gleamed at me. "You really think so?"

"Oh, most definitely. And that is one fine bod you've got."

"You talk nice. And you're cute, too. Can I get you another round?"

"No, thanks. I have to leave soon."

"Don't go. I'm, like, getting into you."

"I thought you were Kev's girlfriend."

"He goes his way, I go mine." She edged up against me, plastering me to the wall, and rubbed her pelvis against mine. "And you're *so* classy. I have such a thing for classy."

"I could tell that about you right away."

"So, listen, you got money?"

"A lot more than I had six months ago."

"Mike has a back room he lets me use. I'll suck your dick like you never had it so good for twenty bucks and swallow every drop. I'll even let you stick your fingers in me. I get soaking wet. Your whole hand will be drenched. What do ya think?"

Mostly, I was thinking about whether she kept a toothbrush, toothpaste, mouthwash, and an ample supply of disposable hand sanitizers back there. "Sounds incredibly tempting, but I'm meeting my lady friend in a few minutes."

"All I *need* is a few minutes to get you off. Trust me."

Kevin came over our way now, looking extremely pissed off at the way the love of his life was practically dry humping me against the wall. In fact, you can forget the word practically.

"Hey, what gives?" he demanded.

"Trying to do some business, will ya?" she shot back.

"Oh . . ." he said glumly.

"What'd Mike say?"

"He won't loan me any more money until I make good on the vig."

"Maybe Mister Classy here will loan you some. I understand he used to hang with your sister."

I said, "Maggie's my friend, and I know what you want the money for. No way."

Her mood did an instant 180, her eyes blazing at me. "In that case, go fuck yourself."

"HEY, DESTINY!" Mike called to her. "I'M PAYING YOU TO SLING DRINKS, REMEMBER?"

She went to the bar, put four full mugs of beer on a tray, and carried them to one of the tables, working her tush.

"You stay away from her," Kevin warned me in a menacing voice.

"Believe me, that won't require a major effort. How much are you into Mike for?"

"Why do you care?" he demanded.

"Destiny just asked me if I'd help you out. I'm curious."

"I'm into him for two hundred on the vig."

"What's the principal?"

"So high I can't even see that far. And don't tell me I should go into a treatment program, or I'll barf all over your shiny shoes."

"I wasn't going to. It's your life. If you want to ruin it, that's your business. I just hate to see

Maggie worrying about you. She's someone I care about."

"Oh, yeah? If you care about her so much, then why'd you dump her?"

"That's not how it went down and you know it. Stop acting childish, Kev. You're a grown man now."

Pete Schlosski made his way over toward us, which sent Kevin heading off in the opposite direction.

"I see you met Destiny," he said to me.

"So up close and personal that I feel as if I need to take a shower now. Forgive me if I'm being out of line, but don't you have a problem with Mike letting her use his back room for quickies?"

"I don't like it but, believe me, that's the least of my worries. I'm much more concerned about home break-ins, car thefts, and—" He broke off as the saloon door opened. "And the fact that Mike associates with *those* two."

He was eyeballing the two young guys who'd just walked in and were sauntering toward the bar with major Don't Mess With Me attitudes.

"Let me go out on a limb. Sly and Shade?"

Pete nodded his head.

"Which is which again?"

"Sly's the one with the slicked-back hair."

He wore a belted black leather jacket to go with his slicked-back hair. Shiny, cheap leather. Black jeans and Frye boots. Shade was a huge bodybuilder. He wore a sleeveless T-shirt with barbed wire tattoos adorning his giant biceps, a pair of workout pants, and sneakers.

Mike poured them two cold ones from the tap. Sly asked him something. Mike shook his head no, which I took to mean that there was no business for them tonight. Kevin was still behind on his vig, just for starters. I didn't know who else in the place they dealt dope to. I assumed there were more than a few.

Sly shrugged and sipped his beer, glanced over at me inquiringly, then murmured something to Mike. Mike murmured a response.

Sly raised his eyebrows, mildly impressed. Shade just stood there drinking his beer, flexing his biceps and doing his best to look scary.

Then Sly glanced at Pete, who responded by striding toward him. I tagged along. Had nothing better to do.

"I've asked you two very politely to stay out of here," Pete said gruffly.

"It's a free country," Sly responded with a toothy grin. "And we're good customers, right, Mike?"

"Sure, whatever, you say." Clearly, Mike wanted no part of this.

"You won't be for long," Pete promised Sly, gazing out the front windows. "See that car idling over at the end of the town green with its lights on?"

"What about it?" demanded Shade, who actually did know how to speak.

"Inside of that car are two members of the state police's Narcotics Task Force. Everywhere you go, they go. They have you under surveillance. You do know that, don't you?"

Sly smirked at him. "What I know is that they're idiots, same as you are. All cops are idiots or on the take, or both." He gestured at me with his chin. "Aren't you going to introduce me to your friend here?"

"He's Stewart Hoag, a high school classmate of mine. Came here for Mrs. McKenna's funeral. He admired her tremendously. He was good friends with Maggie, too. He's a big best-selling author now. Had his picture on the cover of *Time* magazine."

"That a fact? Glad to know you, man. I'm Sly, he's Shade."

"Are those your given names?" I asked him.

"The fuck does that mean?"

"The names that your parents gave you."

"No," Pete informed me. "Sly's is Steve, Shade's is Clarence."

"Which lack a certain panache. I see why you prefer your nicknames."

Sly narrowed his gaze at me, trying to decide if I was someone he was going to hate.

"Hoagy's family owned the brass mill here going back a hundred years," Pete said.

"That's what Mike just told me," Sly said. "Except the mill's gone and Oakmont's nothing but a worthless dump. Where do you live these days?" he asked me.

"Why is that any of your business?"

"Just curious. No need to get hostile. Care for some free advice?"

"That all depends. How much is it going to cost me?"

"I'd go back to wherever you came from. People get killed in this town—like that librarian, Mrs. McKenna."

"Are you implying that you had something to do with it?"

Sly let out a laugh. "No way. I'm not that kind of dumb."

"What kind of dumb are you?"

He didn't respond. Just glared at me.

"So you're simply giving me a friendly warning, is that it?"

"Just telling it like it is, same as Howard Cosell."

"I'm here for Mrs. McKenna's funeral, and I'll leave when I feel like leaving."

"Sure, okay," he said. "Just keep your nose out of my business."

"What makes you think I'm interested in your business?"

He tapped his temple with his index finger. "Instincts. That's the secret of my success."

"Really? So selling crack to a small-time thief and his hooker girlfriend in the blighted remnants of a mill town is your definition of success?"

Sly shook his head at Shade sadly. "Hostile, isn't he? Insulting, even."

"Insulting," Shade agreed, nodding his pinhead.

"Shove off," Pete ordered them. "*Now.*"

"We're leaving," Sly said. "But not because you told us to. We were already going."

"I'm glad we cleared that up," Pete said. "I'll rest a lot easier. Beat it!"

They sauntered ever so slowly out the door.

Kevin followed the two of them, stopped them on the sidewalk and spoke to them urgently, waving his arms in the air.

Sly shook his head at him. When Kevin wouldn't stop pleading his case, Shade shoved him roughly to the ground. Then they got into their car, a black Ford Bronco, and sped off. Their Narcotics Task Force tail stayed where it was for a moment, then followed them.

Kevin got up from the sidewalk, dusted himself off, and came slinking back inside. Destiny was nowhere to be seen. She'd evidently slipped into the back room to take care of some business.

"I'm sorry that Mrs. McKenna had to be around to see Kev make such a mess of his life," I said.

"Me, too. Maggie's position is the same as hers was. She'll help him get treatment. But she refuses to help Destiny. Wants her out of his life."

"I can't imagine why. She seems like such a nice, wholesome girl."

Pete moved over toward Mike Mallory and said, "I've warned you before. If I catch Sly and Shade selling drugs in this place, I'll shut you down."

Mike ran a chubby hand over his bald head and sighed in total misery. "Pete, my boy, at this point in my life you'd be doing me a huge favor."

◆

It was a two-block walk back to our apartment. I needed the fetid night air. It offset the clinging scent of Destiny's patchouli. I did find myself glancing behind me occasionally to see if I was being tailed by a black Bronco. Sly and Shade were small-time punks, but those are the ones you have to watch out for. You learn that if you live in a rough neighborhood in New York. The smaller they are, the more they need to prove themselves worthy of respect. Baiting Sly wasn't the smartest thing I'd ever done, but it felt so damned good I couldn't help myself. Besides, I'd done a lot of stupid things in my life.

But there was no sign of them. They had that Narcotics Task Force tail on them, after all.

Rigby's garage was padlocked shut. The apartment lights were on. I climbed the steps and tapped on the door. Merilee let me in, dressed in yoga pants and one of my old flannel shirts.

"Seven times," I said.

"Seven times as in . . . ?"

"How often I heard the phrase *She looks so lifelike* at the wake."

"It was very brave of you to go." She gave me a big hug before she abruptly pulled back and said, "Darling, I would swear you reek of patchouli. Does Oakmont have a head shop?"

"Nope, it has Destiny. It's her scent of choice. I forgot how awful it is."

Lulu came waddling over, tail thumping. I picked her up and she immediately started sneezing so uncontrollably that I thought her ears might pinwheel around and send her flying around the room like a helicopter.

"What on earth has gotten into her?" Merilee wondered.

"The patchouli. She must be allergic to it."

"May I ask why you smell of it so strongly?"

"You may. I stopped off at Mallory's after the wake for a quick beer and Destiny, Kevin McKenna's classy barmaid girlfriend, plastered me against the wall and offered me a quickie in the back room."

Merilee's green eyes widened in keen interest. "Ooh, tell me more. I want details."

"You really don't, I can assure you," I said as Lulu continued sneezing.

"Hoagy, I'm a performer. This is my raw material. I insist. And I promise I won't be grossed out."

"Okay, you asked for it. She wanted twenty bucks for a blow job. She said she'd swallow every drop and—"

"Is that the going rate?"

"I really wouldn't know."

"Sorry, I interrupted you. And . . . ?"

"I could finger her, too. She said she gets incredibly wet and that my hand would be drenched. That was the word she used. *Drenched.*"

"Okay, I'm totally grossed out."

"Don't say I didn't warn you," I said as Lulu continued to sneeze.

"Darling, why don't you get out of that suit and shirt so that I can hang them in the bathroom to air out."

"I think the garage might be a better choice. I need to take a shower and wash my hair."

She grabbed three hangers from the closet while I took off my shoes, emptied my pockets, and gave her my jacket, pants, and shirt. She held them at arm's length, crinkling her nose, grabbed the keys, and darted outside to open the garage.

The shower wasn't bad. Good water pressure and plenty of hot water. I soaped myself thoroughly and shampooed my hair twice before I felt as if I was getting rid of the smell. I'd put a folded towel down on the bathroom floor in case Lulu wanted to join me in there to steam clean her sinuses. She did. Curled up there on the towel happily and soon stopped sneezing. After I'd dried off, I put on a Sex Pistols T-shirt and jeans and joined Merilee in the kitchen, where she handed me a wineglass filled with Chianti and started inspecting the frying pans that were available for her to use.

I sat down at the table. "How was your expedition to Fulton?" I asked as Lulu climbed up into my lap with a little boost.

"Oh, I had a wonderful time," Merilee said with great enthusiasm. "I love to study body language. Any time go I somewhere I've never been before, it's a terrific opportunity to observe the way people carry themselves."

I took a sip of my wine. "And how do the people at the Fulton A&P carry themselves?"

"With a defeated slump in their shoulders. No one in the entire supermarket was standing up straight. And hardly anyone seems to be trying to stay in shape. I'm talking major potbellies."

"Were you able to find us anything to eat?"

"I most certainly did. A dozen eggs, an onion, and a wonderful selection of fresh mushrooms, as you predicted. I'm going to sauté them right now." She went to work on the mushrooms with a knife on the cutting board. "They also had those Portuguese rolls you mentioned, too, and I got us a couple of gallon jugs of Poland Spring water, because I am *not* drinking what comes out of that tap, orange juice, butter, milk, and so on."

"Would 'and so on' include 9Lives mackerel?"

"A half dozen cans."

"Has she eaten any?"

"She gobbled up a half can just as soon as we got home. I bought a shower cap at the drugstore. My clerk, Gert, was very friendly. The liquor store had a terrible selection of wine but they did have wineglasses. I bought us two, as you can see. There's just something wrong about drinking wine out of a juice glass."

"I couldn't agree more."

"Oh, and I checked out the cineplex."

"What are they showing?"

"A veritable raft of entertainment—*E.T.*, *First Blood*, and *None of the Above*. After I got back, I practiced an hour of yoga while Lulu and I watched reruns of *Barney Miller* and *The Odd Couple*, and then my man came home, stinking of patchouli."

She got the mushrooms and finely chopped onion started in a skillet and broke a half dozen eggs into a mixing bowl before she glanced at me uneasily. "I also used my AT&T calling card to check in with my agent, and it turns out that David Mamet has been trying to reach me all day. So I called him. He's doing an open-book reading of his new play in a rehearsal space downtown tomorrow afternoon and he wants me to read the lead role."

My heart sank right away at the prospect of being stuck in Oakmont without her, but I powered through it. "Merilee, that's fantastic! Have you read it yet?"

"Not a living soul has read it yet. They're sending a town car and driver here to pick me up tomorrow morning at ten thirty in the library parking lot, which seemed like an easy spot for him to find. Supposedly, the driver will be bringing a copy of it for me to pore over on the way home, but it'll still be a cold read. And if David decides to sit up all night rewriting it, there may another cold read Sunday, which means I'm not sure I'll make it back for Mrs. McKenna's funeral. I'm so sorry, darling."

"No, no. Don't be."

"But I feel as if I'll be abandoning you here."

"Not a chance. You can't imagine how much I appreciate that you actually came. You saw the place where I spent the first seventeen years of my life. You visited the library where I learned to love books. Met my closest childhood friend. But your career comes first. Besides, I'll be getting the hell out of here thirty seconds after I shovel a load of dirt on Mrs. McKenna's casket. So don't even think about coming back. Take Lulu with you in her carrier. I'll drive the Jag home."

"I must admit I'm kind of excited about it."

"As well you should be. *Mamet* wants you. How cool is that?"

"Somewhat cool."

"It's totally cool."

"My only worry is that you and Maggie may rekindle your teen romance in my absence. She's vulnerable, what with her mom being dead. You'll be here all by yourself. I want you to know I won't blame you if you sleep with her."

"Are you kidding me, blondie? I'm so madly in love with you that there's zero chance of that happening. Tell me, who else will be reading with you?"

"I have no idea. I don't even know how many roles there are." Her eyes widened. "God, I hope it's not a one-woman show."

"Does it have a title yet?"

"Yes, it's called *Untitled David Mamet*."

She threw the eggs, mushrooms, and onions together in no time and buttered the Portuguese rolls. I got out two plates and forks and we devoured our dinner hungrily with the last of the Chianti.

"Yum. You are going to make somebody a good little wife someday."

Merilee arched an eyebrow at me. "Was that a proposal?"

"It was not. When it's a proposal, you'll know it."

After we'd washed and dried the dishes, I put on my old black Converse Chuck Taylor All Star high-tops, my even older navy blue turtleneck sweater, and my flight jacket. "It's time for your evening constitutional, Lulu," I announced, grabbing her leash.

She let out an eager yip as I hooked it to her collar. "See you shortly."

"Have fun," Merilee called to me from the linen closet. She still had to make the bed.

I walked Lulu in the direction of Mallory's. She stopped and sniffed here, there, everywhere. It was silent and dark out, and the air smelled truly foul. The saloon was still open, though Mike appeared to be all alone in there, sitting behind the bar with his chin resting in the palm of his hand.

"Hey, you're back," he said, mustering a faint smile when I walked in. "Brought your pup, too, I see."

"This is Lulu. I'm supposed to walk her before we go to bed so she doesn't have any accidents in the night."

I plopped down on a stool. Lulu circled around three times at my feet before she curled up there. I had no idea why she did that.

"Pour you a cold one, Hoagy?"

"No, thanks. Just noticed you sitting here and thought I'd say hi. Are Kevin and Destiny out back?"

"Naw, I loaned them my Camry. They went to see *First Blood* for the fourth time. I don't understand the appeal of that Stallone guy. All he does is grunt like a gorilla."

"Kevin doesn't have a car?"

Mike shook his head. "Totaled his old pickup a few months ago. Maggie unloaded her old beater of a Subaru and has been driving Mary's Civic. Mary wasn't well enough to drive anymore, so Maggie drove her to the doctor, the library, and so on. She refuses to loan the Civic to Kev because she's afraid he'll use it while he's committing a crime."

"That doesn't worry you, too?"

"I don't worry about much of anything anymore," he said defeatedly, slumped there behind the bar, looking bleary-eyed. He was wheezing slightly and his complexion didn't look healthy. Not unless you consider gray healthy.

"What's happened to you, Mike? You used to run a nice, friendly place here where a mill hand could bring his girl for a glass of beer. Now you pimp out Destiny in your back room and you're a loan shark who's mixed up with drug dealers. You'd never have let the likes of Sly and Shade in here in the old days."

"Real pieces of work those two, aren't they?" he said sourly. "Sly has a mighty big opinion of himself for someone who's going to get squashed like a bug before long. And Shade couldn't find his own asshole with a flashlight and a detailed map." He shook his head regretfully. "Boy, was Mary furious with me. She knew that I loan out a little money on the side. A lot of people here in town are strapped for cash. But when she found out I was loaning Kev money to buy crack, she really let me have it. Accused me of making a profit out of turning him into a drug addict and career criminal. Mary was a hard woman. She banned me from the library and would no longer speak to me. I know you were really fond of her. Came all of the way back here to put her in the ground. But anyone who ever crossed swords with her will tell you the same thing. She could be a coldhearted bitch."

"Any idea who smashed her head in?"

"Pete Schlosski asked me that, too. How would I know? It sure as hell wasn't me. I'm just trying to keep my head above water. I can barely make the rent on this place. My house around the corner on Beckwith is a wreck. The boiler blew six months ago. I haven't had heat or hot water since. The furnace company wants payment in full. They won't do an installment plan." He ran a hand over his face. "Destiny isn't a bad kid, you know. She's had some rough breaks. Her dad was a mill hand. Died when she was ten. Her mom ran off with some guy and left her to fend for herself when she was sixteen. She dropped out of high school and has been on her own ever since. I'm just giving her a helping hand, same as I've been helping Kevin after Mary threw him out for stealing her TV."

"It doesn't bother you having a pair of crackheads living here with access to your cash register?"

"I don't have much in there. What little I make selling beer, I keep in my wallet in the back pocket of my pants."

"Which I understand are down around your ankles pretty often, courtesy of Destiny."

"That was a cheap shot, Hoagy."

"You're right. I'm sorry."

"I'm not exactly proud of myself, but the truth is I've been going downhill ever since my Greta died three years ago from colon cancer. The medical bills cleaned me out. We'd lost our youngest girl, Tina, the year before that. Too much. It was just too much."

"I'm sorry to hear that, Mike. No one told me."

"Our oldest girl, Nancy, moved to Florida not long after the mill shut down, along with a lot of the young people. She's doing really well down there. Manages a steak house in Boca Raton. Keeps begging me to join her. Boca's got sunshine, blue skies, the beach. She's positive she can get me a job tending bar somewhere. I ought to do that. Move down there, rent a cheap apartment. Just clear the hell out of this place."

"So why don't you?"

"I'm thinking about it."

"Don't think about it. Just do it, before you sink into the toxic ooze along with everyone else here."

"Hey, are you sure I can't buy you a beer?"

"Positive, thanks," I said, getting up off of my stool. Lulu stirred at my feet, yawning. "Good talking to you, Mike."

"Likewise, Hoagy. And, hey, congratulations on your book. I saw you on *Good Morning America* a while back. You looked like . . ." He trailed off into gloomy silence.

"Like what?"

"Like a somebody. Everybody who I know is a nobody."

CHAPTER SIX

Ten-Minute Merilee was packed up and ready well before it was time to meet her town car at the library parking lot at 10:30 A.M. She was in a tense, preoccupied mood that was new to me. She was very . . . inward. I wondered if this was how she was backstage before a performance.

While she paced around the apartment, anxious to go, I took Lulu for a walk. She would be cooped up in her carrier for good long while and the exercise would do her good. Besides, I needed to have words with her.

"I want you to take extra-special care of your mommy, okay? She's really nervous and will need every bit of comfort and support she can get. I won't be around to give it to her, so it falls on you. That's your job, got it?"

Merilee was wringing her hands impatiently by the time we got back. "Shall we go to the library, darling?"

I glanced at Grandfather's Benrus. "We'll be ten minutes early."

"The driver might be ten minutes early."

"Sure, let's do that. But I want a hug first."

She gave me a boa constrictor hug, her eyes tearing up. "Are you going to be okay here all by yourself?"

"Who, me? I'll be fine," I assured her.

"I don't mean to fuss and fret, it's just that we've never been separated for this long before."

"It's true, we haven't. Promise me you'll call me after the reading and let me know how it goes, okay?"

"I promise, but only if you do me a huge favor and wish me luck."

"You don't need luck. You have talent. *And* Mamet specifically asked for you. But I will. Wish you luck, that is."

"Thank you, darling."

I opened the padlock on the garage, which smelled more than faintly of my patchouli-scented suit that was hanging in there, and put her bags in the Jag's boot. She carried Lulu outside in her carrier, locked the apartment door, and got in next to me with Lulu in her lap. I backed out, padlocked the garage, made sure I took the apartment key from Merilee, and drove us to the library. Lulu let out a loud moan in her carrier, which she had never done before.

"Lulu, what did we talk about?" I said to her sternly.

She immediately fell silent.

"Good girl."

Merilee looked at me curiously. "What *did* you talk about?"

"It's strictly between the two of us."

"Oh, I see."

The library was open. Several cars were in the lot. A black Lincoln Town Car was not one of them. We sat in the Jag with the engine running for a minute or two before I finally shut it off and we sat there in silence, holding hands.

The driver got there a half hour late in his black suit, white shirt, and black tie, apologizing profusely. He'd taken the wrong fork in the road before he reached Fulton and got totally lost. "Help you with your bags, Miss Nash?"

I got her bags out of the Jag's boot. He transferred them to the trunk of the Town Car as I lifted Lulu's carrier out of Merilee's lap so that she could get out.

He took one look at the carrier and shook his head. "Sorry, folks, no can do. I'm not allowed to carry pets."

"You have my word that she won't make a mess," Merilee assured him sweetly. "And she doesn't shed."

"And I believe you. And if it was my car, it'd be no problem. But this car service has had an ironclad rule about pets ever since someone's cat vomited on the upholstery a couple of years ago."

"Would an extra fifty bucks change your mind?" I asked him.

"I'm afraid not. Your pup will have to stay behind."

"Merilee, I can catch a train on Sunday. Why don't you drive the Jag home so Lulu can be with you?"

"Because I need to read the play on the way home." She glanced at the driver. "You *do* have the play with you, don't you?"

"I have a big envelope with your name on it. Don't know what's in it."

"Then I guess that settles that." I put the carrier back down on the Jag's passenger seat.

Merilee bent down to say goodbye to Lulu. "Take care of your daddy and make sure he doesn't come home smelling of patchouli, understand?"

Lulu let out a small whoop to indicate that she understood.

The town car's trunk was still open. Merilee removed the cans of cat food that she'd stuffed in her shoulder bag, returned them to the Jag, and gave me a big hug. "Are you sure you'll be okay without me?" she asked, her green eyes searching mine.

"Not to worry. I'll muddle along."

We kissed, a soft, lingering kiss, and then walked hand in hand to the town car. The driver opened and closed the door for her, then he climbed in behind the wheel, closed his door, and eased slowly out of the library's parking lot. Merilee blew me a kiss from the back seat as I stood there, all alone in the last place on earth where I wanted to be.

After they'd driven away, I opened Lulu's carrier, hooked her to her leash and let her out, locking the Jag behind her. Since the library was open, I figured I might as well say hello to Maggie. I let Lulu off her leash as soon as we walked in. She made a beeline for the librarians' lounge in search of Leon's breakfast, but Maggie was a step ahead of her. Leon's bowl was not only empty but washed clean. And Leon was sitting by the fire with Maggie and eight or ten Q-Tips, including our landlady, Pat Dennis. They were holding a meeting of some kind. The yellow police tape surrounding Mrs. McKenna's desk had been removed, but I did not see the murder weapon—her Mark Twain paperweight. Possibly it was being stored in lockup.

I waved to Maggie before I followed Lulu into the lounge to make sure wasn't getting into any trouble. She was nowhere to be seen. Had burrowed underneath the daybed, sniffling and snorting. I got down on my knees and had a look. She was way far underneath it. All I could see was her tail.

"Lulu, what in the heck are you doing under there? Come on out."

She let out an excited yip. Seemed to have found something. And now she was nosing it with some difficulty toward me. I sincerely hoped it wasn't a desiccated mouse corpse. Whatever it was seemed very important to her. She let out a triumphant whoop as she pushed it out into the daylight.

It wasn't a desiccated mouse corpse. It was a piece of gold jewelry. I was so aghast when I got a good look at it that my head started spinning.

"Good girl," I managed to say, stuffing it in the pocket of my jeans. "You just earned yourself an anchovy." Then I joined Maggie and the Q-Tips before the fire, still reeling from Lulu's discovery. Leon was fast asleep in Maggie's lap and paid Lulu no mind at all. "Well, what sort of unholy cabal do we have going on here?" I asked Maggie.

The ladies tittered, all bright-eyed and excited at the sight of me.

"Hoagy, this is the world-famous Oakmont Public Library book club. We read one book a week and meet every Friday from ten until twelve to discuss it. There's coffee and cookies, and Betsy Sherman brought a container of her homemade deviled ham sandwiches."

"I'm sorry, did you say homemade deviled ham sandwiches?"

"Would you care for one?" Betsy asked me, indicating the Tupperware container and paper plates on the coffee table next to Maggie.

"That all depends," I said. "Is the limit one to a customer? For example, what if I wanted two or, say, eleven?"

Which led to more tittering.

"Dig in, by all means," she replied.

They were tea sandwiches with the crusts cut away. I snatched up two, put them on a paper plate and sat in the lone remaining empty chair. Lulu climbed into my lap. "Yum," I said after I'd forced myself not to swallow an entire delicious sandwich in a single bite. "Have you got a husband, Betsy?"

"Why, yes. Burt."

"Damn. The good ones are always taken."

Maggie said, "At first I was worried that Mom would find it disrespectful of us to hold our weekly meeting today, but then I decided she would have been angrier if we'd canceled it."

"You're right, she would have been. What book did you read this week?"

"We chose *Sense and Sensibility* by Jane Austen."

"A fine choice."

"But it isn't often that we have an actual author here with us," Maggie pointed out. "In fact, we never have. Would you—that is, if you're not in a hurry—be willing to join us and read aloud a bit of *Our Family Enterprise*?"

"We all read it and discussed it soon as it came out," Betsy said. "We found your insights about growing up here fascinating. We'd all thought you were a happy young man and that you and your father were great pals. What did we know?"

"Not a whole lot, I'm sorry to say. But I'm afraid I don't have a copy of my book with me," I confessed, munching on my fourth deviled ham sandwich.

Maggie let out a hoot. "Hello . . . ? You're sitting in a public library. We have two copies, not counting the one that you inscribed to Mom. Have yourself a look in the stacks under *H* for *Hoag*."

I lifted Lulu out of my lap and headed off to the stacks. Found one copy of my book there, loving that vanilla scent of the older books, and returned to the fireplace with it. If you've ever wondered whether authors get blasé about holding their first published novel in their hands, the answer is a resounding no.

I sat back down and Lulu immediately climbed back into my lap. I raised the book to eye level. As I cleared my throat, I realized that the ladies were gazing at me, transfixed. They were avid readers who'd never seen a living author read his or her own book aloud before.

I chose to read them my brief introduction, which I'd often taken to doing when I made broadcast appearances:

> *"It wasn't a posh New York City suburb for executives on their way up the corporate ladder.*

It wasn't a Gold Coast shoreline town where people went to sail their yachts and gaze out over Long Island Sound from the decks of their waterfront homes. It was a failing mill town like so many other failing mill towns in the heartsick center of industrial Connecticut, which dated back over a hundred years to when it had been a thriving hub of mills that made everything from clothing to shotguns, brass faucets, wall clocks, and fine furniture. But that was then. Now its rivers were polluted, poisoned by solvents, dyes, lead, and mercury. The workers and their families had become ill, one by one. And the mills had shut down, one by one, leaving nothing but carcinogenic ghost towns behind.

"Young Samuel Hancock knew very little about life at the age of sixteen, but he did know that he loathed his dishonest bully of a father, and that he had no intention of joining the front office of his family's brass mill when he graduated from college, as had the four generations of Hancock men had before him. He refused to devote his life to this fetid, dismal place. He would build a new life for himself somewhere else and swore he would never, ever come back . . ."

I trailed off, closed the book and raised my eyes to them. They applauded me.

"But tell us what you really think of Oakmont," Betsy Sherman quipped.

"Thank you so much, Hoagy," Maggie said, her eyes gleaming at me. "I'm sure you'll be wanting to escape now. We've kept you far too long. I'll show you out. Ladies, I'll be back in a minute. Feel free to start your discussion."

"Would you like to take the rest of the sandwiches, Stewart?" Betsy asked me.

"I wouldn't think of it. Unless, that is, they'll be going to waste."

"Here, take the container with you. Maggie will get it back to me."

I accepted it gratefully and followed Maggie to the front door, pausing to hook Lulu onto her leash.

"Thank you *so* much," she said, her voice cracking with emotion. "You have no idea what a thrill that was for them. How are you and Merilee planning to spend the day?"

"Actually, Merilee's on her way to New York as we speak to do a table reading of David Mamet's newest play in progress. He wants her for the lead role. A Lincoln Town Car picked her up. She'd planned to take Lulu home with her, but the driver refused to allow her in his car."

"Meanie. So what are *you* planning to do?"

"I thought I'd drive down to Bluff Point so Lulu can get a chance to romp around on the beach for her very first time."

Maggie smiled. "What fun. Are you free this evening?"

"Completely."

"Why don't you come over and I'll make you your favorite home-cooked meal?"

"Are we talking meat loaf and mashed potatoes?"

"We are."

"I'd love it."

"Do you remember where I live?"

"Around the corner on Elm, fourth house on the left, as if I could forget. What time should I stroll over?"

"Is six too early for a sophisticated New Yorker?"

"Not in the least. And I have an excellent bottle of Chianti Classico that I can bring. Do you mind if Lulu tags along?"

"I'd love it."

"Great. We'll see you at six," I said as Lulu and I strolled out to the Jag. I unlocked the passenger side door, unhooked her leash and tucked her into her carrier. Then I unlocked my door, started the Jag up with a roar and drove back to the old Hoag homestead. It was when I got out to unlock the padlock on the garage that I discovered that the apartment door had been pried open.

Someone had broken in.

◆

There was zero doubt in my mind as to who the culprits were because Lulu started sneezing her head off as soon as we walked in.

I stood there looking around the living room with my fists clenched angrily, remembering how Mike Mallory had told me that Kevin and Destiny just needed a helping hand. Well, they'd helped themselves. Taken the apartment's only contents of value—starting with its not-nearly-new eighteen-inch Sylvania television. Happily, Merilee had taken her things with her so they hadn't been able to help themselves to any of her valuable wardrobe or jewelry. And my gray flannel suit from Strickland and Sons had been airing out down in the padlocked garage. But they *had* taken my cherished 1933 A-2 Werber flight jacket with my charter member Soupy Sales Society pin on the inside of its collar, Grandfather's gold cuff links and straight razor, the bottle of Chianti Classico I'd intended to take to Maggie's for dinner, and Merilee's French press coffee maker, probably because they didn't know what it was and thought it might be valuable. They hadn't bothered with my dress shirts, silk neckties or my bench-made brogans. Aficionados of men's clothing they were not. Nor had they bothered with the signed first edition of John O'Hara's *Waiting for Winter* that was sitting on my nightstand. Clearly, they had no concept of the value of a signed first edition by a great American author. They'd stowed what they'd taken in my Il Bisonte weekend bag, because that was nowhere to be seen.

By the time I'd finished looking around, Pat Dennis had returned home and parked in front of her unit. I strode up the driveway and tapped on her door.

When she opened it, she gave me a warmer reception than she had yesterday. "Why, hello again, Stewart. How may I—?"

"I'm sorry to report that while we were at the library, someone broke into the apartment and stole your television set and several valuable items of mine, including my grandfather's gold cuff links."

"Oh, dear . . ." Her face furrowed fretfully. "Did Miss Nash lose any valuable jewelry?"

"She had to return to New York City this morning, so there was nothing of hers here."

"Well, that's a small comfort. I'm so terribly sorry. I'll call the locksmith at once. And I'll have to call Trooper Schlosski, too. The landlord will require a police report for insurance purposes."

"Of course," I said. "I'm going to see if I can retrieve what was taken. I have a pretty good idea who took it."

"Kevin McKenna?" Pat shook her Q-Tip head disgustedly. "Be careful, Stewart."

"Kevin doesn't scare me."

"But he consorts with scary people. If you're not back by the time the locksmith finishes, I'll put the new key under my doormat. I'm so sorry about this. It hasn't been much of a welcome home for you, has it?"

"That's okay, I wasn't expecting one."

I unlocked the garage, put my gray flannel suit into my folding garment bag, and stowed it behind the seats in the Jag. I was leaving nothing of value behind. I put Lulu back her in her carrier and set it on the passenger seat. Then I closed the garage door, padlocked it, started up the Jag, and made straight for Mallory's, which opened at noon. The lights were on, but there were no customers inside and no sign of Mike behind the bar.

"I won't be long, girl."

Lulu whimpered in protest.

"You'll be better off if you stay here. I don't want anything to happen to you. Your mommy would kill me."

She fell grudgingly silent.

I locked the car, went inside and found Mike in the back room, where there was a convertible sofa that had not been folded back up into a sofa. The bed sheets and pillowcases were rumpled and didn't smell even remotely fresh. There were cases of Miller and Budweiser stacked back there. There was a filthy lavatory, a small three-drawer dresser and a coatrack that held a few items of Destiny's meager wardrobe, all of which reeked of patchouli. And there was a worktable with a Sylvania TV sitting on it where Mike, Kevin, and Destiny were sorting through the contents of my Il Bisonte weekend bag. I didn't need to search very hard for my Werber's flight jacket. Kevin was wearing it. It was so big on him it looked as if he were wearing his big brother's jacket. If he'd had a big brother.

The three of them looked up when they saw me standing there. Kevin and Destiny had utterly blank expressions on their faces, in sharp contrast to Mike's guilty one. Destiny was wearing the same skintight knit dress with nothing underneath it that she'd been wearing last night. Same boots, too. I didn't want to think about how often she changed her clothes. Or bathed.

"Your life's getting more pathetic by the minute, Mike," I said coldly.

He reddened. "I don't know what you mean, Hoagy. The kids collected some things around town and wondered if I'd be interested in any of them."

"I didn't realize that 'collected' had become synonymous with 'stolen.'"

"We didn't steal them," Kevin insisted with a whiny edge in his voice. "We found them."

"Bullshit. You broke into Rigby's old place, where Merilee and I have been staying, and cleaned out whatever you thought you could sell, like that TV set. And before we go any further, that's *my* antique flight jacket you're wearing. Take it the fuck off and give it to me right now."

"No way. It's mine."

"Oh, really? So you're a charter member of the Soupy Sales Society?"

He looked at me blankly. "Soupy who?"

I grabbed the collar and showed him my pin. "If you don't take it off right now, I'm calling Pete Schlosski."

That put a scare into him. One more bust meant that Kevin would have to do time in a state prison. He took the jacket off and gave it to me. I put it on over my turtleneck sweater. Destiny remained blank-faced and silent.

"Look, we're both hurting this morning, okay?" Kevin tried to explain, his voice growing whiny. "We needed to raise some money fast."

"Not my problem."

"Are you still going to call Schlosski?"

"Actually, Pat Dennis has already called him. You broke the lock and doorframe. To file an insurance claim, the landlord will need a police report. Pete's probably there right now."

"Are you going to tell him we took your stuff?"

"Not if it means I have to come back here to testify at your hearing. I never want to see this place, or you, again."

"Everything's in here." Kevin pushed my Il Bisonte bag toward me. "You could just take it back like this never happened."

"Is that right? Let's see . . ." I began pulling things out of the bag. "Here's my bottle of Chianti Classico, my French press coffee maker, straight razor . . . Hmm, I don't see my cuff links."

"What cuff links?"

Destiny heaved a disgusted sigh and handed them to me. She'd been clutching them in her hot little fist. They felt moist and greasy now. "Those are solid gold," she protested.

"That's why they're mine and not yours." I pocketed them.

"And there's the TV set," Kevin pointed out. "Good as new. Well, not new, but . . ."

"Mike, I'm taking this stuff back to the apartment with me. I hope you're not going to try to stop me."

"Wouldn't think of it, Hoagy," he said defeatedly.

"But I don't have room in my car for the TV."

"I'll swing by later and drop it off," Mike promised. "I didn't know this stuff was yours, Hoagy. Honest, I didn't."

"Boca Raton, Mike. You've got to join your daughter down there. Heed the advice of Eric Burdon: You gotta get outta this place if it's the last thing you ever do."

"Eric who?" asked Kevin, puzzled.

Mike ducked his head, "I know. You're absolutely right."

I zipped my bag shut and glared at Kevin and Destiny. "As for you two, you need to get into a treatment program, get clean, and find something to do with your lives. Otherwise, you'll be dead before you're thirty."

Destiny curled her lip at me. "So what? Everybody dies."

I didn't bother to respond. Just grabbed my bag and headed out of the back room into the saloon. Mike still had no customers, but a black Bronco was parked outside in front of the Jag. Sly and Shade were walking around the Jag and admiring it. Shade was also taunting Lulu by tapping on the window and making scary faces at her. Lulu was yowling, terribly frightened by him.

"Can I help you guys?" I asked as I stood there on the sidewalk with my bag. Lulu quieted down now that I was there. "Let me guess, you just bought a copy of my book at Barnes and Noble and want me to autograph it for you."

"Nice ride," Sly said. "What is it?"

"So that's a no on the autograph?"

He stared at me in hostile silence. He was wearing a belted black leather jacket and black jeans, same as last night. Shade was still dressed for the weight room—tank top, gym shorts, and sneakers.

"It's a vintage Jaguar roadster," I said.

"Jaguar," Sly repeated. That's British, right?"

I unlocked the boot and put my bag inside. "I repeat, can I help you guys?"

"You're messing in our business. I warned you last night to stay out of it."

"Did you? I don't remember that, but I took a lot of psychedelics in the early seventies and suffer from occasional short-term memory losses."

"You want to know something?" Sly said.

"Sure. I'm always interested in finding out new things."

"It'd be a good idea for you to get out of town before something happens to you."

"*Or* to your dog," Shade said, starting his way toward me menacingly.

"Please tell me you didn't just threaten my puppy."

He continued moving toward me, flexing his giant biceps. "Why?"

I grabbed the twenty-four-inch forged steel tire iron that was stowed in the Jag's boot and cracked him across his right kneecap with it as hard as I could. "That's why."

Shade crumpled to the ground, groaning in pain.

In response, Sly came rushing at me angrily right up until his nose ran directly into my right fist, which stopped him cold and sat him down. His nose immediately began gushing blood.

Slowly, he climbed to his feet, reached around in the Bronco for a rag, and held it to his nose, which continued to bleed. "You just made a big mistake."

"I make them all of the time. You should have seen the first six drafts of my novel." I put the tire iron back in the boot and slammed it shut. Shade still lay on the sidewalk, clutching his knee and groaning in pain. "You can threaten me all you want, but do not threaten Lulu. Are we clear about that? And by the way, Sly, if you want to up your game I'd suggest you work on your patter a bit. It's straight out of a bad Brian De Palma movie, which is not to suggest there's such a thing as a good Brian De Palma movie. Try an early Kubrick called *The Killing*. Or John Huston's *Asphalt Jungle*. You're not writing this down. I can't believe you're not writing it down. This is valuable advice I'm giving you."

Shade was still crumpled on the sidewalk, groaning, when I unlocked the Jag and got in. Lulu whimpered at me. "Everything's okay," I said to her reassuringly. "I would never let those bozos hurt you."

She continued to whimper at me. "Oh, were you worried about *me*? No need. I can take care of myself."

I drove back to the apartment but had to pull up short of the garage because it was blocked by a locksmith's van and a Crown Vic. The locksmith was reinforcing the door frame with a steel plate, and Pete Schlosski was chatting with Pat Dennis. I left the Jag in the driveway for now, lifted Lulu out in her carrier, and fetched my garment bag and Il Bisonte bag.

"Here, let me give me give you a hand," Pete said, grabbing the Il Bisonte as we slipped past the locksmith and carried everything inside. I let Lulu out. She immediately went to her dish in search of food. Finding none, she sat and stared at the refrigerator, which was her way of reminding me that I'd promised her an anchovy as a treat for what she'd found under the daybed in the librarians' lounge. Elephants and basset hounds never forget.

I fed her one and said, "I recovered everything that was stolen, Pete. The TV set is still at Mike Mallory's. I didn't have room for it in my car. Mike promised he'd drop it by later."

"Yeah, he promised me, too. Called up a minute ago. Hoagy, did you just kneecap Shade with a tire iron on the sidewalk in front of Mike's saloon *and* give Sly a bloody nose?"

"Had to. Shade was terrorizing Lulu. No one does that to her. I'm assuming they'd stopped by because Kevin had contacted them in the hope that he and Destiny had stolen enough stuff from here to square their vig with Mike."

"Yeah, that sounds about right," Pete said disgustedly. "I understand from Pat Dennis that Miss Nash has gone back to New York City on business."

"Correct. Maggie has invited me over for dinner at six."

"Good. I live right across the street from her and can walk you over there. I'd stay home the rest of the day if I were you."

"But I was going to drive down to Bluff Point."

"I wouldn't. They're liable to follow you. Don't drive anywhere. Don't stroll around town either. Stay put. Sly and Shade are dangerous. They don't have big IQs, but they do have big egos. You knocked them down a peg. They'll try to get even. Count on it. I've alerted the Narcotics Task Force, but they can't devote their manpower to them day and night, so I'll do my best to keep an eye on you. I don't want you to get shot on my watch."

"That makes two of us." On Lulu's whimper I said, "Make that three of us. If it's any help, Shade will probably end up at the hospital in Fulton sometime today to get his knee x-rayed."

Pete's eyes widened. "Are you telling me you *shattered* his kneecap?"

"I have no idea. I'm not a doctor. I don't even play one on television. But he never got up off of that sidewalk or stopped groaning."

Pete shook his head at me. "For a smart guy, you do some pretty stupid things."

"I'm an artist."

"What's that supposed to mean?"

"It means I do some pretty stupid things."

The locksmith was all finished up. He put his tools back in his van, then went to Pat's apartment to give her the new keys and go over the paperwork. After he took off she gave me one of the keys, apologized once more, and returned to her place. I moved the Jag into the garage and padlocked it.

Pete stayed put in the living room, hat on his head, hands resting on his garrison belt. "Do you want to press charges against Kevin and Destiny?"

"Not necessary. I got everything back."

"You got yourself into a serious situation, is what you got."

"I appreciate your concern, Pete. I'll be careful."

"See that you are." And with that he tipped his Smokey hat at me and lumbered out.

Lulu had gone back to staring at the refrigerator. She wanted another anchovy. I had owed her the first one. This one was for the trauma of dealing with Sly and Shade. Being a soft touch, I gave it to her.

"Your mommy wasn't gone for much more than an hour before we got into our first fight. I hope this isn't a harbinger of things to come."

She tilted her head at me curiously, just like Nipper, the RCA Victor dog. "Is harbinger too big a word for you? Sorry, I should have said a *sign* of things to come."

I helped myself to two of Betsy Sherman's home-made deviled ham sandwiches and a glass of milk. I was rinsing out the glass when I heard the steady *thump-thump-thump* of a car stereo's bass idling out front. I went to the window to have a look. It was the black Bronco, Sly behind the wheel, Shade riding shotgun with a big bag of ice on his painful knee. Pete Schlosski hadn't been kidding. They were taking our sidewalk confrontation seriously.

As I stood there watching them, a Crown Vic pulled up behind them and parked. They immediately took off.

It was a newer, shinier Crown Vic than Pete's, and the man who got out, locked it, and strode up the driveway to knock on the apartment door was most definitely not Pete.

CHAPTER SEVEN

Looming there in the doorway was an extremely tall, broad-shouldered black man, about forty, wearing a charcoal gray suit, white shirt and muted tie. He was a good two or three inches taller than I am, which meant he was six feet five or six, and looked extremely trim and fit. His hair was cropped short and showed a few traces of gray. His face was clean-shaven. He had an extremely stern expression on his face, bordering on severe. He would, I imagined, be a very intimidating person to be grilled by.

I was glad he wasn't there to grill me. Or I certainly I hoped he wasn't.

"Stewart Hoag?" he asked me in a baritone voice.

"Yes, that's right."

"Mr. Hoag, I'm Detective Lieutenant Mitry of the Connecticut State Police Major Crime Squad, Eastern District. I'm investigating the homicide of Mary McKenna. I've had several conversations with her daughter, Maggie, and she suggested I speak with you. Said you had been close to the victim and might have some personal insights to share."

"Absolutely. Anything I can do to help." I stuck out my hand. He shook it. His was the largest hand I'd ever shaken in my life. Given his height and the way he carried himself I was curious if he'd played college basketball before he joined the state police, but he did not come across as the sort of man who'd invite a personal inquiry. "Come on in."

He came on in, looming large as he gazed around at the living room. "I understand from Maggie that this entire apartment complex was once your family's home."

"You understand right. This was the caretaker's place."

As he stood there, Lulu whimpered and tried to climbed up his leg. Lieutenant Mitry looked down at her, his facial expression thawing perhaps one degree. "Well, now, look at you." He picked her up and cradled her in the palm of his huge right hand as if she were scarcely bigger than a hamster.

"That's Lulu. I don't know if she'll grow into her ears or if they'll just keep getting bigger. The lady in my life had to go back to New York City this morning on urgent business, so it's just us two for now. After Mrs. McKenna's funeral tomorrow morning, we'll be heading home. This is the first time I've been back in Oakmont since I graduated from high school, but I had to pay my respects to Mrs. McKenna. She meant a lot to me. Have a seat, Lieutenant."

"Thank you." He settled himself on the sofa. "This lady in your life to whom you refer would be Merilee Nash?"

"Correct," I said as I heard the *thump-thump-thump* of the black Bronco's stereo slowly approaching again.

Lieutenant Mitry immediately went to the window to have a look. Sly and Shade didn't linger when they saw his Crown Vic still parked there—and the man himself standing in the window watching them. They sped off.

Mitry remained at the window, gazing out at the street. "I remember driving through this town many times in my youth. It was prosperous, clean, and the town green was lovely. Now it's a blighted, run-down magnet for druggies."

"That's what happens when a mill goes under. Especially a toxic one like my family's brass mill. The owners leave nothing behind but malign neglect."

He turned his gaze from the window to me. "I gather from Maggie that's what your novel is about. It must be quite a feeling of accomplishment, writing a novel and having it be so well received."

"I've been very pleased with the response."

"I also gather that the two of you were very close."

I nodded. "Best buddies. We spent our childhood together seated back-to-back on the floor of that library devouring books and Snickers bars."

He returned to the sofa and sat back down. This time Lulu climbed her way into his lap. He petted her. "Maggie has never married?"

"She told me she came close once. A dentist in Fulton. But she broke it off. Thought he was boring."

"What about you?"

"Couldn't say. I never met the guy."

"No, I mean have you ever been married?"

"Not yet. The closest I came was a wild affair in the seventies with a gifted poet named Regina Aintree. We haunted the punk rock clubs. Tore our way up to after-hours dance clubs in Spanish Harlem on my motorcycle. I had a Norton Commando in those days."

"Had yourself a sheet, too," he said with chilly disapproval, pulling a small notepad from the breast pocket of his suit. "Reckless driving, drunk and disorderly, indecent exposure. You also threw a barstool through the front window of a restaurant called P.J. Clarke's. There was a man sitting on it at the time. Why did you do that, Mr. Hoag?"

"Because he stole my seat. I was an angry young man, Lieutenant. Angry at my father. Angry at everyone. A lot of first novelists are. I needed to write it out of my system."

"And now you're, what, living the life of a prosperous man of letters?"

"Compared to the three years I spent banging my head against the wall of my crummy, unheated apartment, the life I'm living now is like a dream. But when Maggie phoned to tell me about her mom, it brought me right back down to earth. I can't believe that somebody bashed Mrs. McKenna's head in. I understand the weapon was her cast-iron Mark Twain paperweight."

"Correct."

"I gather you didn't find any fingerprints on it or you would have a suspect in custody by now."

"Also correct. It was wiped clean. And no one witnessed anyone leaving the library at the time of her death, which we believe to be a mere few minutes before Maggie arrived at six o'clock to drive her home. It was Maggie who found her there at her desk with multiple wounds to the back of her head."

"Were you able to tell anything from those wounds?"

Lieutenant Mitry raised his chin at me slightly. "Such as . . . ?"

"How tall her killer was, how strong, whether he—or she—was right- or left-handed. Anything of that nature?"

"Mary McKenna was a frail leukemia patient. Two blows would have been enough to kill her, yet she was struck six times with considerable force."

"Does 'considerable force' mean that you think a man killed her?"

"Not necessarily. It could have been a woman who was in a state of extreme rage. The blows were struck from several different angles so it's very difficult to determine the height of her assailant, especially if she was collapsing over the desk when the final blows were being inflicted. Same as to whether her assailant was right- or left-handed. That's a myth they sell on TV cop shows."

"Is an enraged killer likely to carefully wipe their prints from the murder weapon?"

"That's a fair question. You'd think they would be in a hurry to get the hell out of there. But the answer is yes. I've seen it happen more times than I care to recall." He paused, narrowing his gaze slightly. "You wondered if a woman might have killed her. Have someone in mind?"

"Destiny, her son Kevin's so-called girlfriend. I'm sure you're aware by now that both Destiny and Kevin freebase crack."

"I am. I'm also aware that freebasing can lead to sudden mood swings, including rage."

"Mrs. McKenna tried repeatedly to get Kevin into a drug treatment program but he wouldn't go because she refused to extend the same helping hand to Destiny, whom she detested. Kevin became so desperate for drug money that he stole his mother's television set and handgun. She responded by throwing him out of the house and changing the locks. He moved in with Destiny in the back room of Mike Mallory's saloon, where she slings drinks and gives blow jobs. She was deeply resentful that Mrs. McKenna was anxious to help Kevin but didn't give a damn about her. That much I know."

"I'm sure you know a whole lot more."

"Okay. I know that Mrs. McKenna was a beloved figure in Oakmont but that she'd also made her share of enemies. She was furious with Mike Mallory, who dabbles as a loan shark, for loaning Kevin drug money. They had angry words recently, and she banned Mike from the library. He told me she could be a very hard woman. I believe the words he used were 'coldhearted bitch.'"

Mitry's jaw muscles tightened. "Would you consider him a suspect?"

"I would. His life is a total mess right now and he's capable of just about anything. So is Kevin, who hated his mother bitterly. So are Sly and Shade. Could be they showed up at the library when she was there alone and demanded the drug money Kevin owed them. Could be she said no, reached for the phone to report them to Trooper Schlosski, and Shade bashed her head in."

"Evidently, *you've* made enemies of Sly and Shade. I understand you scuffled on the sidewalk in front of Mallory's with them today. That was reckless of you."

"I didn't consider it reckless. I felt physically threatened, so I caught them by surprise by striking the first blow. Best thing to do if you're outnumbered."

"Perhaps," he allowed. "But you've stripped them of their precious manhood. They're small-time punks with big-time ambitions. If I were you, I'd clear out of Oakmont as soon as you can."

"Believe me, I'll be gone tomorrow just as soon as my shovel of dirt hits Mrs. McKenna's coffin."

"And I'd stay home this afternoon, if I were you."

"Trooper Schlosski suggested the very same thing. I'm having dinner around the corner at Maggie's at six. He lives right across the street from her. He intends to walk me over there and escort me home."

"Good," the lieutenant said approvingly.

"Pete and I were high school classmates. I never imagined he'd turn out to be a state trooper. He seems to be a good one."

"That he is. Won't surprise me one bit if he ends up on the Major Crime Squad before long."

"But it so happens that *he* tangled with Mrs. McKenna himself back when we were in high school. She tore up his library card and banned him for a year."

Lieutenant Mitry soaked this in, intensely interested. "Why was that?"

"This is a bit awkward, but Trooper Schlosski's nickname in those days was Peter the Beater."

He furrowed his brow. "And why was that?"

"Because he used to drift off in class and flog his meat."

"You're kidding me."

"I wish I were. Every boy in the school called him Peter the Beater. In fact, it's hard for me not to call him that now. Mrs. McKenna caught him doing it in the library one afternoon when he was drifting off over his homework, threw him out, and banned him. He was incredibly hurt because the library was the only place in town he could go and be left in peace."

"You're not suggesting *he* may have something to do with her death, are you?"

"Just sharing some of my personal insights, as you requested. Most of the boys used to head for Super Drug for chocolate milkshakes after school. It was on the town green. Doesn't exist anymore. Nor does Gene Dennis, who owned it. When my father shut down the mill, people started clearing out of town and Gene saw his profits fall so dramatically that he had trouble paying his rent. My shithead father evicted him. A few days later Gene took his pistol into the woods and blew his brains out. His widow, Pat, manages this apartment complex."

"So she harbors no love for your father, I suppose."

"You suppose right. She wasn't exactly thrilled about renting this place to me when I showed up for here for Mrs. McKenna's funeral, what with me being his son. She did it strictly as a favor to Maggie."

He sat there in silence for a long moment, his wheels turning.

"Is there anything else I can help you with, Lieutenant?"

"Sum it up for me, if you don't mind. Who you think might have killed Mary McKenna and why. In no particular order."

"Okay, if you think it'll help."

"It'll help," he assured me.

"It could be that Kevin and Destiny stopped by the library, wanted drug money from her, she wouldn't give them any, and one of them brained her. Was her purse robbed?"

"Good question. Yes, it was. Its contents were dumped on the desk. According to Maggie, her mother rarely carried more than fifty dollars in cash, but whatever she had was gone. Nothing else was taken. Her credit cards weren't touched and she wore no valuable jewelry. Who's next on your list?"

"Mike Mallory, the saloon keeper. He never struck me as the violent type, but he also doesn't strike me as someone who'd be pimping out Destiny and moonlighting as a loan shark and fence. He's awfully cozy with Sly and Shade, too, and feels none too proud of what's happened to his life. Has a daughter in Boca Raton who wants him to join her down there. He should, but if I were a betting man, which I'm not, I'd say he'll probably never leave this place. Mike and Mrs. McKenna exchanged angry words recently over Mike loaning Kevin money for drugs. He won't loan Kevin another nickel until Kevin makes good on the two hundred dollars of vig for what he's already loaned him. Kevin and Destiny broke into my apartment this morning and took whatever they thought they could fence. I knew it was them right away."

"How did you know that?"

"Lulu sneezed."

"Sorry?"

"She's allergic to patchouli, Destiny's scent of choice. They stole Pat's television. They stole my antique leather flight jacket and my grandfather's gold cuff links and a few other things that they thought might be of value. I headed straight for Mallory's Saloon and found the three of them in the back room sorting through it."

"Trooper Schlosski told me you've declined to press charges. Why is that?"

"Because I got my possessions back and I don't want to have to come back here for a criminal hearing."

"It was outside of Mallory's, after you'd loaded up your car, that you got into your ill-advised altercation with Sly and Shade, formally known as Steven Romano and Clarence Sadowski. Oakmont is one of several small towns where those two sell drugs. They're by no means big-money dealers yet, but they're hooked up with a rough gang in Willimantic and are hoping to go places. Does anyone else come to mind? Possibly from Mary McKenna's past?"

"Not really. She had a circle of devoted friends, all of them older ladies like Pat Dennis, whom I encountered at her reading club this morning. Maggie's keeping the club going. They were extremely fond of her."

"And you were fond of her yourself, I gather."

"I was. She gave me the confidence to believe that I could achieve my dream to be a writer. She was like an antidote to my father, who demanded I take a position at the mill when I graduated from Harvard. He refused to allow me to think of doing anything else with my life. And he refused to believe that the mill was about to go belly up—which it did two years after I graduated. He blamed *me* for that as if I could have stopped the flow of history. All of the brass mills were failing. He took no responsibility for the lead poisoning that took the lives of so many mill workers and their families and continues to do so to this very day. He even went so far as to renege on their health and pension benefits. Just took off for Vero Beach with my mom and never came back."

"How well do you get along with him now?"

"I don't."

"Are you on speaking terms with him?"

"That would be a no."

"Must be a lot of mixed emotions for you, being back here," he observed.

I nodded.

"Is there anything more you care to share with me?"

My thoughts strayed back to that discovery Lulu had made underneath the daybed in the librarians' lounge that morning. But that wasn't something I was ready to talk to him about yet. "Nothing that that I can think of."

He peered at me. "Sure about that?"

"Why are you asking?"

"Seemed as if you were turning something over in your mind."

"Oh, that. I'm a writer. Happens all of the time."

"I see," he said, unconvinced. His own mind was very sharp.

Again I heard the *thump-thump-thump* of a car stereo out on the street, but since Mitry's Crown Vic was still parked there, Sly and Shade kept right on going.

He got up off of the sofa and rose to his full height. "I'm tempted to put you under police protection until you leave for New York City, but as long as you stay here and have Trooper Schlosski nearby to keep an eye on you, I don't think it's necessary. If those two try to get even with you today, they'll end up behind bars. They're not that stupid."

"Are you sure about that?"

He allowed himself a faint smile. Very faint. "Have a safe trip back to New York City tomorrow. And thank you for your time and your insights."

"I can't imagine I told you anything you haven't already thought of."

"You'd be wrong about that. You gave me some fresh perspective, and a lot to chew on. I appreciate it."

"In that case it was my pleasure, Lieutenant," I said, before I quickly added, "our pleasure."

CHAPTER EIGHT

I t wasn't long after Lieutenant Mitry took off that I heard the steady *thump-thump-thump* of the black Bronco's sound system outside of my window yet again. It was impossible to make out any melody but if I were a betting man, which I'm not, I'd wager that Sly and Shade were major Twisted Sister fans.

I looked out the window at them idling out there at the curb, trying to scare me. They were failing miserably. Okay, I just lied. Being harassed by two armed, pissed-off drug dealers with gang ties didn't exactly soothe my soul. Mind you, they didn't get a chance to idle out there for long before Pete Schlosski pulled up next to them, got out of his cruiser, and tapped on Sly's window. Sly lowered it. Pete said something to him. I couldn't hear what it was, but it prompted Sly to roll up his window and drive off down the street. As soon as the Bronco was gone Pete steered his cruiser into the driveway and parked. I opened the door and invited him in.

"Hiya, Hoagy." He bent down to pat Lulu, who thumped her tail. "You sure did make a pair of real pals for yourself today."

"Lieutenant Mitry was just here. He thinks I'm going to have a problem with them."

"He's not wrong," Pete responded. "They're steaming mad. Shade's knee hurts so much he can barely put any weight on it. You can expect some payback, no question."

"What did you say to them?"

"That if I see them idling here again, I'm going to run them in for harassment. Sly said, 'Hey, it's a free country.' And I said, 'Whoever told you that was lying to you.'" Pete tilted his Smokey hat back on his head an inch and said, "I'm supposed to keep an eye on you. What time are you heading over to Maggie's for dinner?"

"Six."

"I'll drive you over there."

"It's just around the corner."

"Okay, then I'll walk you over there."

"Pete, that's really not necessary. I'll be fine."

"I'm walking you over there," he said, leaving no room for argument. "I'll see you a few minutes before six." He gave Lulu another pat on the head and took off.

As he drove away, I felt an overwhelming sense of despair wash over me. They say you can't go home again. They're wrong about that. You can. It's just a totally unpleasant experience. That was why I'd never come back. It took Mrs. McKenna's death to force my hand. And now that Merilee was no longer with me, the novelty of showing her around was gone. So was her determination to be upbeat about the experience. Plus, I missed her. We hadn't been apart for more than a couple of hours at a stretch since that night when we'd first set eyes on each other in the Blue Mill.

I kicked off my sneakers and stretched out on the bed with a notepad and my Waterman fountain pen. Lulu made use of the stool we'd positioned at the foot of the bed, climbed up onto my chest, licked my face, and made contented little noises.

"Lulu, is it just me or do you think we're bonding? Are you in the mood for a nap? How would that be?"

Lulu seemed to like that idea very much. She nestled on my chest and went to sleep in no time while I jotted down a few bullet points for the eulogy I was to deliver tomorrow at Mrs. McKenna's funeral. Then I set the pad and pen aside, followed Lulu's example, and dozed for a little while myself. It had been a hectic day.

It was a few minutes past four when I woke up, according to Grandfather's Benrus. Lulu woke up, too, climbed down off of the bed and treated me to her new "feed me" howl. I figured it would be a good idea to feed her now so she wouldn't have an urgent need to take care of personal business in the middle of dinner at Maggie's. Got up and gave her a half can of 9Lives mackerel and stood there watching her, pleased, as she devoured it hungrily. She was turning into a real nose bowl champ. After she'd licked her bowl clean, she lapped up some water and then took something akin to a victory lap around the living room, whooping playfully.

Me, I took a quick shower and dressed in a Ramones T-shirt, burgundy cashmere crewneck sweater, jeans, and my Chuck Taylors. Turned on the porch light. Found a grocery bag and put the bottle of Chianti Classico in it. At exactly ten minutes before six I heard heavy footsteps out on the driveway and a tap at the door.

Lulu let out a bark. She had herself a big bark on her for someone with no legs.

"It's me, Hoagy!" Pete Schlosski called out.

I let him in. He was still in full uniform. On duty.

I put on my flight jacket, fetched Lulu's leash, and hooked it to her collar. "Come on, girl, we're about to have dinner with another woman. But it's okay, your mommy won't mind." I left a living room and porch light on, grabbed the wine bottle, and locked the door behind us, pausing to make sure that the garage was padlocked before we strolled in silence down to the sidewalk and started in the direction of Elm Street. It was a cloudy night with no moonlight to illuminate the darkness and rather dim streetlights. The evening air gave off that *eau de Oakmont* scent of dead fish and toxic chemicals.

"Get any more drive-by visits from your new pals?" Pete asked me.

"I didn't hear any, now that you mention it."

"Possibly that's because I just heard that Shade's at the hospital in Fulton getting his knee x-rayed. It must have hurt like hell for a muscle-bound tough guy like him to give in and go to the hospital. The security guard there said that Shade even had to use a wheelchair. Let me tell you, if you shattered his kneecap, you will be even less popular with those two than you are now."

"He wanted to provoke a confrontation. He got one. Did I break Sly's nose while I was at it?"

"Don't believe so. He didn't ask for medical attention."

"Too bad."

We rounded the corner onto Elm, which I remembered as being a nice mill workers' street of small, well-kept houses with neatly tended front yards. That was no longer the case. As we strolled our way along, we passed two houses that had fallen into such disrepair that they'd been boarded up, another that had burned to the ground and another that needed a new roof so badly that big blue tarps were stretched across it and held in place with bricks. There were four beat-up old pickups clustered in front.

"Do you remember the Pardo brothers from Mary McKenna's wake?" Pete said. "That's the place they share with those two other losers who were with them out on the front steps of the mortuary. Not one steady job between the four of them, but they manage to scrape enough bucks together to pay the rent and party like there's no tomorrow. Sly and Shade sell them loads of weed. Not that I can prove it. I just know it."

There were heaps of fallen maple leaves on the sidewalks and most of the lawns. No one was bothering to rake them up. Lulu thoroughly enjoyed crashing her way through them. I heard a car ease by us. So did Pete, who stiffened immediately, but it was just someone coming home in their Jeep and pulling into a driveway down the block.

My feet remembered where Maggie's small brick house was without any help from my so-called brain. Her leaves had been raked up and bagged. The lawn was mowed, too.

"Well, here we are," he said. "Have a nice evening. Maggie certainly deserves to enjoy herself with an old friend. She's had a rough time of it between taking care of her mom, the library, that crackhead jerk Kevin, and his trampy crackhead girlfriend. But Maggie's one tough lady, just like her mom was."

"Yes, she is."

"That's me, Mary Ellen, and the girls right over there," he said, gesturing toward the place directly across the street, where the lawn was also mowed and the leaves raked up and bagged. My guess was that Pete had taken care of Maggie's yard for her while he was at it. "When you're ready to head back, just flick the porch light on and off and I'll be right over."

"It's nice of you to offer, Pete, but I really don't think you need to—"

"Don't try to talk me out of it, Hoagy. I'm following Mitry's orders."

"In that case, thanks."

He strode across the street to his house while I walked up the familiar steps to the porch, used the door knocker, and waited there with Lulu.

Maggie opened the door and stood there with a wistful smile on her face.

She'd changed into jeans and a silk blouse that accentuated her breasts with a discreet bit of cleavage. She'd also dabbed on some perfume. It was the same perfume she used to wear in high school. Jean Naté. I recognized it instantly.

"Hi, Hoagy."

"Hi, back at you. I brought a friend. Also some Chianti Classico."

"Not to mention a resident trooper escort."

"Pete insisted. I had a bit of an altercation this afternoon."

"I heard. The word's all over town. What on earth were you thinking, mixing it up with Sly and Shade?"

"Lulu was in the Jag in her carrier and that big baboon Shade was frightening her. I put a stop to it. It was over very fast."

She shook her head at me. "I'll never understand men."

"We're complex, but we're not deep."

"Your timing is perfect. I was just about to put the meat loaf in the oven. Come on in."

We went on in. I unhooked Lulu's leash and she roamed her way around, nose to the carpet.

"I sure do love your vintage leather jacket," Maggie said, admiring it.

"If you detect a faint odor of patchouli, it's because it was stolen briefly today by Kevin and Destiny."

She looked at me in dismay. "How did . . . ?"

"They broke into the apartment while I was at the library with you and took whatever they thought was of value. Pat's television. My grandfather's gold cuff links. This jacket . . . Lulu started sneezing as soon as we walked in the door. She's allergic to Destiny's patchouli. So I drove straight to Mike's saloon and found them in his back room trying to sell him what they'd stolen to raise enough money to buy crack.

Mike sure has fallen on hard times. Not only loan sharking, but fencing stolen goods. But I got there in time to get everything back."

"I'm glad for that, but *damn* Kev and Destiny. They make my life hell. I wish . . ." She broke off into angry silence. "Tell you what, let's not talk about them. And now I'd better put our meat loaf in the oven."

She darted into the kitchen while I stood there in the living room, taking it all in. It was as if time had stopped here. Everything was exactly the same. Same matching cocoa-colored corduroy sofa and easy chair. Same coffee table. Same pictures on the walls—framed still life drawings that Maggie had done in a high school art class. She'd had talent, but never pursued it.

She returned, wiping her hands on a dish towel.

"I can't believe that everything's exactly the same," I said.

"Well, not everything. The TV's brand new, courtesy of Kevin."

"Shall I open the wine?"

"Please. The corkscrew's in the drawer to the left of the sink."

The kitchen was the same, too. Same pink-and-charcoal tile counters, a color combination that had been all the rage back in the fifties. Same blue-and-gold linoleum floor, which had been equally popular. Same Formica kitchen table and vinyl chairs that looked almost exactly like the table and chairs in Rigby's place except that these were bright blue instead of bright yellow. The table was set for two. The McKennas had always eaten dinner in the kitchen. The was no dining area in the living room. I dug the corkscrew out of the drawer and opened the wine, then found a couple of wineglasses in a cupboard and poured us some.

By the time I returned to the living room Lulu had made herself at home in Maggie's lap on the sofa. "Lulu, you are absolutely *the* cutest puppy I've ever seen. Yes, you are." Which earned her a thorough nose licking. Maggie drew back, slightly aghast. "Hoagy, her breath is . . ."

"You have only yourself to blame for that. Or I should say Leon does, as does Rigby."

"How does Rigby enter into this?"

"There was a prehistoric jar of anchovies in his fridge. When I opened it, Lulu started raising a fuss, so I rinsed one off and nearly lost a finger feeding it to her. She loves them."

I handed Maggie one of the wineglasses and joined them on the sofa. Lulu rolled over onto her back and got a belly rub from Maggie, her tail thumping happily. Lulu's, that is, not Maggie's.

I sniffed at the air as the meat loaf began to bake. "Now my sense memories are really in a time warp. That's your mom's recipe. Sauteed bacon, onion, and . . . one more ingredient. What is it?"

"Bell pepper."

"Bell pepper, right. I'm so glad we're doing this."

"So am I, Hoagy."

I raised my glass. "What shall we drink to?"

"How about old times?"

"That'll do, although I was going to suggest the daybed in the librarians' lounge."

She swatted me playfully. "Now you're being naughty."

"I've always been naughty. Just ask Lieutenant Mitry. He has my sheet from when I first moved to New York and was in punk rock heaven. My record includes reckless driving, drunk and disorderly, destruction of public property, indecent exposure . . ."

Her eyes widened. "*Indecent exposure*? No details, please. I don't ever want to know."

"He paid me a visit this afternoon. Was not at all pleased that I got into that altercation with Sly and Shade. He seems to think I'm in mortal danger for making them look like a couple of wimps. Suggested I leave town as soon as possible. I assured him I'd be packed and ready to leave right after the graveside ceremony."

Maggie's face fell, as if the prospect of my leaving so soon saddened her. "Is that why Lieutenant Mitry paid you a visit?"

"No, he mostly wanted the benefit of any insights I cared to share about who might have wanted your mom dead."

"Meaning he still has no idea who killed her?"

"If he does, he's sure playing it close to the vest. The man's a serious pro. Didn't share much with me, other than that the blows could have been struck by a man or a woman. I know we promised not to discuss them, but I sensed that he likes Kevin and Destiny for it."

Maggie sighed. "Kevin thinks Destiny's the great love of his life, but she's nothing but a drugged-out whore. Mom despised her." She paused to take a sip of her wine. "Destiny's such a tiny thing. Could she have bashed Mom's head in with that paperweight?"

"She and Kevin freebase crack, which makes people speedy and crazed. Also desperate, because it's so highly addictive. Mitry didn't come out and say it, but he gave me the impression that if Destiny got strung out and enraged enough, she definitely could have done it. He also mentioned that whoever killed her stole all of the cash from her purse. No credit cards. Just cash."

"He mentioned that to me, too. Mom didn't usually carry very much, but Kevin and Destiny would have taken it, that's for sure."

"Mitry also has Mike Mallory in his sights. Mike sure has fallen far. He used to run a nice, decent saloon. Now he's a loan shark who pimps out Destiny, fences stolen goods and does business with Sly and Shade. Not that he's happy about it. The man's consumed by self-loathing and shame. He told me your mom hollered at him up, down, and sideways for loaning Kevin crack money. She even banned him from the library. Did you know that?"

"I did," Maggy replied unhappily. "And you're right. Mike's fallen a long way. When he lost his wife, he lost his moral compass. He's no longer a reputable person."

A timer went off in the kitchen.

"That means it's time for me to put the macaroni and cheese in."

"You made your mom's mac and cheese, too?" I asked, unable to keep the excitement out of my voice. It was the best I'd ever eaten. Her secret was that she used twice the amount of extra sharp cheddar that the recipe called for. "You're spoiling me."

"Just treating you to some good old-fashioned Oakmont hospitality. Back in a sec." Maggie set her wineglass on the coffee table, then went into the kitchen and made an assortment of stovetop and oven-door noises. She returned a moment later, sat back down, retrieved her wineglass, and said, "I meant to tell you—that was awfully nice of you to visit with the book club this morning."

"Are you kidding me? It's a real pleasure to talk to people who've read my book. Plus I got a supply of homemade deviled ham sandwiches out of it."

"I have to confess that I read it in a state of total terror. I thought you might have made me a character and that it would be about our relationship. Instead, you made up that affair with Mrs. Allen, our English teacher. You *did* make that part up, didn't you?"

"Of course, silly. And I would never have mentioned anything about what you and I shared together. That's private."

"I appreciate that. It's just that your protagonist, Samuel, is *so* you. A loner who lives inside of his own head. I can still remember how guarded and private you were when we first became friends at the library. It wasn't long before you were spending all of your time at the library with me. You didn't have many guy friends at school, did you?"

"I didn't have *any*. I was Boss Hoag's son. They hated me. I was rich and smart and they were none of the above. You were my only friend when we were kids."

"Why me?"

"Because you were smart and funny and you loved to read. And then, when puberty arrived, I realized you were kind of cute, too."

She blushed. "I'm surprised your folks didn't send you off to a fancy prep school."

"They wanted to, but I didn't want to go."

"Why not?"

"Because of you."

Now her eyes began to well up with tears.

"Looking at that daybed in the librarians' lounge yesterday sure brought back some memories. The first time I saw your bare breasts in the moonlight. The first time we held each other naked. Your skin was so smooth. I never knew that anything could feel so wonderful."

"Stop it, you're going to make me sob." She took a sip of her wine. "Can I ask you something rather awkward?"

"You can ask me anything."

"You never wrote me after you left for Harvard. Not once. You never came home for the summer. You just . . . vanished. I was so hurt. You were my first love and you totally abandoned me. Why did you?"

"I'm so sorry it seemed that way to you. It wasn't you. The day I left for Harvard, my dad told me he expected me to join the front office of the mill when I graduated and I told him I had no intention of doing so. We got into a huge shouting match. Haven't spoken since. My vanishing was strictly about him. How much I hated him and wanted to flee this place. I was only thinking about myself. Looking back on it now, I should have handled it so much better. Called you, written you. But I was a seventeen-year-old jerk. I didn't think about how much it would hurt you that I didn't come home for a single summer to be with you. All I could think about was how much I wanted to be *gone*. Can you understand?"

"I can now, but I couldn't back then."

"Can you forgive me?"

She patted my knee. "Of course I can. I forgave you years ago. We were seventeen, like you said. I was just curious, that's all."

The kitchen timer went off again. This time I joined her in there, bringing our wineglasses along. She took the succulent, perfectly browned meat loaf out of the oven, smelling of bacon, onions, and bell pepper, followed by the covered baking dish of molten mac and cheese. She let them cool a bit on the stove while she boiled some water for string beans, cooked them in a jiff, and dumped them in a strainer. She cut two slices of meat loaf for each of us and plated them along with generous heaps of mac and cheese and the string beans.

"Sit," she commanded me.

We'd gone through half of the bottle of wine. I topped off our glasses and sat. Lulu circled around three times at my feet and sat, too.

"Dig in," she said as joined me with our plates.

"Yum," I said as I sampled my first forkful of meat loaf. "I would swear yours is better than your mom's."

"Never. But I did make enough for a family of eight. I'll make you a couple of sandwiches that you can eat in the car on your way home tomorrow."

"You've had worse ideas." I sampled the mac and cheese and found it equally tasty and comforting. As I sat there devouring my favorite childhood meal with my high school sweetheart in her kitchen just as I had so many times years and years ago, I had a surreal moment when it occurred to me that *this* was reality and that the spectacular success of my novel and torrid romance with Merilee Nash were nothing but an aspiring writer's schoolboy fantasy. But the weight of the former Princess Flavia on my feet under the table was real. I sneaked a peek just to make sure.

As we ate, we both heard a car start up across the street.

"That'll be Pete," she murmured as he backed out of his driveway and went speeding off. "The poor man has to go rushing off day and night. He's usually not gone for long, but if he's not back by the time you want to go home, I'll walk you back."

"You don't have to do that. I'll be okay."

"I'm walking you back," she insisted.

We ate in silence for a moment before I said, "Now that your mom is gone, have *you* thought about fleeing this place? Finding yourself a job in one of the libraries on the eastern shoreline? There are all sorts of lovely towns, like Mystic and Stonington. You could walk on the beach every day. Meet a bright, funny guy who has a beard and a dog. I totally understand that you didn't want to leave your mom. You were being a good daughter. But you don't have to be anymore."

"I can't leave Kevin. I'm responsible for him."

"What if it turns out that Lieutenant Mitry's instincts are correct and Kevin killed your mom? What if he ends up in jail for decades? Would you still stay here and waste your life away?"

"I wouldn't be wasting it," she said with an edge in her voice. "I have the Oakmont Library to think of. Who would take care of it if I left town? I feel as if it's my legacy, not only because it meant so much to my mom but because it's the only place left where decent people can congregate. Your grandfather always put money into the library to keep it in one piece. And your father did, too, even though the mill was failing. He cared about it."

"Are you sure it was just the library that he cared about?"

Maggie looked at me uncomfortably before she said, "I don't know what you mean by that."

"Lulu found something in the librarians' lounge this morning when she was burrowing around underneath the daybed. It was way back near the wall. She nosed it out to me."

"Please don't tell me it was a dead mouse."

"I almost wish it had been." I reached into the pocket of my jeans and put a monogrammed gold cuff link on the table between us. The initials were MBH, as in Montgomery Brainard Hoag, known as Monty by one and all, excluding the one person on the planet who called him Dad. "Why was one of my father's cuff links underneath that daybed?"

"Hoagy, are you telling me you really don't know?"

"Don't know what?"

"My mom and your dad were lovers for years. She was only thirty-eight when my dad died. Still young and attractive. And very lonely. Your dad and your mom were not happy together. *That* much you must have known."

"Maggie, I didn't know my parents at all. Three strangers lived in that giant house. All I knew was that he worked all of the time."

She put her hand over mine. "Not all of the time, sweetie," she said gently. "He needed someone to talk to. That someone was my mom. It started with him stopping by the library several times a week at closing time to check on a leak in the roof or a toilet that wouldn't stop running. They'd sit and talk. One thing led to another and they took up together."

"How did you find out?"

"One evening, when I came back for a school-book I'd forgotten, I walked in on them in the librarians' lounge with most of their clothes off. They were totally mortified. I was horrified. Later that night, my mom tried to explain to me that sometimes two lonely people find each other and these things just *happen*. But I didn't understand. Not really."

"How old were you?"

"Fifteen."

"Why on earth didn't you tell me?"

"I was afraid to. You were already so filled with hatred for your father that I thought you might explode and run away from home. Just drop out of school, thumb a ride out of town and disappear. I—I didn't want to lose you. So I kept quiet."

I sat there, stunned. "How often did they . . . ?"

"Once or twice a week after closing hours."

"We were sixteen when we started having sex on that same daybed."

She nodded. "We'd sneak out of our houses late at night and I'd use my key to the library. It was our special place. Looking back, it's kind of amazing that we never ran into them there."

"I must admit that it gives me the creeps to realize we used the same bed."

Maggie said, "You and I slept *on* it, wrapped in a blanket, not *in* it the way they did, if that makes you feel any less creeped out."

"It doesn't. Tell me, how could she be with him? He was a total asshole who treated people like shit."

"He didn't treat her that way. He was nice to her. He showed an interest in her. She was lonely, like I said. And I gather that he was, too."

"I knew nothing about my parents' marriage. My dad ran the mill. That's all he did. He didn't play golf or fish or sail. What my mom did with her time was always a mystery to me, since we had a maid and a cook. She didn't have to shop for groceries or clean house or do the laundry. I know she got her hair and nails done every Friday. Played bridge at the country club in Norwich. I suppose you're going to tell me that she had a lover, too."

"Not that I'm aware of." She reached for the wine bottle and emptied it into our glasses.

I sipped my wine, shaking my head. "Here I am taking victory laps all across the country for my keen insights into a dying New England mill town, and the whole time you knew what was really going on here and I didn't."

"Strictly because you and your father didn't speak and my mom and I did. We confided in each other."

"Does that mean she knew about us?"

Maggie nodded. "She was okay with it, as long we were being careful."

"Which we were. I still remember riding my bike to Fulton to buy condoms from the pharmacist at the drugstore there. I didn't dare buy them from Gene at Super Drug. He would have ratted me out to my father. What did your mom say when I didn't write you from Harvard or come home for the summer?"

"Pretty much what you just said—that you were angry at your dad, self-absorbed, and totally unaware of how painful it was for me. She loved you dearly, you know. You were like a second son to her. Vastly preferable to Kevin. She was so proud of you when you published your first short story in the *New Yorker*. Couldn't stop beaming. And when your novel was such a huge success she kept saying, 'I always knew he had greatness in him.' She never said anything remotely like that about me. The most

I ever got out of her was 'You have heart and soul and goodness.'"

I reached across the table and put my hand over hers, gazing at her fondly. "Which you do."

We'd polished off the last of the wine. I can say with total certainty that if I hadn't been so madly in love with Merilee, I would be telling you right now all about how Maggie and I ended up in her bed together making sweet love for old times' sake. But we didn't. There was no way I'd cheat on Merilee. Neither would Maggie. There are two kinds of women in this world—the ones who sleep with another woman's man and the ones who don't. Maggie was a don't.

"You should keep that cuff link, sweetie."

"I don't want it."

"Someday you might."

"Hard to imagine, but okay," I said, pocketing it.

She got up out of her chair, ruffled my hair, and began making me two meat loaf sandwiches to wrap in wax paper for my drive home. "Don't tell me . . . ketchup and mayo, right?"

"I can't believe you remember that."

"It's the librarian's curse. We have memories for details that most normal people forget."

"I'll help you with the dishes," I said, stirring from my chair.

"Like hell you will. You're my guest."

"Maggie, I'm so glad we did this. And not just because the meal was so awesome. It's been great talking to you again. It feels as if we just picked up right where we left off. Best friends."

"Best friends," she agreed, placing the sandwiches in a Ziploc bag. "And now, best friend, I'm going to walk you and Lulu home, because I haven't heard Pete come back."

I got up and went to the front door. "I'm supposed to flick your porch light on and off. Maybe he's just waiting out there in his cruiser."

I flicked the porch light on and off and opened the front door. Halfway down the block I saw a Crown Vic idling. Pete flashed his high beams on and off at me. "Yeah, there he is, all right, keeping a protective eye on the street." I put on my flight jacket and hooked Lulu's leash to her collar. Maggie joined me and handed me my sandwiches.

I gazed at her and said, "I'm going to need a hug."

She smiled at me, her eyes shining. "And you're going to get one."

We held on to each other for a good long minute, neither of us wanting to let go. Finally, I released her and gave her a soft kiss on the lips. "You'll always be my first sweetie."

"And you'll always be mine."

"What time will you be at the Fulton Congregational church in the morning?"

"The funeral service starts at ten. I'll probably be there by nine."

"In that case, so will I."

"And after the graveside ceremony you'll be on your way back to New York?"

"I will. Only this time I promise it won't be eleven years until you hear from me. I'll pepper you with phone calls."

"No, you won't," she said solemnly. "But it's a pretty thought. And I'll remember this evening for as long as I live."

"So will I." I kissed her again before Lulu and I headed down the front steps.

Pete eased his cruiser up to the driveway. "Did you save any leftovers for me, Maggie?" he called out.

She let out a laugh. "Dream on, Pete. Not a crumb."

I had to pause for a moment to let Lulu take care of personal business in the bushes under state police supervision before we got in his car. Lulu rode between us on the bench seat.

"Busy night?" I asked him, waving goodnight to Maggie. She waved back before she went inside and closed the door.

"A half dozen cars got broken into in the parking lot of the Fulton cineplex. All of the radios were stolen, and the cassette players were taken from two of the newer cars. Some department store bags that had brand new sweaters and pants in them were also lifted, complete with receipts. Also two bottles of Southern Comfort that were in a bag from the liquor store."

My stomach did an involuntary half gainer. I drank way too much Southern Comfort at my twenty-first birthday party and spent most of the night on the bathroom floor. To this day, even hearing the name sets off hurl alerts.

"Any idea who your thief is?"

"Pretty good idea," Pete said as he backed out of Maggie's driveway and headed back to my old house. I saw no one out walking or driving. All was quiet. "Mike Mallory loaned Kevin his Camry because he and Destiny wanted to go see a movie in Fulton."

"Have they brought the Camry back yet?"

"Yeah, it's parked behind the saloon. It's not as if they stayed to see the movie. I have no doubt they unlocked his back door and delivered their haul. Chances are that Mike's already unloaded the car stereos and cassette players to whoever he deals with, which means Kevin may have raised enough so that Mike will call Sly for him. That reminds me, the X-ray results on Shade's knee weren't good. You shattered his kneecap into so many pieces that he's been in orthopedic surgery for hours."

"One thing the Brits know how to make is tire irons."

"Sly's definitely going to be looking to make you pay. If I were you . . ."

"Not to worry. I'm clearing out of town just as soon as Mrs. McKenna's in the dirt. I'll be packed and ready to go. Maggie even made me a lunch."

He made a left, pulled into my old driveway, got out and checked to make sure the front door hadn't been tampered with again before he gave me two thumbs up.

Lulu and I got out. "Thanks for the ride, Pete," I said as I unlocked the door. "Appreciate it."

"Not a problem. Did you enjoy your evening?"

"I did. We both did. And Maggie's meat loaf may even be better than her mom's, not to speak ill of the recently departed."

"I'll see you at the funeral in the morning. But if you hear the slightest peep tonight you call me, okay?"

"I'll do that," I said as Pete got back in his cruiser and took off.

The phone was ringing as Lulu and I went inside. I locked the door behind us and answered it.

"Hello, darling," said Merilee from the city that never sleeps.

Lulu immediately started whimpering. She'd learned to recognize her mommy's voice over the phone. Don't ask me how.

"I was hoping you'd call. I just walked in. Maggie took pity on me and made me her mom's awesome recipes for meat loaf and macaroni and cheese."

"Ooh, two of my all-time favorites. We'll have to discuss the complete details when you get home."

"*And* I had a police escort to and from her house."

Briefly, she fell silent. "Why on earth did you need a police escort?"

"Kevin and Destiny broke into our apartment while I was at the library after you left and made off with everything of value, including my flight jacket."

"With your Soupy Sales Society membership pin?"

"*Charter* membership pin," I pointed out.

"Oh, right. Sorry, I forgot that part. But how awful, darling."

"Not to worry. I managed to get it all back, although not without some difficulty. I've made some enemies since you left town."

"Enemies? What sort of enemies?"

"A couple of small-time drug dealers, one of whom I put in the hospital with a shattered kneecap."

She let out a gasp. "Hoagy!"

"He was terrorizing Lulu. No one does that to the former Princess Flavia. But enough about my day. Tell me about Mamet. How did the reading go?"

"Well, it's still a work in progress, and David knows it, but it has the makings of a wonderful play filled with brutal emotional honesty. He *seemed* very pleased with my take on the lead character. Kept telling me I was bringing new dimensions to her and that he couldn't wait to get back to work on it."

"Sounds like you aced it."

"I think so. I hope so. People in my business don't always say what they mean, or mean what they say, but I choose to believe him. He said it'll probably be about two months before he's ready for another reading."

"Who else read with you?"

"Mary Beth Hurt, whom I adore, and Al Pacino."

"As in *The Godfather* Al Pacino? That's impressive. He's a huge film star."

"Yet he still thinks of himself as a stage actor. We're a lot alike, setting aside the fact that I'm six inches taller. Meow, listen to me, will you? I should warn you that I get catty when I'm exhausted and hyper. The trouble is, I don't know if I can get to sleep without you holding me in your arms."

"I was just thinking the same thing."

"But you're not all alone. You have Lulu."

"It's true. I do. She was a very good girl today. And an excellent dinner guest."

"Was it fun reminiscing with Maggie?"

"It was. I also learned something about our parents that I can't wait to share with you. It was highly educational."

"How so?"

"Let me put it this way. If I'd known four years ago what I found out tonight, I might have written a different book."

"That's rather amazing. I can't wait to hear the details. And now that I've heard your voice, I'll be able to get to sleep. Goodnight, darling. I love you."

"Not as much as I love you."

"You, sir, could not be more wrong."

After I'd hung up, I put my carefully wrapped sandwiches in the fridge, turned off the kitchen and living room lights, and glanced out the front window. The street was deserted. I brushed my teeth, stripped down to my Ramones T-shirt and boxers, and climbed into bed with my collection of John O'Hara stories and Lulu. My head was still spinning over the revelation about my father's long love affair with Mary McKenna, over how clueless I'd been, over how Maggie had shielded me from the truth to protect me from my angry adolescent self—for which I'd repaid her by leaving town and never writing or speaking to her again.

Is there a bigger fool on the planet than a seventeen-year-old-boy who thinks he knows everything?

I hadn't read more than the first page of my favorite O'Hara Hollywood novella, "Natica Jackson," when I felt my eyes getting heavy. As soon as I turned out the light and got comfy, Lulu crept her way up closer to my pillow—actually *onto* my pillow, her floppy-eared head practically atop mine. She settled in with a snort and fell instantly to sleep. I know this because she snored like a little steam locomotive. Plus her breath gave off the fragrance of the Fulton Fish Market. All of this was new to me. When Merilee and I slept together, we were wrapped in each other's arms and Lulu usually nestled between us in relative silence. Briefly, I was convinced I wouldn't get a wink of sleep all night. But I soon adjusted to my new pillow mate and fell fast asleep.

I just hoped this didn't develop into a regular habit of hers.

It was before dawn when Lulu nudged me awake with that sense of urgency I'd grown accustomed to on Charlton Street.

"Okay, girl . . ." I said hoarsely, yawning. "Good girl. Just give me a quick sec." Even though we weren't on bustling Charlton Street, I was not comfortable with the idea of letting her outside without me. I turned on the nightstand lamp, threw on my old navy blue turtleneck sweater and jeans, and laced on my Chuck Taylor high-tops. With my eyes half open, I stumbled into the darkened living room, groping around until I found a lamp to flick on. Lulu whimpered eagerly as I hooked her leash onto her collar. Then I turned on the porch light and out the door we went, Lulu tugging me down the driveway to the weedy parkway strip next to the sidewalk. She was plenty strong for a little pup. I didn't dare imagine how much of a tugger she'd be when she was fully grown.

She sniffed and snuffled around until she found some weeds that suited her and relieved herself while I stood there in the chilly purple predawn darkness of my silent hometown, inhaling the putrid scent of the Oakmont River. Then she moved over to a different location a few feet away to take care of the rest of her business, sniffing daintily for *just* the right spot to make her precious morning deposit. She was in no hurry. Took her sweet time about it.

As I stood there, yawning, my semi-awake mind returned to what Maggie had told me last night about how my horrible father and her wonderful mother had carried on a secret affair for years. Secret, that is, except that Maggie knew about it and kept it from me for fear that I'd freak out and run away from home. Which I suppose was wise of her. I might have done that very thing. Girls are more insightful at that age than boys are. Hell, woodchucks are more insightful at that age than boys are. I thought about my novel and all of the praise I'd received for my remarkable insights into this place. All bullshit. I hadn't known a thing about what was going on.

That's what I was thinking about when I suddenly heard rapid footsteps on the sidewalk behind me. As I turned to see who it was, a gun went off in the silence and I felt a searing pain in the left side of my neck that sent me pitching over, cracking my head on the sidewalk. I remember I heard those footsteps running away. I remember that Lulu was standing over me, whimpering.

I don't remember anything at all after that.

CHAPTER NINE

My brain kicked in very slowly when I came to. I noticed that I was in a brightly lit room with windows and that it was dark outside. I noticed the sort of noises you hear in a hospital and became aware that I was lying in a hospital bed that had been cranked up to a 45-degree angle. I felt numb all over. Drugged to the gills.

When I tried to turn my head, I discovered I couldn't. By glancing sidelong to my left I was able to see that my left shoulder and upper chest were swaddled in bandages. Then, I became aware that my left arm was folded across my stomach and held in place by a cumbersome sling that seemed to be fastened around the back of my neck. By glancing to my right, I saw that I had two IV feeds in the crook of my forearm with tape slapped over them. By looking down, I became aware that Lulu was curled up in my lap gazing at me with eager anticipation. She let out a whimper and pawed gently at my tummy.

"Hey, girl," I said. When no sound came out, I swallowed and tried again. This time I managed to get the words out hoarsely.

Then I realized that Merilee was sitting in a chair in the corner of the room wearing a powder blue turtleneck sweater, jeans, and a stricken expression on her lovely face. When she heard me speak, she immediately darted out into the hall and said, "Nancy, he's awake." Then she returned and kissed me gently, mustering a smile. "Hey there, my brave boy."

"You know, you look a lot like that movie star, Merilee Nash."

"You would be amazed how often I hear that."

A sturdy young nurse came in and said, "Welcome back to the land of the living, Mister Hoag."

"He answers to Hoagy," Merilee said, so that I didn't have to.

"We've been pumping you full of fluids, but your mouth must be incredibly dry." The nurse moved a tray table over next to my right arm and put a Styrofoam cup of water on it. The cup had a lid with a straw inserted in it. "Can you manage that by yourself?"

She watched me carefully as I lifted the arm that was hooked up to the IV feeds, but otherwise functional, raised the cup toward my mouth, and took a sip from the straw. Then another. She took the cup from me and set it on the tray table. "Is that better?"

"Much. Thanks."

"You're in Fulton Hospital. You've been here since about six o'clock yesterday morning. It's now two A.M. on Monday. I'm Nancy. Doctor Joe will be here soon to explain what's happened. Just relax and try not to move around too much. Let me tell you, this whole hospital has been buzzing ever since your lady friend arrived yesterday afternoon."

Nurse Nancy took my temperature and checked my pulse and blood pressure before she left us. Lulu inched her way a bit closer to my right hand so that I was able to pet her. She let out a soft whoop and thumped her tail.

"Shall I fill in a few blanks for you while we're waiting for Doctor Joe?" Merilee asked.

I tried to nod, but discovered I couldn't. "Please."

She settled back down in her chair. "What's the last thing you remember?"

"I was on the sidewalk taking Lulu for her predawn walk and . . . um, I heard footsteps, started to turn to see who it was, and somebody shot me in—in my neck, I guess. I hit the pavement, cracked my head on the sidewalk and . . . wait, that was yesterday?"

"It was."

"Does that mean I came home to Oakmont for Mrs. McKenna's funeral and missed it?"

"I'm afraid so, darling."

"I'm sure I'll find some irony buried in there somewhere when my head clears up. It *will* clear up, won't it?"

"No one has said otherwise."

"How did I get here?"

"Do you remember Pat Dennis?"

"Our Q-Tip landlady? Sure."

"She heard the shot. Flicked on her porch light and saw you lying there on the sidewalk with Lulu making a terrible fuss over you. Pat immediately called an ambulance and Resident Trooper Schlosski, although he keeps insisting I call him Pete."

"He also answers to Peter the Beater."

"We'll pretend you didn't just say that. The ambulance got there right away. So did Pete. The only trouble was that Lulu wouldn't let anyone near you. She's gotten *so* protective of you. And she was covered with your blood. Pat fetched a bath towel and Pete managed to wrestle her off of you so that the EMTs could put you in the ambulance and whisk you here. Then Pat asked Pete to carry Lulu into her apartment so she could give her a bath in her tub. Our place only has a stall shower, remember? After she dried her off, she found a can of her food in our kitchen, fed her breakfast, and kept Lulu in her place until I was able to get here."

"Nice of her."

"Yes, it was. Meanwhile, Pete was placing phone calls to his troop commander and to Lieutenant Mitry. Also Maggie, who he said let out a shriek when he told her what had happened. Pete knew that Maggie had managed to phone you in New York to tell you about her mom's death, so he wondered if she knew how to reach me, too, which she did because she'd called you on your line at the Charlton Street house. So Pete called, woke me up, and told me what had happened. When I asked him if you were going to die, he said he wasn't a doctor but you were in pretty bad shape and that I might want to get back here. I ordered a town car right away, threw some things in a bag and tried not to give in to total hysteria on the way out here. I swear, that was the longest three-hour drive of my life. Lulu was *so* relieved to see me. Yipped and yapped her head off. Pat loaned me her spare key to our apartment. I wanted to drive over here right away, but when I couldn't find the keys to the Jag, I realized they must have been in the pocket of your jeans when you were shot. Pete drove me over here and I found them in your clothing locker. He's so upset about what happened. Blames himself, I think. He and Maggie both stopped by yesterday afternoon while you were still in surgery. She was in tears. I imagine she'll stop by again today."

"I was in surgery?"

"Boy, were you in surgery. I'm talking *hours*, darling. The longer it went on, the more convinced I became that you weren't going to make it. Not that I'm trying to turn this into a movie about me, but I've been on an emotional roller coaster since six o'clock yesterday morning. Haven't slept a wink. I swear, I'm never, ever falling in love again. It's too painful."

"Does this mean you're dumping me?"

"No, silly, it means you're my one and only."

"Oh, okay. I like the sound of that better. So you've been here at the hospital all day and night?"

"Pretty much. Pete drove me back to the apartment so I could fetch the Jag and reclaim Lulu from Pat. I also found some incredibly tasty homemade deviled ham sandwiches in the fridge that are gone now and I want to know more about when it's convenient. I took Lulu for a walk, and then we drove back here and waited. And waited. When they finally brought you in here from post-op, Lulu insisted on curling up on your tummy. She would not be denied."

I glanced down at her. "Were you worried about me, Lulu?"

She responded with another low whoop and thump of her tail.

"Merilee . . . ?"

"Yes, darling?"

"Will you kiss me again?"

"Gladly." She got to her feet and gave me a longer, more lingering kiss this time.

That was when a short, roly-poly man with a goatee came bursting in and said, "Good morning, Hoagy. I hate to break in on love scenes but I'm your surgeon, Doctor Moeller. Pretty much everyone here calls me Doctor Joe. And you, sir, are one super lucky fellow."

"Don't feel super lucky."

"You could *not* be more wrong. You must have a million questions. I'll try to explain what's happened using small words because you're still heavily sedated. For starters, those IVs that are hooked to your right forearm are glucose and antibiotics. You also needed a pint of blood when they brought you in. But that was yesterday morning. I'm talking ages and ages ago . . ." He trailed off, gawking up at Merilee as she towered over him in her cowboy boots. "Sorry, I still can't believe I'm standing in a hospital room in Fulton with a world-famous movie star. You're an even luckier guy than I imagined possible. And I see you have a living, breathing teddy bear in your lap, too."

"That's Lulu," Merilee said. "She wants to be with him. It's okay, isn't it?"

"As long as she stays calm, Miss Nash."

"It's Merilee. And she will."

"She's got to be the cutest puppy I've ever seen, with those floppy ears and big black nose. Basset hound, isn't she?"

"Yes, she is," Merilee said.

"What a cutie. If my daughter ever saw her, she'd grab her and you'd never—"

"Um, can we talk about me?" I broke in.

"Getting to that, Hoagy. You insisted that I call you that, as opposed to Mister Hoag, yesterday when you were briefly semiconscious."

"Mister Hoag was my father."

"You were brought in with a gunshot wound from a handgun shortly before dawn."

"Still waiting to hear the lucky part."

"You'd been shot through your left trapezius muscle just above your clavicle and beneath your earlobe. The trapezius—or trap, as we docs call it—is a very important muscle. It wraps around your back and secures your arm in place, rotates it, you name it. You wouldn't have a functioning arm without it. Moving on to the lucky part, the wound was a through-and-through, meaning the bullet went in the front and out the back and hit absolutely nothing vital on its way. If it had entered your body an inch lower, it would have shattered your clavicle and very likely nicked the top of your lung, which is serious stuff."

"That's how I breathe."

"Correct. Say, you really know your anatomy, don't you?"

"I'm a published author."

"So I've been told. And you do hospital room love scenes with gorgeous movie stars, too. In my next life

I'm going to skip med school and become an author. Now, stay with me here . . ."

"I'm not going anywhere, trust me."

"That's it. Don't lose your sense of humor. I was just making sure you're not drifting off. If the bullet had entered your body a mere inch to the to the right, it would have gone directly through your carotid artery, which carries blood from the heart to the brain, and we wouldn't be having this conversation right now because you would have bled out on the sidewalk before the ambulance made it out of the hospital driveway. If it had entered, say, another half inch to the right, it would have shattered any number of cervical vertebrae, and once again we probably wouldn't be having this conversation because it very likely would have severed your respiratory nerves and you would have stopped breathing instantly. If it had entered your body an inch higher, well, then we'd be looking at what we call a headshot, which means it would have entered one of two possible lobes in your brain and—"

"Okay, you've convinced me, Doctor Joe. I'm one lucky guy. But I think I've taken in as much human anatomy as I can right now."

"Understood. After we gave you a pint of our finest blood and stabilized you, I thoroughly disinfected the through-and-through hole in your body because bullets are dirty, nasty things, and we didn't want the bullet hole to get infected. That's why you're getting intravenous antibiotics and will continue to do so until we release you, followed by at least two more weeks of oral antibiotics. I did not stitch the wounds closed in case you develop a fever and we detect festering, which means we'll need to go back in and disinfect that bullet hole again. So right now you're just gauzed and bandaged, front and back."

"And why am I wearing this clumsy sling thingie?"

"The reason you're wearing that clumsy sling thingie is that you suffered extensive muscle tears from the bullet and your arm has to be immobilized for now. In fact, you'd better get used to wearing a sling. Recovery will take many, many weeks. I'm talking intensive physical therapy and strength training. Since you appear to be right-handed, you got lucky once again. But the bad news is that it's going to hurt like hell. I'll be giving you a prescription for pain medication, although I'll want you to get off it as soon as possible so you don't get addicted. It'll also make you loopy, although not as loopy as you are now. Did I forget anything? Oh, right, you also suffered a slight concussion when your head hit the sidewalk." He flashed a tiny flashlight in my eyes. "Look up, please . . . Now look down . . ." He flicked off the light. "Your pupils are responsive. I think the concussion's the least of your worries right now, since you're not going anywhere. But any time you jolt your brain it's something that, well, you don't want to do that."

"How long will I have stay here like this?"

"At least forty-eight hours. When I'm positive your wounds are clean and beginning to heal, I can stitch them up and outfit you with a slightly less cumbersome sling so that you'll be able to get around. I understand that you live in New York City. We'll transfer all of your records to your personal physician, and he or she can take it from there. You're a young, healthy guy with good muscle tone. The torn muscle should heal quickly compared to someone who's older or in poor health. I realize that Fulton isn't Mount Sinai or Lenox Hill, but I'm a Yale medical school graduate, I've been here two years, and I can assure you it's a fine hospital. We'll take very good care of you."

"Of course you will," Merilee said with great conviction. "Doctor Joe?"

"Yes?"

"Why is there a state trooper seated in the hallway outside of Hoagy's room?"

I looked at her in surprise. "There's a trooper out there?"

"Standard procedure in a gunshot case, I'm sorry to say," he answered uncomfortably.

I said, "You mean whoever shot me might try again?"

He didn't bother to answer me.

"Did you admit a patient yesterday or, I guess the night before that, with a shattered kneecap that required surgery?" I asked him.

"That would have been performed by our orthopedic surgeon, not me."

"Understood. I was just wondering if he's still here. He goes by the nickname of Shade. His last name is . . . give me a second . . . Sadowski. Is he still here?"

"I'll check at the desk. Be right back." He went bustling out, returned a moment later, and said, "Mr. Sadowski is on the second floor. Scheduled to be released at noon to the Bendix Recovery Center in Norwich. Friend of yours?"

"Not exactly. I'm the person who shattered his kneecap."

He looked at me in surprise. "What did you use, a baseball bat?"

"Tire iron."

"I'm surprised he hasn't filed criminal assault charges against you."

"Not too likely. He's a drug dealer."

Doctor Joe's eyes widened. "And the state police are concerned that one of his associates might try to pay you back. You surprise me, Hoagy. I'm accustomed to thinking of authors as cerebral intellectuals."

"I'm a different kind."

"I'll be back to see you in a while. For now, just try to get some sleep."

"That shouldn't be too hard."

And out the door he went.

"Well, if nothing else, you now have a vivid demonstration of why I left Oakmont and swore I'd never come back," I said to Merilee. "Although I hadn't anticipated getting shot. Plunged into deep despair was more like it—which I was, after I had dinner at Maggie's house."

"Why, what happened?"

"After your town car whisked you off to New York for the Mamet reading, I decided to go inside the library. Not surprisingly, Lulu headed straight for the librarians' lounge to raid Leon's dish. She came up empty, but she did find a monogrammed gold cuff link way, way underneath the daybed in there. One of my dad's cuff links. Turns out he and Mrs. McKenna were lovers for years. Maggie knew about it, but she kept it a secret from me."

"Because she knew how you felt about your father and that you would freak out and do God knows what if you found out. She was protecting you from yourself, darling, because she cared about you. Still does. You're quite the catch, you know."

My eyes suddenly felt very heavy. "Don't . . . feel like one right now."

"I should let you get some rest. It's nearly time for Lulu's predawn walk, anyway. I can feed her, too. I brought a can of her food and her dish. We'll be back soon."

"Why don't you just go back to the apartment and crawl into bed? You look exhausted."

"I don't want to leave you." Lulu let out a low whoop of protest. "*We* don't want to leave you."

"But I'll be out cold for hours, and I'm in good hands. Seriously, go get some sleep."

"Well, maybe I will," she conceded. "Can I bring you anything when I come back?"

"I wouldn't say no to a thermos of your French press espresso. Hospital coffee is famously bad. And there should be a bag with two of Maggie's meat loaf sandwiches that we can eat for lunch."

"Consider it done." She hoisted Lulu out of my lap and took off.

I was asleep instantly.

I awoke at nine thirty A.M. in desperate need of my bedpan. I rang for my nurse, a different one from the middle of the night—Judy, not Nancy—but equally young and sturdy. Judy took care of my urgent need to pee with efficient professional dispatch. Took my temperature, which was normal, checked my pulse, my blood pressure, and my IV bags. She freed me from the glucose bag, then asked me if I was hungry. I realized I was, which shouldn't have come as a big surprise given that I hadn't eaten since dinner at Maggie's. I was also in a great deal of pain from the bullet that had gone through me and I had a nasty headache.

"I'll get you your meds and see if I can snag you some breakfast," she said. "Would you like some coffee?"

"Please."

She returned a few minutes later with a food tray. Cranked up my bed so that I was more vertical and set the tray on a cart next to my right hand. "This little paper cup has your pain meds and anti-inflammatories in it." There were four pills in all. "But you should wait to take them on a full stomach, okay? Just buzz me if you need me."

I thanked her and sampled the coffee first, which was not actually coffee at all but lukewarm brown water. I set that aside and dug into my breakfast, which consisted of orange juice, rubbery room-temperature scrambled eggs, buttered whole wheat toast, and a fruit cup. It was a sign of how hungry I was that I devoured it all. Then I took my pills with a gulp of that lukewarm brown water and settled back, hoping that the pain meds would take effect soon.

After Nurse Judy had taken away my tray I heard heavy footsteps in the hall outside of my room, and then Pete Schlosski appeared in the doorway in his Smokey hat.

"Morning, Hoagy. How are you feeling?"

"Groggy, and anxious for my meds to kick in. Hey, thanks for reaching out to Merilee and taking such good care of her once she got here."

"Not a problem. This morning I'm relieving the trooper who's been on guard detail in the hall. Not that anyone asked me my opinion, but there's no way Sly is dumb enough to try to attack right here. He'll wait until you're released and blast you outside in the parking lot. But I have to follow protocol, so here I am. We could chat for a few minutes if you're up to it."

"Sure, okay." As he parked himself in Merilee's chair it dawned upon me that an extremely large man was now looming in the doorway. It was Lieutenant Mitry, looking stern, severe, and supremely pissed off. I certainly hoped he wasn't pissed off at me. "Hello, Lieutenant . . ."

Before he could respond, Nurse Judy said, "Excuse me!" in a loud, clear voice because the lieutenant was doing such an excellent job of blocking the entire doorway. After he'd stepped aside and she'd fetched my tray she said, "I know you officers have an important job to do, but so do I. Mine is to protect the health of my patient, who is in no condition to be answering a lot of questions yet. I am in charge of this room, and I am ordering you to leave."

Lieutenant Mitry said, "Understood. I just need to ask him a quick couple of questions and then I'll be gone." He turned to me and said, "Any idea what happened?"

"Well, I was shot."

"That's one," Nurse Judy said.

"I mean, do you have any idea *who* shot you?"

"None. Do you?"

"Not yet, I'm sorry to say."

"Okay, out the door you go, Lieutenant."

"Nurse Judy, may *I* ask *him* a question before he goes?"

She tapped her foot impatiently. "Go ahead."

"Lieutenant, in your professional opinion, did the same person who beat Mary McKenna's brains in take that shot at me?"

"Good question. In my opinion, yes."

"But why?"

"Possibly because you know something."

"How could I? I've been gone for eleven years."

"Well, did anyone have a grudge against you?"

"I was Boss Hoag's son. Everyone who I went to high school with hated me. The only friend I had was Maggie." My pain pills were kicking in now. I could feel my eyelids growing heavy.

"Okay, that's it, end of conversation," Nurse Judy said firmly, shooing the lieutenant and Pete out of the room. "Try coming back this afternoon, okay?"

The lieutenant spoke briefly to Pete out in the hallway before he waved goodbye to me. I raised my right hand a few inches as Nurse Judy cranked my bed down to a reclining position. I don't remember

anything until three hours later, when a remark-
ably fresh-faced Merilee returned with Lulu and a
shoulder bag, which she unpacked to reveal a thermos
of espresso, a genuine non-Styrofoam coffee cup, and
those two meat loaf sandwiches that Maggie had made
for me. She deposited Lulu in my lap, where Lulu
wriggled around happily and let out a contented *argle-
bargle*. Then Merilee kissed me gently, cranked my bed
back up so I was in a seated position, poured me a cup
of espresso, and put my right hand around it.

"Have you got hold of it, darling?"

"Got it." I raised the cup to my mouth and took a
grateful gulp. "God, this tastes good. Thank you so
much. You're a lifesaver. Are you having some?"

"Already chug-a-lugged mine before I got here. It's
all for you."

"And you got some sleep, too, didn't you?"

"Does it show?"

"It does. You looked so tired the last time I saw you."

"Only because I was. Also terribly worried. But I'm
not anymore because you're out of danger and on the
mend. It's lunch time. Are you hungry?"

"I am."

"Meat loaf sandwiches aren't nearly as good cold
as hot. I've managed to befriend the nurses and they

said I could heat them in the microwave in their lounge."

"I can't imagine that they were tough to persuade. They must be thrilled beyond belief to have you around."

"Well, I must admit the Polaroids have come out and we've taken a lot of pictures together. But I've promised to do my part. This afternoon I'll be performing my world-famous hand puppet show for the kids in the pediatric cancer ward. Lulu's going to be my assistant."

"This I would pay to see."

"And I understand there's an elderly heart patient named Helen who's a fan of mine and could use some cheering up. I'm doing what I can to pitch in while I'm here. It lifts my spirits."

"You're an awfully good sport. Can I ask you something?"

"Anything, darling."

"How did I get so lucky?"

"You didn't, silly man. I'm the one who did. Okay, off I go to heat up our sandwiches. Be back soon."

I finished off my coffee, which did a remarkable job of reviving me, and patted Lulu, who rolled around happily on her back. True to her word, Merilee returned

soon with a tray laden with our sandwiches, two chocolate chip cookies, and two individual-sized cartons of
milk. She placed it on my tray table, shoved her chair
over next to me, and dug in as hungrily as I did.

"Yum," she said. "Let me tell you, Maggie makes
a mean meat loaf."

"It was her mom's recipe."

"I'm going to make it when we get home. I may
try it with pancetta instead of bacon, and possibly
caramelize the onions and bell pepper a bit longer,
but this is *good*." After her sandwich had vanished,
she ate her cookie and drank her milk, then emptied
the thermos of espresso into my cup and returned
the tray to wherever it had come from.

While she was gone, Nurse Judy came in to take
my temperature, check my pulse and blood pressure,
check my IV bags, and tell me that Doctor Joe would
be in to visit me soon. Then Merilee returned, sat
next to me and held my hand until Doctor Joe strode
in, beaming.

"So, did you miss me, Hoagy?"

"Terribly."

He examined my chart. "No fever, good." He
gently pressed a hand against my bandages, front and
back. "The wounds feel nice and cool. Also good. Are

you experiencing any kind of throbbing sensation, or is it more like an ache?"

"An ache. Is that also good?"

"That's a yes. But I'd still like to remove the bandages, examine the wounds, and make sure they're clean. I always like to err on the side of caution."

"Of course. And bonus points for the correct pronunciation of the word *err*."

"Merilee, it means we'll have to move him to a different room, but he won't be gone long. Hoagy, have you been up on your feet since we deposited you in here?"

"No, I have not."

He called for Nurse Judy and they got me up, my gown flapping open in back.

"Try to control yourself," I said to Nurse Judy.

"Trust me, hon, it's nothing I haven't seen. Although you're not in bad shape. You have pretty good taste in butts, Merilee."

"I certainly think so."

Nurse Judy tied the gown closed as I wavered there on weak legs. "Are you feeling dizzy?" she asked me.

"I'm fine."

She slid my feet into those stupid little hospital slippers and Doctor Joe gripped me tightly by my good arm while she wheeled the pole with my IV hookup along. Slowly, we headed out of the room, my sling feeling huge and clumsy.

"Still okay?" she asked me.

"Fine. Just a little wobbly," I said as Pete gave me a thumbs-up from his perch outside of my door. People went rushing past us at what seemed to be warp factor seven. Monitors beeped, lights at the nurses' station blinked on and off. It was an assault on my senses.

"Just let me know if you're going to faint on us, okay?" Dr. Joe said. "I hate surprises."

"Haven't been very fond of them myself lately."

We only moved across the hall and three rooms over, but it felt like trekking all of the way down to Battery Park from my apartment on West Ninety-third Street. We ended up in a small examination room. Dr. Joe had me sit up on a paper-covered stainless-steel table with my legs dangling over the edge. Both he and Nurse Judy washed and dried their hands, then donned surgical gloves and masks.

"I'm not going to put you under while we check you over, Hoagy, but I am going to shoot you up with Novocain, which I should warn you is going to burn for a few seconds and then *really* hurt—but, again, only for a few seconds. Then it'll numb the whole area. I'm doing the exit wound first." He removed my sling and placed my left arm, which no longer seemed connected to the rest of my body, in my lap. Carefully, he removed the bandage and gauze. "I haven't read your book yet. Understand it's about Oakmont."

"Are you trying to take my mind off of the pain you're about to inflict?"

"Can't put anything over on you, can I?" He jabbed me with the needle, which did burn and then *really* hurt. "Just relax and breathe, it'll stop hurting in a few seconds . . . There, isn't that better? I'll have to read it. What's the story about?"

"Partly it's about all of the lead poisoning caused by my family's brass mill."

"A subject I'm all too familiar with," he said grimly. "We've got two floors of cancer and leukemia patients here. An appalling number of them are children." He tapped my exit wound with his finger. "Feel anything?"

"Nope."

"Nurse, can you tidy him up for me, please?"

Nurse Judy dabbed at what I assumed was dried blood with a cotton ball drenched in alcohol.

Dr. Joe said, "It looks nice and clean, Hoagy. No puffiness or swelling, no festering. But even though we have you on an intravenous antibiotic, I'm going to go in and disinfect it again just to play it safe. This won't hurt a bit."

"Is he lying to me?" I asked Nurse Judy.

"Doctor Joe never lies."

"Will you be able to stitch it closed now?"

"Not yet. You've suffered a serious gunshot wound. I'm going to dress you again with gauze and bandages and keep you on the IV antibiotic bag, which means you get to spend another night here with us. But I'd like to see you start walking around a bit, okay? If everything looks good tomorrow, we'll stitch you up and switch you to an oral antibiotic. Then we can talk about you going home."

"To New York?"

"Not yet. I'll want to see you again before I let you go home to New York."

He moved me sideways on the table so that he could face me and removed the bandage and gauze. Nurse Judy tidied me up again. Then he shot up the entrance wound with Novocain. After that had stopped burning and *really* hurting, he said, "Looks nice and clean here, too. Good, good." After he was done disinfecting the entrance wound he dressed it with gauze and bandages, put my arm back in its sling, and took off.

Nurse Judy helped me down off of the table, gripping me by my good arm, and grabbed my IV pole. We slowly made our way back to my room, where I discovered that not only were Merilee and Lulu waiting for me, but so were Pete and Lieutenant Mitry. It was practically a convention.

"Doctor Moeller granted us permission to question Mr. Hoag at greater length," the lieutenant said to Nurse Judy with an official edge in his voice. "He said he's quite alert."

"Yes, he is," Nurse Judy said. "But he also tires easily, so please bear that in mind."

Merilee lifted Lulu off of the bed and held her in her arms while Nurse Judy helped me into it, wheeled my IV pole into place, and made sure my sling was comfortable. Then she left us.

Merilee lowered Lulu gently into my lap. I patted her. "I'm doing real well," I reported. "No sign of swelling or infection. But he wants to wait until tomorrow before he stitches the wounds shut, disconnects me from the IV antibiotic, and sets me free. And I'll still have to come back again the following day to be examined one more time before we can go home to Charlton Street."

"Whatever it takes, darling. As long as you're healing."

I sat back with a sigh and looked at the lieutenant and Pete. "So . . ."

It was Pete who spoke first. "Hoagy, when I picked you up after you'd had dinner at Maggie's, I told you I'd just come from the parking lot of the cineplex here in Fulton where a half dozen cars had been broken into, remember?"

"Um . . . vaguely."

"The radios and a couple of cassette players were stolen, along with some newly purchased clothing and two bottles of Southern Comfort."

"Okay, now I remember." It was the mention of the Southern Comfort that brought it back, loud, clear, and ulpy.

"After I dropped you off at Rigby's apartment I headed over to Mallory's. Mike's Camry, which he told me he'd loaned to Kevin and Destiny, was parked in back. He said the kids had returned it and gone strolling off with two bottles of Southern Comfort to hang with the Pardo brothers. When I asked him if he'd heard anything about a bunch of car radios and other items being stolen that evening from the parking lot of the Fulton cineplex, he played dumb."

"Just out of curiosity, what would Mike do with stolen car radios?" I asked.

"He probably knows a guy who unloads them to low-end used car lots," Lieutenant Mitry answered. "We're guessing that Kevin's parking lot score got him even on the vig he owed Mike and that Mike floated him another loan. Kevin then called around to the local bars until he connected up with Sly, who swung by the Pardos' sometime later with a fresh supply of crack along with anything the Pardos wanted. Not that there was a thing we could do about that. We had no search warrant to enter their home, no probable cause."

"After you were shot early the next morning," Pete said, "I arrived at the scene and had to wrap Lulu in a towel and wrestle her off of you so that the ambulance could whisk you away. Boy, she is one loyal little pup. Strong, too. Pat Dennis washed your blood off of her in her bathtub, and Maggie gave me your phone number in New York so I could contact Merilee to tell her what had happened."

"It was so thoughtful of you to call," Merilee said to him.

"Just doing my job," Pete said, blushing slightly. "I left Pat's and started home to get breakfast and kiss my girls before the school bus picked them up. As I was driving along I noticed that the Pardos' front door was wide open. It still wasn't much past six A.M., mind you. Their porch light was on and Kevin was sitting there on the porch weeping and carrying on. I pulled over and said 'Hey, Kev, what's going on?' And he sobbed, 'She's gone! Destiny's gone!' I said, 'Maybe she just went home to Mallory's back room. Want me to give you a lift?' And he said, 'No, you don't understand! When Sly stopped by here last night, she started cozying up to him big time. I got pissed. She told me to fuck off, and when Sly took off she left with him. Found a better deal for herself and dumped me. She's a whore. A no-good whore.'"

"Are you trying to tell me he wasn't aware of that?" I asked Pete.

He looked at me in dismay. "Hoagy, I'm just telling you what he told me. Ronnie Pardo heard our voices and came out onto the porch and said that after Destiny took off with Sly, Kevin got roaring drunk and passed out on the living room floor in a puddle of his own vomit."

"Better his own than someone else's," I said.

"I left Kevin there on the porch, sobbing, moaning, and smelling none too sweet, and went on home."

"Approximately one hour later," Mitry said, "two detectives from the Major Crime Squad headquarters in Tolland found Kevin passed out on the sofa in Mallory's back room. He has his own key, evidently. They woke him up and asked him to submit to a paraffin test to determine if there was any gunpowder residue on either of his hands, which, as you know, would indicate that it was he who'd fired that shot at you. They didn't for one second think that he was in any condition to hit the side of a barn from more than three feet away, but we have to be thorough. He consented to the test and passed it. He wasn't the shooter. They then went to Mike Mallory's house, which is walking distance from the scene of the shooting."

"Mike's life is a train wreck," I said. "He and Mary McKenna had quarreled bitterly over him loaning Kevin drug money. I got pretty rough on him myself. Told him he used to be a decent guy and that he wasn't anymore."

"The detectives said that the man's house is practically falling down," Mitry said with a disapproving shake of his head. "But he was cooperative. Agreed to submit to a paraffin test and passed it. He wasn't the shooter either."

"What about Sly?" I asked. "He and Shade had been cruising our apartment all day after I beat the crap out of them and put Shade in the orthopedic ward. Seems to me that he'd be your prime suspect."

"So it would seem," Mitry conceded. "I sent two more detectives to his apartment in Willimantic, which is about a fifteen-minute drive from Oakmont. He rents a small studio apartment in a converted Victorian house there. When the detectives arrived they heard the creaking of bed springs, moaning, and groaning, and they surmised that Sly was not only home in bed but that he wasn't alone. They knocked. He demanded to know who it was. When they responded he demanded to know what they wanted. One of the detectives told him there'd been a violent incident and that it would be a good idea for him to open the door. After some muttering and cursing he unlocked the door, wearing just boxer shorts. He was covered in sweat and reeked of sex and some sort of awful perfume."

"Patchouli," Merilee informed him.

He glanced at her. "Excuse me?"

"Destiny bathes in patchouli."

"She was right there sitting up in bed, stark naked, covered in sweat and high as a kite. Both detectives felt she had no idea they were even standing there. She had numerous scratches and bite marks on her body and—pardon me, Miss Nash—they noticed two used condoms on the floor next to the bed. It was obvious to them that she and Sly had been having sex for a good long while and were still going at it."

"Thereby confirming that she and Kevin McKenna are history," I said.

Mitry nodded. "Sly's a crack dealer. Destiny's a crack whore. She'll do anything to keep him satisfied as long as he feeds her habit. When Sly asked the detectives what they wanted they told him that you'd just been shot in Oakmont. 'Is he dead?' Sly asked them. When they said that you were still alive Sly said, 'Too bad. What do you want me with me?' They told him they wanted him to submit to a paraffin test. That it was strictly voluntary, but that if he wasn't involved in the shooting it would be in his best interest to cooperate. They could administer it at police headquarters right there in Willimantic, it would only take a few minutes, and they'd bring him right back." Mitry paused before he added, "He told them to go to hell."

"So much for cooperation," I said.

"Indeed. As a result of his hostile attitude the detectives responded that, while they had no warrant to search his apartment, there was a half smoked joint on the nightstand next to his bed in plain view from the doorway. Therefore, they were placing him under arrest for suspicion of illegal drug possession. 'This is bullshit!' he roared. 'No, this is what happens when you refuse to cooperate,' they told him."

"I'm starting to like these guys," I said.

"They ordered him to get dressed, then cuffed him and took him in. He gave Destiny a big kiss before he left and said, 'Don't go anywhere, baby. I'm not through with you yet.' Then they drove him to police headquarters. 'This is bullshit,' he kept saying from the back seat of the cruiser. 'One of these days I'm going to be a major player and, trust me, you'll be sorry.' To which one of the detectives replied, 'One of these days you're going to be found dead with a bullet in the back of your head and, trust me, absolutely no one will be sorry.' Then they threw him in a holding cell and made him stew for an hour before they administered the test."

I gazed at Mitry, whose facial expression gave away nothing. "And . . . ?"

"And he passed it. Whoever it was that shot you, it wasn't Sly."

"I gather from what you've said that he didn't have an opportunity to wash his hands."

"You gather correctly."

"Lieutenant, have your people found the bullet that passed through me?"

"We have a team of recruits combing the area, but I wouldn't count on it. Could have ended up in an overgrown bush three houses away, or in the tall weeds halfway down the block. There's no telling how far it traveled or what the trajectory was. We haven't found the shell casing, either."

"Would you expect to?"

"Frankly? Yes. It was dark out. The shooter was in a hurry to get away—yet paused to pick it up, which means we're dealing with someone mighty careful. Either that or it bounced into the storm drain next to the sidewalk, in which case we'll never find it."

The hospital room fell silent as I lay there in my bed mulling it over. "What if . . . we come at this from a completely different direction?" I asked.

Mitry narrowed his gaze at me. "And what direction would that be?"

"What if I wasn't the intended target at all?"

CHAPTER TEN

Mitry peered at me dubiously. "What are you suggesting—that Lulu was the intended target?"

"No, I'm suggesting that my father was. Did you administer a paraffin test to our landlady, Pat Dennis?"

"Why are you asking?"

"Because her apartment's right there on the scene. It was she who phoned it in, I'm told. She no doubt owns a gun—Maggie told me that everyone in Oakmont does. And she *hates* my father. Blames him for her husband Gene's suicide. Meanwhile, he's still living the sweet life with my mom in Vero Beach. And now, all of these years later, I show up to attend Mary McKenna's funeral and to serve as a highly suitable stand-in for him."

The lieutenant considered this before he said, "We didn't. Give her a paraffin test, that is."

Pete said, "And she gave Lulu a thorough bath right after you were shot, which would have washed off the gunpowder residue, assuming there was any."

Nurse Judy stuck her head in the door and said, "Trooper Schlosski? The Bendix Recovery Center van is here to pick up Mister Sadowski. You asked me to let you know."

"Yes, I did. Thank you." Pete hustled to his feet. "I want to see if Sly stops by to see his buddy off. Be right back." And off he went.

The lieutenant sat there in silence for a long moment. "Still, that's an interesting theory. You have an unusual mind, Hoagy."

"I've been told that before, although seldom so politely."

"People in my line of work are trained to work a case from point A to point B. There's a term for that. It's called—"

"Linear thought."

He raised his eyebrows. "Why, yes, that's right. But your mind leaps all over the place. Is that because you're a writer?"

"Partly that, and partly that I happen to be heavily medicated."

Pete returned now, slightly out of breath. "Sly's black Bronco pulled up behind the white Bendix Recovery Center van just as an orderly was wheeling Shade out. Shade's got one of those one of those huge Aircasts on his knee. He was thrilled to see Sly, who gave him a soul brother handshake and told him he had the world's greatest present for him when Shade was ready to go home."

"I wonder what you give the man who has nothing," I said. "Wait a second, no, I don't. I know exactly what Sly meant."

"As do I," said Mitry. "He's going to pass Destiny along to him. And then, when Shade's had enough of her, he'll pass her along to another dealer."

"That's . . . horrible," said Merilee, totally aghast. "What will end up happening to her? Will she go back to Kevin?"

Mitry's face tightened. "Miss Nash, in another few weeks she won't even remember who Kevin was."

I said, "Lieutenant, you mentioned earlier today that in your opinion the same person who shot me is responsible for murdering Mary McKenna. That would mean there's a link between the two incidents, correct?"

"In a town this size? Has to be."

"If it's Pat Dennis who shot me, then that would mean it's Pat who beat Mrs. McKenna's brains in."

Mitry turned to Pete. "Are you aware of any bad blood between the two of them?"

"None at all. They were good friends. Pat was a member of the book club. Still is, in fact. Maggie is keeping it going. And please don't ask me to pump those old ladies for dirt about Pat, because it would be like setting off a hand grenade in the middle of the library. None of them will ever speak to me again."

"They'll speak to me," Merilee said.

Mitry frowned at her. "Excuse me?"

"Ladies say all sorts of things to other ladies that they would never say to men. And it won't occur to any of them that I'm playing Nancy Drew. They'll just be tickled to talk to me and ask me a million questions about Robert Redford. I can be very cagey. Maybe I can dig up some old gossip."

"I appreciate the offer," Mitry said, "but I can't allow you to get involved."

"But I *am* involved, Lieutenant. Cast your eyes upon the man I love."

"Merilee . . . ?"

"Yes, darling?"

"You're an awfully good sport. I could imagine spending the rest of my life with you."

"You're not getting all sloppy and sentimental on me, are you?"

"Trying not to, but if Pat *is* responsible for what's happened, then I'm starting to wonder if it's safe for you to be staying all by yourself right across the driveway from her. Since she struck out with me, she might go after you. What better way to punish me?"

"You're scaring me, darling," she said as Lulu began to whimper softly in my lap. "And not just me."

"Good. I think you should be scared," I said as Nurse Judy came in to take my temperature and check my blood pressure again.

Merilee looked at Mitry. "Do you think I should check into a motel, Lieutenant?"

"If you feel at all concerned about being there alone, then it might not be a bad idea."

"I don't mean to eavesdrop," Nurse Judy said, "but the hospital always keeps a couple of guest rooms available for out-of-town relatives of intensive care patients. They're nothing fancy. Just a room with a bed and a restroom, with a shower across the hall."

Merilee let out a hoot. "Compared to some of the fleabags I used to stay in when I worked the old Keith-Orpheum circuit—four of us to a room—it sounds like the Plaza Hotel. Do you think they'd let me use one?"

"I'm sure they would. And that way you and Lulu will be right here close to Hoagy around the clock."

"What do you think, darling?"

"I think . . ." I stifled a yawn, suddenly feeling a wave of weariness wash over me. "You should go get your stuff."

Mitry said, "I'm on my way over there right now to see if the recruits have made any progress finding the bullet. You can ride with me, pick up your things, and I'll bring you right back here. That'll attract Pat's attention much less than if she sees you loading up your Jaguar."

"Judy, who do I speak to about a room?" Merilee asked.

"Don't worry your pretty head, hon. I'll take care of it."

"Thank you."

"And *you*, sir, need some rest," Judy said to me. "I'm afraid I'll have to ask you gentlemen to leave."

Which I'm assuming they did, but I honestly can't say for sure. I was already asleep.

❖

When I woke up it was more than two hours later, and Lulu was no longer dozing in my lap. But I was not completely alone in the room. Maggie was sitting in Merilee's chair. No sign of Merilee, just Maggie, who was wearing a signature Oakmont buffalo plaid wool shirt, jeans, and hiking shoes. She looked drained and exhausted. Had circles of fatigue under her eyes, which were red from crying. She also looked utterly distraught at the sight of me there in my hospital bed with my left arm in its padded sling and my right hooked up to the IV bag on its pole.

"Hey, carrot top," I said to her hoarsely.

She immediately started to cry. "Oh, Hoagy, I'm *so* sorry."

"So am I. I came all of this way for your mom's funeral. Had an incredibly moving eulogy all prepared, and I didn't show up. Plus I have two bullet holes in me."

She dabbed at her eyes with a Kleenex from the box in her lap. "Are you going to be okay?"

"It'll take a while, but Doctor Joe seems to think I will. Merilee and Lulu have been keeping me company, although I have no idea where they are now."

"The nurse told me she's giving a hand puppet show for the kids in the pediatric cancer ward. Lulu's helping her. She's such a sweet woman."

"Big, big fan of your meat loaf sandwiches, too. We devoured them for lunch. She'll be sorry she missed you, but you'll see her again. I'm not going anywhere until Doctor Joe is positive that the wound's not infected."

Maggie started to blubber again.

"You've got to stop that or I'm going to kick you out. Come over here and hold my hand, will you?"

She got up and came over to the bed. I held my good hand out to her and gave hers a squeeze. "I'm awfully glad to see you. I understand you were here yesterday while I was in surgery. You must have had such a long, trying day."

"I did," she allowed, lowering her eyes.

"Tell me about it."

"Well, the funeral was at the Congregational church right here in Fulton. We had a good turnout. At least fifty people, which is a lot for our little semi-abandoned ghost town. Mom . . . everyone loved Mom. All of the library patrons, everyone who knew her. The pastor gave a lovely eulogy. And then I gave mine, which I worked on all night. I broke down and sobbed in the middle of it, which I was afraid would happen, but I made it through to the end somehow. And Pat Dennis spoke on behalf of the book club ladies."

"How about Kevin?"

Her faced dropped. "He told me he wouldn't be able to pull it off, or some cowardly crap like that. I told him, 'Just get up there and say she was your mother, you loved her, and you'll always miss her.' He refused."

"If it makes you feel any better, Destiny has dumped him for Sly, so she's out of his life."

"So I've heard. Kev's a total wreck. Imagine him thinking that she actually cared about him. All she cares about is getting high."

"And Sly is a much better deal for her. In fact, she was in bed with him in his apartment in Willimantic when I got shot."

Maggie frowned. "So that means he didn't do it. I guess I just assumed he did. That it was payback for you shattering Shade's kneecap."

"Nope. Somebody else did it. Tell me more about the funeral. Were there any other eulogies?"

"Mike Mallory asked me at the last minute if he could say a few words, believe it or not."

"What did he say?"

"How much Mom had meant to Oakmont. He got very sentimental. Kind of surprised me, because I know they'd exchanged angry words about him loaning Kevin drug money."

"Mike's struggling now, but he used to be a decent guy."

"I suppose. We left the church at about noon, got in our cars and made the long, slow procession to the cemetery. Pete led the way with his lights flashing. The graveside ceremony was brief, and then we had a potluck luncheon inside Huffman's Mortuary. Tables and chairs were set up, and people brought tons of food. My refrigerator is stuffed. It felt . . ." Maggie released my hand and sat back down. "I don't know, it felt like more than a funeral just for Mom. It was as if she was the last thread holding Oakmont together."

"I don't agree. There's still someone else."

"Who?"

"There's you."

"Hoagy, that's sweet of you to say but—"

"You've been running the library for how many years now?"

"That doesn't matter. People still thought of Mom as the *real* library director." She heaved a sigh. "I can't say it was the happiest day of my life. And I'm not feeling super happy today either. All I want to do is curl up in a little ball on my bed and sob."

"I'm sorry."

"No, don't be, Hoagy. I'm the one who's sorry."

"For what?"

"Calling you in New York and telling you about Mom. I mean, look at you. You were almost killed, and it's my fault."

"Now you're just being silly. It was my decision to come. And okay, it's true that I got shot. And it's true that this place is even more dismal than I thought possible. But I'm still glad I came. I got a chance to see you again and, wow, what you told me about your mom and my dad—that will stay with me forever. I was so bewildered as to why you'd kept it a secret from me that I told Merilee about it. She thinks you were protecting me. That it meant you cared about me."

"I did care about you. I still do."

"Same goes for me."

"Will I see you again before you head home to New York?"

"You betcha. And I sure wish I'd made it to the funeral."

"It wasn't exactly your fault that you didn't."

"And yet, somehow, I have a feeling that it was."

Maggie peered at me. "Why would you say that?"

"Because someone didn't want me to be there."

"You don't really believe that, do you?"

"What I believe is that the reason I'm lying here has something to do with the past. I'm not sure why, maybe because I'm all drugged up, but in a weird sort of way that's how it feels."

She came over to me, ruffled my hair, and gave me a hesitant kiss on the forehead. "Go back to sleep, sweetie."

❖

It was dark out by the time I woke up. Lulu was back in my lap, dozing contentedly, and Merilee was sitting in her chair with her shoulder bag at her feet. She had tears streaming down her face. It was a day for tears. We were running out of Kleenex.

"Hey there, blond person."

"Hey back at you," she said, sniffling.

"I seem to have fallen asleep again. That's all I've been doing today."

"Because your body is recovering."

"How did your hand puppet show go, and why are you crying?"

"Because it's so *sad*. That pediatric cancer ward is *filled* with bald-headed little kids on chemo who've been sickened by the lead in the water."

"That's my family's legacy, it pains me to say. Did you cheer them up?"

"Oh, sure. I made them laugh their heads off, and they absolutely adored 'Roo-Roo.' She's now their official mascot. But what are their chances? Are they *all* going to die?"

I didn't answer. Couldn't. "Maggie stopped by in between my naps. We had a chance to talk about the funeral."

"I'm sorry I missed her. How is she?"

"Sad. Lonely."

"She's still in love with you, you know."

"Merilee, that was a long, long time ago."

"Maybe for you, but not for her. I could see it in her eyes as soon as I met her."

"Did you manage to move into your room here?"

"I did. Lieutenant Mitry was nice enough to give me a lift back. Pat's car wasn't there when I was grabbing my stuff so I don't think she even knows I've taken temporary quarters here. The room's perfectly nice. I'm one floor down from you."

"Good. I feel better with you staying here."

"That makes two of us. Excuse me, three of us. I've just fed Lulu and I'll take her for a walk before I go to bed. There's a security guard at the front desk, so there's no need for you to worry about us."

"Did Mitry's recruits find the bullet?"

"Not yet. They haven't found the shell casing either."

"That's too bad."

"He didn't seem too worked up about it. Not that he'd let on if he were. That man's a whole new definition of stoic. I wonder if he ever smiles."

I shifted around in the bed, dislodging Lulu from my lap. "Lulu, my friend, I have to pee. And then Doctor Joe wants me up and walking."

"How may I help, darling?"

"Would you mind cranking my bed up higher, please?"

"No problem. I'm getting very good at it." She cranked me up to a sitting position.

"Now I need to turn sideways and stand up. If you'll grab my right bicep and give me a little boost up, that would be a big help."

She helped me to my feet. A weakling Merilee was not.

I stepped into my stupid hospital slippers on my own and stood there on my slightly rubbery legs. "Now, if you wouldn't mind trailing me into the john with my rolling IV pole, that would be great. You don't have to stay in there with me. You can even close the door. I'll let you know when I need you."

"You'll be okay by yourself?"

"Assume I'm okay unless you hear a loud thud."

But there was no loud thud. I stood there like a manly man all by myself and peed. After I finished I did have to ask her to return so she could wash and dry my one functioning hand for me and help me and my rolling IV pole out of there.

"Okay, now I intend to take a lap around the entire fifth floor," I announced boldly.

"Wait, not so fast . . ." Merilee reached into her shoulder bag. "I brought you my robe. Call me old fashioned, but I don't want every woman on the floor staring at your bare butt. This is actually quite big on me, and it's cashmere." Navy blue cashmere, to be exact. "Here, you can wear it over your shoulders like a cape and I'll tie the belt loosely around your waist like this so you'll be nice and toasty warm." She stepped back to admire her handiwork. "You look quite dashing, actually. I should have brought you an ascot. So, the idea is that I walk alongside you and wheel the IV pole?"

"Correct. And grip my arm if I seem to be faltering."

"Got it. Lulu, would you like to come with us?"

She let out a little yip, jumped down from the bed and waited out in the hallway for us as we made our way slowly out the door and started down the corridor, one small step for mankind at a time.

"Pick up those feet, Hoag!" I growled at myself.

"What's that, darling?"

"Oh, just something that the track coach at Harvard used to yell at us after we'd run a couple of miles and were starting to scuff our feet."

"You were on the track team?"

"Young miss, I'll have you know that I was the third-best javelin hurler in the entire Ivy League."

"I'm awestruck. I had no idea that you were such a star athlete."

"Well, I don't like to brag."

As we neared the nurse's station I spotted a familiar face. "It's Nurse Nancy! I missed you. Not to take anything away from Nurse Judy but you were my first, you know."

She let out a laugh. "Look at you, up and about with your celebrity escort and Roo-Roo."

"Doctor Joe's orders. He wants me to walk. I'm aiming to take a full lap of the entire floor. Besides, I don't want Merilee to think I'm a wimp or she'll dump me for that pretty boy Redford."

"Not a chance," Nancy assured me. "You're stuck with her."

One of the other nurses grabbed her Polaroid and took our picture.

"I understand you were quite a hit with the kids this afternoon," Nurse Nancy said to Merilee as we walked and wheeled our way slowly past the station.

"Honestly? It was one of the most emotionally draining experiences I've ever had," Merilee said. "I don't know how you nurses can do it every day."

"It's not easy," Nancy conceded. "The job takes everything you've got, and then demands more. I love what I do, but a lot of nurses leave the job after a few years because they can't hack it."

As we moved our way along the busy corridor, Merilee said, "You know what, darling? I'm going to make a movie about it someday."

And she did just that in 1987—*The Third Floor,* a major tearjerker hit about the trials and tribulations of a pediatric cancer ward nurse that earned her a Best Actress Oscar nomination.

By the time the Charlton Street team had made a complete lap of the fifth floor, I was totally exhausted.

"I have no stamina at all," I gasped as Merilee helped me remove my cashmere cape and get back into bed.

"You seem to have forgotten that you have two bullet holes in you, sir."

"Believe me, I haven't forgotten."

"But you did very well. I'm proud of you."

Nurse Nancy appeared in the doorway and said, "Are you two lovebirds ready for your dinners now?"

"Absolutely," Merilee said.

"So you've signed up for the full meal plan?" I asked her.

"Whatever you eat, I eat."

We watched *Barney Miller* and *The Odd Couple* together on my TV while we supped on Salisbury steak, mixed vegetables, mashed potatoes, and a fruit cup. The portions were small and flavorless.

Nonetheless, Merilee cleaned her plate hungrily and said, "That was *the* best Salisbury steak I've had in years."

"You'll get no argument from me," I said as I cleaned my own plate. "Vastly superior to the Salisbury steak they served at the Oakmont High cafeteria. Merilee . . . ?"

"Yes, darling?"

"Exactly what *is* Salisbury steak?"

"I believe it's a flavored—or in our case, non-flavored—hamburger patty with some form of gravy on it. This may have been mushroom, but that's just a stab in the dark."

"Have I told you today how much I adore you?"

"You've never told me that you adore me."

"Have so."

"Have not."

"Have so."

"Have not."

"Well, I do."

"I'm glad to hear it, because it so happens that *I* adore *you*."

An orderly with a cart came by to take away our trays. I found myself starting to yawn. Our wild evening of revelry on the fifth floor of Fulton Hospital was starting to wind down.

Merilee turned off the TV and said, "I'll take Lulu for another walk and bring her back soon." And off they went.

Nurse Nancy came in to take my temperature, check my blood pressure, and give me my pain and sleeping pills. "Hoagy, have you defecated today?"

"I'm not sure our relationship has evolved to such a degree of intimacy."

"It's just that the pain pills plug people up. If you haven't, then I ought to give you an overnight laxative."

"I haven't, now that you mention it."

"Be right back." She returned with a pill in a little paper cup. I swallowed it with a gulp of water. "I've also brought you a disposable razor and a can of Barbasol for tomorrow morning. Can't have you parading around the fifth floor with the great Merilee Nash looking like an Oakmont swamp Yankee. Would you like to get up and brush your teeth and micturate before you go to sleep?"

"I love it when you get all spontaneous and zany, Nancy. Let's do it."

"Hoagy, you're a hoot."

"That's what all the girls say."

I made it into the bathroom on my own power, but Nancy still needed to stay with me to wheel my IV pole. After I'd peed, she washed my hand for me, squeezed some of the contents of the miniature tube of toothpaste onto my miniature toothbrush, and waited patiently for me to brush, spit, and rinse. Then it was back to bed, which she cranked to a lower angle.

"Will Lulu be spending the night with her mommy?"

"No, Merilee's taking her for her bedtime walk. She'll be back."

"I think it's so sweet the way Lulu stays with you."

"She's guarding me. We've only had her for a couple of weeks, but the two of us seem to have bonded, which is a bit unexpected because she's supposed to be Merilee's dog."

"She's so well behaved. Smart, too."

"Merilee or Lulu?"

"Lulu, silly. We're going to miss the three of you. We don't often get such colorful sorts here. Not to mention famous ones."

My eyes were starting to feel heavy.

"Would you like your bedside light on or off?"

"Off, please."

She flicked it off, which is not to say that it's ever really dark in a hospital room, because your door has to stay open so they can keep an eye on you. But I was fast asleep by the time Merilee brought Lulu back. I did awaken once in the middle of the night when I tried to turn over onto my side, felt a shooting pain in my neck, and groaned, which woke Lulu up. I reached down and patted her. She made a soft, contented noise and we both went back to sleep.

CHAPTER ELEVEN

Merilee woke me shortly before dawn with a kiss and whisked Lulu out of my lap for her walk. Nurse Judy came in and took my temperature, which was normal, then helped me and my IV pole into the bathroom so that I could take care of personal business. When I was done, she asked me if I'd experienced a bowel movement. I reported that I'd not only experienced it but enjoyed it. After I'd brushed my teeth, she gave me a brisk but thorough sponge bath. She also gave me a pretty decent shave with the disposable razor and can of Barbasol that Nurse

Nancy had left me, working carefully around my bandaged neck. It was by no means as smooth as when I shaved myself with Grandfather's straight razor and the shaving soap that I worked into a rich lather with my badger brush, but I looked very presentable.

"Washing your hair is going to be a challenge for a while," she said as she toweled me dry. "Merilee will have to wash it for you in the kitchen sink."

"We'll have loads of fun with that. Maybe I can even talk her into dying it purple."

When we were done with my ablutions, Nurse Judy helped me and my IV pole back to bed just as Merilee returned with Lulu and the two cups of steaming hot turbo-charged espresso she'd made in the nurse's lounge. Nurse Judy cranked me up to a sitting position and left us to savor our morning coffee together while Lulu thumped her tail contentedly in my lap.

"She just had her breakfast in my room," Merilee reported. "She certainly has a healthy appetite."

"That's because she's a growing girl. Why, before we know it, she's going to grow into her ears."

"Darling . . . ?"

"Yes, Merilee?"

"She's never going to grow into her ears."

Soon it was our own breakfast time. An orderly brought in our trays and placed them on my rolling cart table so that I could reach mine. They were not big on variety at Fulton. It was the same orange juice, rubbery, room-temperature scrambled eggs, buttered white toast, and fruit cup that I'd enjoyed yesterday. The only difference was that yesterday I'd been starved. Today, I managed only two forkfuls of eggs before I shoved the rest around on the plate and contented myself with the toast and my coffee.

"Would you like my fruit cup?" I offered Merilee, who'd only managed to swallow one forkful of the scrambled eggs before she, too, settled for toast and coffee.

"No, thank you. And, speaking for both Lulu and myself, I hope I never hear you say those words again."

"Were you able to get some sleep?"

"Off and on. I missed you. When I'm not in your arms, I feel as if my whole world is awry."

"So do I."

Doctor Joe came breezing in and wished us a good morning as he looked at my chart. "Temperature normal, no throbbing. Good, good. I'm about to make you a happy man, Hoagy. I'm going to stitch up your wounds and discharge you."

I brightened considerably. "I can go home?"

"Home to where you're staying in Oakmont. Not home to Gotham City. I'll want to examine you again tomorrow before I'll feel comfortable sending you and your medical records on your merry way. But, just for starters, how would you like to be liberated from that IV bag?"

"You're not toying with me, are you?"

He wasn't. Nurse Judy came in, yanked off the bandage that had been holding the intravenous antibiotic in the crook of my arm since I'd arrived there, applied some alcohol with a cotton ball to the area, and slapped a fresh bandage over it. My right arm was now free. And I no longer had to drag around that damned pole on wheels.

Doctor Joe said, "Okay, now we're going to pay a visit to that same little room where we had so much good, clean fun yesterday. I'm going to disinfect your wounds one more time, sew them up, and put padded bandages over them. I'll be sending you and Miss Nash home with a big supply of those. And cotton balls and a bottle of alcohol so that she can keep the wounds clean. Also a thermometer, because I want her to take your temperature every four hours."

"Oral or rectal?"

Merilee snorted. "Dream on, writer boy."

"I'm also giving you a prescription for oral antibiotics, pain pills, and something to help you sleep. You can fill those at the pharmacy downstairs. And, best of all, you're getting a lighter-weight sling that will still do the job of holding your left arm in place without being quite so cumbersome."

"Will I be able to shower?"

"That's a no. Your arm still needs to be fully supported, meaning you can't take the sling off and won't want to get it wet. Short term, Miss Nash will have to give you sponge baths."

"You get to wash my hair, too," I said, grinning at her. "Admit it, when you first set eyes on me in the Blue Mill, you had *no* idea we were going to have this much fun together."

"No idea at all," she admitted, her green eyes shining at me.

"Are you ready to get stitched up?" Doctor Joe asked me.

"You bet."

Merilee said, "While you're doing that, Roo-Roo and I are going to pay another visit to the pediatric cancer ward. I'll pick up your prescriptions, too. See you soon." She hoisted Lulu out of my lap and off they went.

I swung my legs out of bed and Nurse Judy helped me to my feet with her hand around my right bicep. She had a grip on her like a plumber. But now that I was no longer attached to the IV pole I was able to walk on my own to the examination room, although my legs still felt a bit wobbly. When we arrived, she sat me on the edge of the examination table, removed my sling, and held my flopping left arm firmly in place in my lap while Doctor Joe got ready to poke me with a syringe. Both of them wore surgical gloves and masks again.

"Okay, round two of the Novocain," he said to me. "We'll start with the exit wound again. You'll be happy to know it's always less painful the second time."

"Are you lying to me?"

"Of course I am."

I was prepared this time for the burning sensation followed by the ten seconds of incredible pain. But it made no difference whatsoever. He still had to exhort me to relax and breathe until the pain passed.

"I imagine you're anxious to get back to New York," he said while we waited for the wound to become numb to the touch.

"I am. The day I graduated from high school I swore I'd never come home to Oakmont again, and I haven't. The only reason I broke my promise to myself was because I wanted to attend Mary McKenna's funeral. But I missed the funeral because I got shot, so my trip home has been a giant bust—which isn't to say I'm not thoroughly enjoying myself right now."

A second masked nurse joined us now to assist him.

"You may feel a bit of poking or tugging," he said to me. "Just try to hold as still as possible."

"Will do."

He stitched up the bullet hole slowly and carefully. "A very neat job, if I do say so myself," he told me when he was done. "I don't think you'll have much of a scar at all." The nurse swabbed it with alcohol, then put a padded bandage over it. "Now that I've honed my technique, let's go to work on the one above your clavicle, which might actually show during tank top season. Ready for your next shot of Novocain?"

"I'm not only ready, I'm looking forward to it."

Again, he had to exhort me to breathe until the pain subsided. Again, Nurse Judy cradled my arm. The other nurse held my neck gently but firmly in place.

"Just close your eyes and think deep, writerly thoughts," Doctor Joe said as he moved in closer and went to work stitching up the hole in the front of my neck. "This won't take long at all . . . Not long . . . Heck, this one's turning out even better. I should turn pro, you know? Quit that job at Sears Automotive Center and go to work here full time . . . There, all done. In a few months it'll hardly be visible at all."

The other nurse swabbed it with alcohol and put another padded bandage over it.

Doctor Joe stripped off his mask and gloves, beaming at me.

"Good to go?" I asked him.

"Good to go. If you experience any throbbing or swelling later on today, or if your temperature spikes, I want you to call us and come right back. I don't think you will, but I'm supposed to tell you that. I want you to do nothing today but rest. You're still weak and it'll take you a while to get your stamina back."

And with that, he and the other nurse went darting off. People moved really fast in that place. Nurse Judy stayed with me so that she could fit me with my new sling, which did a fine job of securing my forearm against my chest without the bulkiness of the one I'd been wearing. Then she led me back to my room and helped me back into bed. Before she left me, she handed me an appointment card for the next morning at nine A.M.

Merilee and Lulu joined me a few minutes later. "How did it go?" she asked as Lulu wriggled around in my lap.

"Dr. Joe seems pleased. We have an appointment for nine o'clock tomorrow morning, as you can see," I said, handing her the card. "But he did correct himself. He wants you to take my temperature four times a day with a *rectal* thermometer, not oral."

"Is he at all concerned that you're turning back into a thirteen-year-old boy?"

"Doesn't seem to be."

Nurse Judy returned with a plastic bag loaded with bandages, cotton balls, a plastic bottle of alcohol, a truly disappointing oral thermometer, and a second sling. "You'll need two of them so you can alternate them and wash them," she explained. "They get kind of smelly after a few days."

Merilee said, "And here are his prescriptions." She produced three bottles from her shoulder bag. Into the plastic bag they went.

Then Nurse Judy used her key on my locker and Merilee grabbed my black high-top Chuck Taylor

All Stars, which were its only contents. Everything else I'd been wearing when I was admitted had been blood soaked.

"I'm sure glad I wasn't wearing my flight jacket, but I'm going to miss my old navy blue turtleneck sweater. We'd been through a lot together."

"I'll hold onto it for you, darling. My dry cleaner's a miracle worker. Maybe he can rescue it."

Merilee had brought me fresh boxer shorts and a clean pair of jeans. I stood up and she helped me put them on. She also gave me my wallet, which she'd been holding on to. I sat down to put on my Chuck Taylors, which wasn't much of a challenge, although tying the laces with one hand was. Merilee had to kneel and do that for me, which gave me an eerie, distant flashback memory to being four years old and my mom tying them for me. Then she and Nurse Judy discussed how to clothe my upper body. T-shirts and pullover sweaters of any kind were a no-no because I couldn't raise my wounded arm over my head. Nurse Judy showed Merilee how to remove the sling and cradle my wounded arm by placing her palm beneath my elbow. First they maneuvered that arm, then my healthy one, into a soft tattersall flannel shirt, then into Grandfather's half-century-old, tan-and-gray

277

argyle cardigan sweater, which I was exceedingly glad I'd brought with me as an afterthought. I was able to button that myself with the fingers of my right hand while Merilee carefully followed Nurse Judy's instructions for how to put my sling back on. Then she gently draped my flight jacket over my shoulders.

"Merilee, did you check to see if—?"

"No one has touched your Soupy Sales pin," she assured me.

"Would you believe that when Kevin McKenna stole this jacket, he had no idea what a valuable collectible that charter-member pin is? He'd never even heard of Soupy Sales."

Nurse Judy frowned at me. "Soupy *who*?"

I turned to Merilee and said, "That settles it. Time for us to go."

I wasn't allowed to leave on foot. A wheelchair had to deliver me to the front entrance. And it wasn't any old orderly who showed up to push my wheelchair. It was Resident Trooper Pete Schlosski.

"Hey, Pete. Nice of you stop by," I said as Nurse Judy helped me into the wheelchair.

"When I heard you were being discharged this morning, I wanted to make sure Sly didn't try to take a shot at you in the parking lot."

"Oh, right," I said, feeling my pulse suddenly quicken. "Did you spot his black Bronco in the lot when you got here?"

He shook his head. "It would be a stupid move on his part. Heck, it's broad daylight. There would be a ton of witnesses. But Sly is pissed off and he doesn't have Shade riding shotgun for him like he usually does, so there's no telling what he'll do, although the Narcotics Task Force told me he's spent most of the past twenty-four hours holed up in his apartment with Destiny."

"Young love is a wonderful thing," I said.

"It sure is good to see you up and about, Hoagy. Ready to go for a ride?"

"We most certainly are."

"Who's this *we*?"

As soon as Lulu let out a whoop he smiled, picked her up, and settled her into my lap along my plastic bag of supplies. Ten-Minute Merilee had already packed up, moved out of her room, and was set to go. Even though I had an appointment to return the next morning, she still paused at their nurses' station to thank the nurses. Out came the Polaroids again.

Then we proceeded to the elevator and rode down to the lobby. The glass front doors opened automatically and Pete pushed me out into the day-light. It was a chilly day. His Crown Vic was parked in a No Parking zone near the door. Again, I felt my pulse quicken as my eyes searched the parking lot for the black Bronco. I saw no sign of it. The Jag was in a parking space across the lot. Merilee hoisted Lulu out of my lap and put her on her leash. The two of them headed for the Jag while I waited with Pete, who was keeping his eyes open for someone, anyone sitting in a parked car or hanging around watching us. There was always a chance that Sly had phoned a running buddy and asked him to blast my head off.

Merilee pulled up quickly in the Jag and got out. Lulu was now in her carrier in the passenger seat. Merilee moved her to the driver's seat and opened the passenger door for me.

Pete helped me out of the wheelchair and walked me to the Jag, gripping me firmly by my right arm, before he hesitated and said, "I love this car, but it's built awfully low to the ground. I wonder if it might be easier to get Hoagy in and out of my cruiser. It's much higher and roomier."

"I think you're right, Pete," Merilee agreed. "Lulu and I will meet you at Rigby's."

She returned Lulu's carrier to the Jag's passenger seat, climbed in, and took off with a throaty roar. Pete opened the passenger door of the cruiser. I swiveled around and perched on its bench seat, butt first. He helped me get my legs in. When I was good and settled in, he closed the door, pushed the wheelchair back to the lobby, and climbed in behind the wheel, his eyes continuing to scan the parking lot.

"All set?" he asked me.

"All set."

We headed out. The autumn sunlight seemed uncommonly bright after so many hours of artificial hospital light.

"You've been a good friend, Pete. Thanks."

"Just doing what they pay me to do. Besides, you'd do the same for me."

"You're right, I would." I sniffed the air in the cruiser. "Is it just me, or are we surrounded by uncommonly fragrant food smells?"

"That's courtesy of Maggie," he said as he pulled out of the parking lot and started toward Oakmont. "She ended up with a ton of food from the potluck luncheon at the mortuary and brought it home with her. She thought you folks would want something to eat, so there's a whole roast chicken, sliced pot roast, homemade potato salad, coleslaw, all kinds of stuff."

"That was nice of her. I'll have to call and thank her. Did she go back to work today?"

Pete let out a laugh. "It's Tuesday. What do you think?"

By the time we got to Rigby's and pulled around to the door Merilee had already parked the Jag, padlocked the garage, opened the front door, and carried Lulu inside in her carrier. She must have floored it all of the way there. She opened the passenger door of the cruiser for me. I swung around and planted my feet on the ground. She took me firmly by my right arm and I climbed out without too much difficulty.

Pat Dennis spotted us from her window, opened her front door, and called out, "Welcome home!"

I thanked her as I headed into the apartment under my own power. Pete was ready to grab me if I faltered, but I didn't.

He set the bags from Maggie's potluck feast on the dinette table.

"What's all this?" Merilee asked.

"Major eats from the graveside ceremony courtesy of Maggie," I said. "We will not go hungry. Hey, thanks again for the ride, Pete."

"Yes, thank you," Merilee chimed in.

"You bet." He tipped his Smokey hat to her, got back in his cruiser, and drove off.

I sat down on the sofa, a bit tired out. Lulu climbed her way up there and curled up next to me.

"How about another cup of espresso, darling?" Merilee asked as she went through the bags of food and deposited them in the fridge.

"Please."

While she filled the kettle with bottled water and put it on to boil, I remembered to get up and call the library. When Maggie answered the phone, I thanked her for the care package. "There's enough for three. Would you like to join us for dinner? I'm back at Rigby's. They discharged me."

"That's wonderful, Hoagy! And thanks for the invite, but I'm afraid I'm not very good company right now. I'm still recovering from the funeral. All of those people and emotions. I need some alone time."

"Sure, I understand. What's the word on Kevin?"

"Latest I heard was he's hanging out with the Pardo brothers, totally bombed. He still can't believe that Destiny flat out dumped him and moved on."

"Best thing that could have happened to him."

"I agree. Maybe now I'll be able to talk him into getting some treatment."

"I wonder if this means Mike Mallory will need a new barmaid."

"Oh, is that what he called her? Enough about them. Tell me about you. How do you feel?"

"I still get tired easily, but I'm improving. My wounds are stitched up. I have a new sling and a truly hot live-in nurse." Merilee stuck her tongue out at me. "I'll need to stay on oral antibiotics for a while, and also pain pills. I go back tomorrow morning to get checked over again. If Doctor Joe gives me the okay, we'll be heading back to New York."

Maggie let out what sounded like a cross between a sigh and a sob.

"Are you okay?"

"I just . . . I still can't believe how close I came to getting you killed when I called you to let you know about Mom. I didn't imagine you'd actually come home for her funeral. I feel responsible for what happened to you."

"You're not. It's not your fault."

"I keep thinking it is."

"Well, quit it." I heard twittering voices in the background now.

"My knitting circle has arrived. I have to let you go."

"Take care of yourself, Maggie."

"You take care of *yourself."*

I hung up as Merilee made our espresso and poured us each a cup. We sat together on the sofa while Lulu climbed around on us.

I took a grateful gulp and said, "That is one sad, lonely woman."

"Think she'll be okay?"

"I hope so. She was always smart and tough. But she needs to move on. Meet some people who aren't eighty years old or total losers. She's only twenty-eight. She's a good catch for the right guy."

"She's only interested in one guy, darling."

"Please don't start with that again. She's a part of my past—not my present and certainly not my future. It's kind of amazing to think about—I didn't even know you three weeks ago. And now you're the single most important person in my life. How nuts is that?"

"Plenty nuts, but I feel the same way about you. It's as if my life didn't start until the night you walked into the Blue Mill and stood there looking at me."

We kissed softly before she abruptly turned Nurse Ratched on me and took my temperature, which was normal. Then she insisted I sit down at the dinette and eat a plate of cold chicken, potato salad, and coleslaw. She made me drink a glass of milk with it and then take my pills. By then I was starting to feel sleepy.

"You, sir, need a nap. I'll pile some pillows on the bed and get you good and comfy."

"I won't fight you."

After she'd arranged the pillows and helped me off with my sneakers I sat down sideways on the bed, swung my legs up all by myself and stretched out with my slinged arm in a comfortable position, or as comfortable as it got. She put a blanket over me. Lulu nestled against my hip with her head on my tummy. I stroked her.

"What are you planning to do?" I recall asking Merilee.

I have no recollection of her response. I was already asleep by the time she answered me.

◆

When I woke up it was two hours later and Lulu was jumping off the bed to greet Merilee as she came in the front door. She poked her head in the bedroom doorway to see if I was awake.

"For future reference," I said, "you're supposed to call out, 'Honey, I'm home!'"

"Did you get some sleep?"

"Lots. I just woke up."

Her cheeks were flushed from the autumn cold and her eyes bright with excitement.

"Do tell, where have you been?"

"I took a power walk over to the library to return Betsy Sherman's deviled ham Tupperware dish. I needed the exercise. I've been spending so much time sitting in your hospital room that my butt's starting to turn to flab."

"Beg to differ."

"And once my butt goes, poof, there goes my career—unless they're looking to cast the lead role for a Totie Fields biopic."

"Are you sure it was wise to walk there? There's no telling who might be the killer's next target."

"I've always refused to live my life in fear. If I did, I would never have had the nerve to set foot on a Broadway stage. Or fly to Bozeman to star in a major Hollywood film opposite Robert Redford."

"Did he have to stand on a box when the two of you kissed?"

"I just bent my knees a little. He's not *that* short."

"He's not that tall, either."

"His authorized bio says he's five feet ten."

"Which means he's actually five eight."

"Darling, can we talk about what we were talking about?"

"Which was . . . ?"

"Betsy Sherman. She was coffee-klatsching in front of the fire with a few other Q-Tips, and guess what she gave me."

"Her deviled ham recipe?"

"Bingo! She wrote it all down for me. Insists that the secret is using an old-fashioned hand-operated meat grinder, not a Cuisinart, which means we're in business, mister, because my folks happen to have one. I intend to experiment as soon as we get home to Charlton Street."

"What are the other ingredients?"

"We can discuss that on our drive home. It'll give us something exciting to talk about."

"You have an eager look in your fetching green eyes. You found out some juicy gossip, didn't you?"

"I did, now that you mention it." She sat down on the edge of the bed. "It so happens that Betsy is a world-class blabbermouth. She pulled me aside and asked me how we were doing having Pat Dennis as our landlady. I said she'd been very hostile toward you when we first arrived, because she blames your father for her husband's suicide, but you seem to be winning her over and she took wonderful care of Lulu after you'd been shot."

"But . . . ?"

"How did you know there's a but?"

"There's always a but."

"But Betsy said Pat is well known for bearing long-term grudges, and that she never, ever forgave Mary McKenna when she found out that Mary was having an affair with your father—or Monty, as Betsy called him. Pat was livid. Furious with Mary. And, cue the drumroll, she never stopped being furious with her."

"Meaning *Pat* might be the one who brained her with the Mark Twain paperweight?"

"Exactly so."

"Hmm . . . I wonder how she found out about the two of them."

"Apparently it wasn't *that* deep a secret. A select few of the library regulars were aware of the way your dad was always dropping by, and that Mary would blush and act all girlish when he did. They knew *something* was going on between the two of them, especially because he went out of his way to give money to the library for repairs, books, anything Mary asked for."

As I lay there mulling this over a car pulled into the driveway and someone got out and knocked on the door. I got up off of the bed and onto my feet while Merilee went and answered it.

Lieutenant Mitry was standing there hugely in the doorway in his standard dark gray suit, white shirt, and muted tie.

"Come on in, Lieutenant," she said to him warmly.

He came on in. "I hope I'm not disturbing you folks, but when I stopped by the hospital they told me Hoagy had been discharged."

"I have indeed," I said as I made my way to the sofa and sat down. "Furthermore, your timing is perfect. I just took a good, long nap. Have a seat, Lieutenant."

He settled in the armchair and responded to Lulu's pleas for attention by picking her up with one hand and stroking her ears. She walked around happily in his lap for a moment before she jumped down and joined me on the sofa.

"How are you feeling?" he asked me.

"Much better now that my wounds are stitched up and I'm not connected to that damned IV pole. Although it still hurts like hell."

"That's because you're overdue for your pills," Merilee said, aghast. "I forgot to give them to you. What a terrible nurse I am." She fetched the pills and brought them to me with a glass of water.

I thanked her and swallowed them. "I have to continue taking antibiotics for several weeks, but I'm supposed to get off of these pain pills and make do with Tylenol after ten days because Doctor Joe said these pills can be highly addictive. I'd end up having to move back here and becoming one of Sly and Shade's customers."

He stared at me with a blank look on his face. "This is you being ironic, I gather."

"It is."

"I'm still getting used to you, I must admit."

"So am I, Lieutenant," Merilee confessed. "Hoagy's something of an acquired taste. Can I offer you anything? Coffee?"

"I'm fine, thank you. How long will you need to wear a sling?" he asked me.

"A good long while, unfortunately. My left arm will remain completely useless until the torn muscles heal. Then I'll need physical therapy to get my strength and range of motion back. But, as Doctor Joe pointed out, I'm a lucky man."

"How so?"

"I'm alive."

"Good point," he said, nodding his head. "I wanted to update you on what we know so far."

"By all means. And it so happens that Merilee just picked up some choice gossip at the library herself. But you first."

He arched an eyebrow at her curiously before he removed his notepad from the breast pocket of his jacket and glanced at it. "Aside from highly reluctantly agreeing to take that paraffin test, Sly has barely left his apartment ever since he spirited Destiny away from Kevin on Sunday night. He can't get enough of her, it seems. Shade has taken up full-time residence at the Bendix Recovery Center in Norwich, since he needs crutches to get around, lives alone in a walk-up apartment, and has no one to look after him."

"So he's hanging out with the wild and crazy party hearty crowd?"

The lieutenant nodded. "For one to two weeks."

"He must be loving that."

"He could, if he chose to, file criminal assault charges against you. But that's not his style."

"You say that as if he has a style, Lieutenant."

"As to the break-in here, are you still declining to file criminal charges against Kevin and Destiny?"

"I am. I got everything back, and have no desire to return here as a witness should they have to stand trial."

"Kevin and Destiny are still considered suspects in Mary McKenna's bludgeoning death. I've ruled out Destiny as a suspect in your attempted murder because she was in bed with Sly in his apartment at the time. But I'm still not ruling out Kevin, unlikely as that sounds. The Pardos live right around the corner from the scene of the shooting. Who's to say he didn't wake up in a blind rage over Destiny dumping him, snatch a gun from the Pardos' house, go stumbling out of there in the predawn darkness, covered in vomit, and take out his anger with a lucky shot at the first person he ran into—who just happened to be you."

"Whom, it so happens, he bitterly resents because my last name is Hoag. Kevin's father was one of my father's mill hands. The poor bastard barely made it to forty before he died of liver cancer. Plus, it never sat right with Kevin that Maggie and I were high school sweeties. At their mom's wake the other night he made it clear to me that he still resents the way I 'bailed' on Maggie, as it put it."

"Bailed on her how?"

"After I left Oakmont for Harvard, I not only never came back here but I never called her or wrote her a single letter. It's something I still feel bad about. Forgive me, Lieutenant, but there's one small discrepancy here. You told me that Kevin *passed* the paraffin test, didn't you?"

"It's true, I did. But he has a nodding acquaintance with soap and water, and had ample time to make it back to the Pardo brothers' house and wash his hands. We obtained a search warrant for the house, but we haven't turned up the gun."

"Well, that one's a no-brainer. All he had to do was toss it into the Oakmont River. The toxic chemicals would have dissolved it overnight."

He *almost* allowed himself a faint smile. "Does Maggie still resent it, too? That you disappeared from her life, I mean."

"We talked about that over meat loaf the other night. She was sad and hurt at the time, but not angry. She understood how much I hated my father. She also understood that if you have a chance to get out of a place like Oakmont, you have to take it. She didn't have the nerve herself, plus she was incredibly loyal to her mom and to the library. As to whether she still feels any resentment toward me now, I don't believe so. In fact, I don't see how she can after the bomb she dropped on me the other night."

Mitry narrowed his gaze at me. "Which was . . . ?"

"My father had been having an affair with her mother for years. I have Lulu to thank for learning about that. She found one of his monogrammed cuff links way, way under the daybed in the librarians' lounge. I showed it to Maggie when we were eating dinner and asked her what the hell it was doing there. It turned out that she'd known about their affair for years but hadn't told me because she was afraid I wouldn't be able to deal with it emotionally."

"She was protecting you, darling," Merilee said.

"Maybe so."

"There's no maybe about it," Merilee insisted. "I would have done the same thing if I'd been in Maggie's shoes. You were a teenaged boy boiling over with rage toward your father. There's no telling how you would have reacted if you'd found out he was cheating on your mother with a woman whom you admired. Rebelled, dropped out of school, run away from home, maybe all of the above."

Lieutenant Mitry raised his chin at me. "You've had yourself quite some experience since you came back, haven't you?"

"I have, Lieutenant, and I'm really sorry I did. I would have been a lot happier never finding out that my favorite librarian was having an affair with my least favorite father. Also a lot happier if I didn't have two bullet holes in me."

Lieutenant Mitry glanced through his note pad. "I believe that brings us up to date."

"Not quite. Merilee, do tell the lieutenant what you found out at the library today while I was napping."

"Gladly," she said, her green eyes twinkling. "It seems that the deep, dark secret affair between Mary McKenna and Monty Hoag may not have been so deep and dark. According to Betsy Sherman, who is a world-class gossip, Pat Dennis got wind of it somehow and was utterly furious that Mary, whom she considered a close friend, was sleeping with the ruthless businessman who evicted Super Drug when her husband, Gene, fell behind on his rent. Gene lost a huge percentage of his business after Monty shut down the mill and reneged on his promise to continue providing health and pension benefits to his former employees. As far as Pat was concerned, it was Monty who drove Gene to commit suicide. Pat even went so far as to confront Mary about it and demand she break off the affair. Mary told Pat to mind her own damned business, or words to that effect, and the two ladies were never friends again. Pat still belonged to the book club and remained a steady patron, but she never forgave Mary. Betsy went so far as to say she despised her. Pat certainly detested Hoagy on sight when we showed up to stay here. She's thawed slightly toward Hoagy, but I can definitely see her taking that shot at him when he took Lulu out for her predawn walk."

"She was first on the scene, don't forget," I said.

"I haven't," Lieutenant Mitry said thoughtfully, running a hand over his close-cropped salt-and-pepper hair. "And shooting him would be a perfect opportunity for her to finally get even with the Hoag family. Interesting theory," he said. "But I'm afraid that's all it is. A theory. In fact, I'm afraid that's all that this entire case is. We have one murder, one attempted murder, a grab bag of theories, but no hard evidence. Frankly, it's beginning to exasperate the heck out of me, because I happen to be in the results business."

"Do you trust me, Lieutenant?" I asked.

He studied me with a stony expression on his face. "I don't know you very well, but I have no reason not to trust you. Why do you ask?"

"Because I've been spending a lot of time lying in bed turning things over in my head, as you can well imagine, and . . ."

"And . . . ?"

"I believe I know who killed Mary and put these two holes in me. Proving it will require some organizational effort on your part. But unless I'm wrong, and I don't think I am, I believe I've come up with a foolproof scheme for blowing this case wide open."

He let out a heavy sigh. "Mister Hoag . . ."

"It's Hoagy, remember?"

"Hoagy, I do things by the book. I don't play games with the law."

"I'm not playing games, Lieutenant. In fact, I couldn't be more serious. If that bullet had entered my body a mere inch to the right, then you would be sitting here right now having this conversation with only Merilee and Lulu. I simply want to know whether or not you'll listen to what I have to say."

He folded his huge hands in his lap, staring at me with a grim expression on his face. "Okay, fine. I'll listen."

CHAPTER TWELVE

I felt a wave of weariness wash over me after the lieutenant left, so I used my good arm to push myself off of the sofa and started for the bedroom.

"Going to lie down for a while, darling?"

"I think so. That was a bit draining."

"Care for some company?"

"Are we talking tall, blond company?"

"We are."

"I'd love nothing better."

She joined me in the bedroom, propped up my pillows, helped me off with my shoes, and put a blanket over me. Then she took off her cowboy boots and snuggled under the blanket next to me on my right side so that I could put my arm around her and hold her close, feel her warmth, and inhale her scent. Lulu climbed up onto the bed using her stool and walked around for a minute, trying to decide where she wanted to be, before she finally settled herself on Merilee's hip.

"I've missed this so much, darling."

"Are you talking to Lulu or me?"

"You, silly wabbit."

"So have I. More than you can possibly imagine." I kissed her gently, stroking her silky golden hair. "I think we should get married."

"So do I. But can we wait until we get back to the city? I don't think the karma here is good for us."

"Or anyone else. So . . . it's settled?"

"What's settled?"

"I kind of just proposed to you, in case you didn't notice."

"Oh, I see. Of course. Yes, I accept your proposal."

"Whew, that's good. I'm glad. We'll have to get our own place, you know. We can't stay in your folks' Charlton Street house."

"Do you have a dream apartment in mind?"

"I do."

"Somehow I had a feeling you would."

"It's in a prewar high-rise doorman building on Central Park West somewhere near the Museum of Natural History. It has lots and lots of rooms and at least eight windows overlooking the park. Could you live with that?"

"Yes, I think I could manage quite nicely."

Blissfully, I dozed off with Merilee snuggling there with me under the blanket.

I had only been asleep for a few minutes when the phone rang in the kitchen. It was Merilee who got up and answered it. She was moving a lot faster than I was.

"Yes? Oh, hello, Lieutenant," I heard her say. "No, you're not disturbing us at all. Let me get him for you."

She returned to the bedroom and helped me up off of the bed with a firm grip around my good arm. As I made my way into the kitchen and reached for the phone, Merilee was right there next me, keenly interested.

"This is Hoagy. Has there been a new development, Lieutenant?"

"Not exactly," he responded. "I've been thinking over that—that *scheme* of yours."

"Ah, I see. And . . . ?"

"I have to tell you it's quite a bit out of my comfort zone."

"Of course, I understand. I had a feeling you'd—"

"But let's go for it."

"Wait, you mean you're in?"

Merilee's eyes widened excitedly.

"I'm in, though I may live to regret it."

"You won't regret it, Lieutenant."

"Oh, I'll regret it, I'm sure. But I agree with you. It's the only way to put all of the pieces together. I've just spoken to Maggie and she's all for it, too. The library closes at six. That's when we'll gather there."

"Today?"

"Today. I've already mobilized several troopers to make sure that it happens."

I glanced at Grandfather's Benrus. It was just past four thirty. "You don't believe in wasting time, do you?"

"No, I do not." Then he hesitated. "Perhaps I should have checked with you first. Do you need another day of rest?"

"Nope. One cup of Merilee's high-octane espresso and I'll be fine." She started for the tea kettle immediately. "We'll see you at six o'clock, unless you want us there a few minutes earlier."

"No, six will be fine. Actually, a few minutes after six would be even better. Um, Hoagy?"

"Yes, Lieutenant?"

"I'm putting a lot of faith in you. I don't know why I am. Maybe it's because you've been called the first major new literary voice of the nineteen eighties, which tells me you have keen insights into people. You certainly have keen insights into Oakmont. But if this scheme backfires, it's my neck that'll be on the chopping block."

"Put that thought out of your mind, Lieutenant. I have total confidence that it will succeed. See you soon," I said as I hung up.

Lulu was sitting directly in front of the fridge, staring at it.

"I think one of us wants an anchovy," I pointed out.

Merilee smiled at her. "At least she's subtle about it." She fetched the jar out of the door, opened it, rinsed the crusted, ancient salt from a choice anchovy, and fed Lulu her treat. "Darling, do you mind if I ask you a somewhat awkward question?"

"Not at all. What is it?"

"Do you really have total confidence that it'll succeed?"

"What are you, kidding me? Hell no. But I couldn't tell *him* that, could I?"

◆

The Oakmont Public Library's parking lot was crammed with cars when we arrived at a few minutes after six P.M. On an ordinary weekday, the lot would have been empty except for Maggie's Honda. A library director always stays around for another fifteen or twenty minutes after closing to tidy up.

But this was not an ordinary weekday.

Crowded alongside Maggie's Honda were Lieutenant Mitry's shiny Crown Vic, Pete Schlosski's weathered tan Crown Vic as well as two more Crown Vics, Mike Mallory's Toyota Camry, Sly's black Bronco, Pat Dennis's green Mazda, and a white van from the Bendix Recovery Center. Lieutenant Mitry had requested the presence of quite a few people. Everyone had complied, because a request from a homicide detective is not something that anyone would mistake for a request. But they had not been aware that anyone and everyone who might be connected to Mary McKenna's bludgeoning death and my attempted murder would also be there. Each of them had been led to believe that he or she alone would be meeting the lieutenant at the library. Possibly Shade, who had to be wheeled into the Bendix

Recovery Center's van and hauled there from Nor-wich, suspected something. After all, it would have been a whole lot more convenient for Lieutenant Mitry to question him at the recovery center. But since Shade was not the proud owner of a triple-digit IQ, I highly doubt he suspected anything when he was told by the Bendix staff that he was going for a ride to Oakmont. He was probably happy to be going for a ride anywhere.

Merilee drove us there in the Jag. I rode shotgun with Lulu on my lap in her carrier, my slinged arm resting atop it. I wore my same flannel shirt with Grandfather's argyle cashmere cardigan, jeans, and my Chuck Taylor All Stars. My flight jacket was thrown over my shoulders. Merilee wore her powder blue cashmere turtleneck, faded jeans, buckskin jacket, and suede cowboy boots.

She pulled into a parking space that was not so much a parking space as it was the weedy lawn next to the full lot, but didn't turn off the engine. Just idled there, staring straight ahead. "Darling, I love you more than you can imagine, so you'll please forgive me if I ask you another somewhat awkward question."

"Go right ahead."

"What's your backup plan if this doesn't work?"

"Haven't got one. Don't need one. I have an ace up my sleeve."

"I see . . ." she said slowly. "Well, actually, I don't see."

"It'll be fine. Just act as if you're in complete command of the room. The premise of this scene is *confidence*."

She exhaled slowly and said, "Okay." Then shut off the engine and got out of the car so she could come around to open my door and let me out. First, she had to lift Lulu and her carrier out of my lap. She set it down on the ground and started to open it.

"Actually, we're going to leave Lulu here in the car for a while."

"Why?" she wondered. "Never mind. Whatever you say."

She returned Lulu's carrier to my seat, locked the Jag, and the two of us started toward the library. Lulu, who was not happy about being left behind, let out a howl of protest.

"My God, there are four state police cars here," Merilee observed.

"Lieutenant Mitry is risk averse."

"You think?"

Maggie was seated at her desk waiting for us, looking calm albeit a bit confused by what was taking place. She wore the bulky cable-stitched sweater that the library knitting group had made for her, and she needed it. It was chilly in there, despite the fire that was roaring in the fireplace and the crowd of warm bodies seated on folding chairs facing her desk—with the exception of Shade, who was sitting in a wheelchair with an orderly beside him. There was a lot of murmuring going on. Ill-at-ease murmuring.

"You made it," Maggie exclaimed as we approached her desk. "How are you doing, Hoagy?"

"Considering that I have two highly unwelcome holes in my left trapezius, or *trap* as we pros call it, I'm doing just fine. Plus I fully intend to have a good checkup tomorrow morning, which means we'll be able to leave for home."

"That's great. I'm really happy for you." Maggie's smile was tinged with sadness. "Although I'm sure going to miss you."

"I know. I'll miss you, too. But this time I'm going to stay in touch."

Her eyes searched my face. "You really promise?"

"I really promise."

She looked around, frowning. "Where's Lulu?"

"She blew us off. Had a hot date with a six-month-old schnauzer named Moe. We haven't seen her for hours."

"Lulu was acting up," Merilee explained. "She's having a time-out in the car."

I noticed that the librarians' lounge door was shut.

"Has Leon retired for the night?"

"Yep. He's accustomed to me putting him in there at closing time. He's got his food, his litter box, and a comfy blanket. And that's where the mice get in. He'll be on duty guarding his territory most of the night."

Pete Schlosski produced two more folding chairs. Merilee and I sat next to Maggie, facing the occupants of the other chairs. I could smell Destiny's patchouli from fifteen feet away. She and Sly were seated together. She was wearing the only dress she seemed to own, her skintight knit minidress, and sat sideways in her chair so that her bare legs were slung over his and she was able to nuzzle his neck and run her hands over his chest. He ran one of his hands up her bare thigh.

A trooper sat parked between them and Kevin, who kept sneaking sullen glances at them like a despondent little boy. I think he was still in a state of utter disbelief that Destiny, the great love of his life, had ditched him for Sly faster than you can say "Obi-Wan Kenobi" *and* was practically humping the guy without paying Kevin the slightest bit of attention. I'm not sure she even noticed him there.

Mike Mallory sat next to Kevin. He seemed highly uncomfortable. His face was flushed and sweaty despite the chill in the room.

Shade sat in front of Mike and a few feet off to one side in his size-huge wheelchair so that he didn't block Mike's or anyone else's view. The Aircast he wore around his knee was also huge, as was the Bendix orderly who'd accompanied him. Shade alternated between staring at Merilee with undisguised sexual desire and staring at me with undisguised hatred.

"How's your knee, Shade?" I asked him.

"Hurts like hell, and I'm stuck in this cast for weeks. You'll pay for this, man. Count on it."

"You're not actually threatening me aloud in front of two, three, four members of the state police, are you?"

He didn't respond. Just peered at my sling. "I hear somebody shot you."

"It's true, somebody did."

"Good."

"I had a feeling you'd say that."

"Too bad they only wounded you."

"I had a feeling you'd say that, too. I have to say, you don't disappoint. How's life at the Bendix Recovery Center?"

"Sucks. Everybody there except for me is like a hundred years old and there's nothing to do but watch TV."

"You could try reading a book. They must have a library. I would imagine that some of the books have pictures."

He glowered at me. "You trying to be funny?"

"No, helpful."

"Shade . . . ?" Merilee interjected, "Do you mind if I ask you what your name is?"

He frowned at her, confused. "It's Shade."

"But surely that's not your given name."

"His real name is Clarence," Pete spoke up with a mocking grin.

Merilee smiled. "I think Clarence is a sweet name."

"I was named after my uncle who got killed in 'Nam," he muttered, reddening.

"I much prefer it to Shade. *Shade* is rather trite, no offense."

He looked at her in surprise. "You really like Clarence better?"

"Absolutely. It has charm and authenticity. *Shade* is the sort of nickname that they give to would-be tough guys in second-rate melodramas. I played in a total rip-off of *The Petrified Forest* in Woonsocket back when I was working the Keith-Orpheum circuit. It was awful. And I still can't believe the so-called playwright wasn't sued for plagiarism."

"Moving right along . . ." I said.

"Sorry, darling. I digressed, didn't I?"

"Little bit. That's okay."

"Do you know what's not okay, sir?"

"What?"

"That I don't have an engagement ring. You proposed to me this afternoon, I accepted, and you didn't give me one."

"Where was I going to get it—at the hospital gift shop?"

"You're *engaged*?" Maggie beamed at us in delight. "That's wonderful! I'm so happy for both of you. I've saved my mother's engagement ring, you know. She stopped wearing it years ago after Dad died. I'd be honored to give it you. It's nothing fancy. Dad was a mill hand. But it would mean a lot to me if you'd accept it."

"Thank you, Maggie," I said. "That's such a generous offer."

"Truly, it is," Merilee said. "But you should keep it for when *you* get engaged."

"I can't imagine that ever happening," Maggie said glumly.

"Forgive me for eavesdropping," said Pat Dennis, who was seated up front next to one of the troopers, "but I think it's wonderful news too. You're such a lovely young couple. Gifted and famous, but not stuck up."

Pete had been eavesdropping too. "Way to go, Hoagy. Just think, I knew you when we were kids on the playground, and now you're going to marry a movie star."

"And *I'm* going to marry the first major new literary voice of the nineteen eighties," Merilee pointed out. "Although I can guarantee you that he's getting awfully sick of that label."

"No, I'm really not," I assured her.

And then, as so often happens after a great deal of chattering, the library suddenly fell silent, except for the crackle of the fire in the fireplace.

I made eye contact with Lieutenant Mitry, who was pacing back and forth behind the assembled group like a caged panther, his jaw muscles clenching.

"Did you wish to say a few words, Lieutenant?"

"No, you go right ahead," he said, his voice taut.

"As you wish. First of all, thanks to each of you for coming."

"It's not like we had a choice," Sly grumbled. "This trooper pounded on my door, made us get out of bed, put our clothes on, and follow him here."

"Likewise," Mike Mallory said. "Aside from the being in bed naked part."

"So what's the deal?" Kevin demanded angrily. "Why are we are sitting here freezing our asses off in Mom's library?"

"I'm not cold at all," Destiny said to him in a naughty little girl voice as she hugged Sly tightly.

Kevin glared at her angrily. "Shut your fucking mouth, you filthy slut."

"Watch your language, Kevin," Pete said harshly as he got up and put two more logs on the fire. "There are ladies here."

"And, in case you haven't noticed, it's actually your sister's library now," I said to him. "So try to keep your eye on the ball, okay?"

"Ball?" Kevin shook his head at me, baffled. "What ball? What are you talking about?"

"Here's what I'd like to know," said Sly said in a low voice that I imagine he thought was menacing. "Why are we all here?"

"Because one of you beat Mary McKenna's head in with her Mark Twain paperweight," I said as my eyes scanned the room, from Shade to Mike Mallory and Kevin, to Sly and Destiny, to Pete Schlosski and Pat Dennis. "And then came within an inch of killing me on the sidewalk outside of Rigby's apartment when I was walking Lulu before dawn two days ago. Ultimately, it's Lieutenant Mitry's vast experience as a homicide detective that is responsible for you being here."

The lieutenant looked at me inquiringly. "In what sense?"

"You told me that the odds of two different people murdering Mary McKenna and attempting to murder me are nil. You're convinced that the same person is responsible for both. I suggested we bring everyone together and see if we can sort it out, and you went along with the idea."

Merilee nodded knowingly. "I've played in one of these, too, at the Ivoryton Playhouse while I was still at Yale drama school."

"One of what?" Lieutenant Mitry asked, frowning at her.

"A creaky murder mystery from the nineteen twenties. I was the rich, virginal young heiress. The denouement took place in a scary mansion on a dark and stormy night, complete with lightning and thunder and the electricity going out. The butler did it, of course. He had to be subdued by the handsome young hero, who wore brilliantine in his hair and sported a trim little moustache." She tilted her head at me curiously. "Darling, have you ever worn a moustache?"

"I have. Looked like a gigolo. Please don't ask me to grow one."

"Not if you don't want to, but it means you'll have to write me a creaky mystery play, and this time *I* want to be the murderer. Or is it murderess?"

"Merilee, I'm a novelist, not a playwright. And I don't have the slightest idea how to write a mystery. I can't even imagine how those goofballs can concoct such byzantine plots. They must be idiot savants, and can we talk about this later? We're starting to digress again."

"Of course, darling."

I turned back to the people who were gathered before us. "The lieutenant and I have gone over Mary McKenna's murder from every possible angle, and we both believe that her killer has to be someone who is currently sitting here in this room. There's no one else who had a motive for beating her brains in with that paperweight. Kevin . . . ?"

He gulped, his eyes widening. "Yeah . . . ?"

"When your mother refused to give you drug money, you stole her television as well as the handgun she kept in her bedroom dresser. In response, she kicked you out of the house and changed the locks on the doors. You moved into the back room of Mallory's with Destiny. The two of you were so broke, strung out, and desperate that I have no trouble imagining you showing up here and begging her for money. When she refused, one of you bashed her brains in for the cash in her purse—what little there was of it. Destiny . . . ?"

She glared at me. "What?"

"I doubt that you weigh a hundred pounds, but in a drugged-out frenzy I have no doubt you'd possess the strength to smash a frail leukemia patient's head in. Furthermore, you possess such low moral character that I can picture you killing her for the sheer pleasure of it, seeing as how you hated her just as much as she hated you."

Destiny peered at me curiously. "What's 'low moral character' mean?"

"It means you're a crack whore, honey," Maggie spoke up. "You give blow jobs in Mike's back room, remember?"

Destiny turned to Sly, her eyes blazing. "You gonna let her talk like that to me?"

"What do we care what she says?" he replied, running his hand under her dress and up, up, up her thigh until she let out a soft groan of pleasure.

I turned to Merilee and said, "You don't by any chance have any hand sanitizers with you, do you?"

"I'm afraid not. Why are you asking?"

"No reason. Moving right along to, Sly and Shade . . . or should I say Sly and Clarence?"

"Much better, darling."

"You could have shown up here and demanded that Mary give you the crack money Mike had loaned Kevin that Kevin was having so much trouble paying back. He wasn't even keeping up on the vig. It's not hard to imagine how things might have turned ugly."

"That never happened," Sly said coldly. "This is the first time I've ever set foot in this place."

"Mike? You told me you quarreled bitterly with Mary for the very same reason. Yet she refused to bail Kevin out financially. Just sat here at this desk and berated you for profiting from his crack addiction. You told me she was a cold, hard woman. In fact, you called her a bitch."

"Because she was one," he acknowledged. "But I didn't kill her, I swear."

"Pete? I'm sorry to bring you into this, but back when we were in high school Mary once caught you in here flogging your meat while you were dozing over a textbook. She tore up your library card and banned you for a year. You were very upset because this was the only place where you could go after school and not be taunted by other boys in town—including me, I'm ashamed to say—for the proclivity that earned you the infamous nickname Peter the Beater."

Pete shifted uncomfortably in his chair. "That's ancient history, Hoagy."

"Then again, maybe it isn't. It's entirely possible you've never gotten over the grudge you held against her."

"But I *have*, Hoagy," he protested heatedly.

"Maybe yes, maybe no."

"What's up with the Q-Tip?" Sly wanted to know. "What's *she* doing here?"

"Do you mean Pat Dennis? It seems there's been bad blood between she and the late Mary McKenna for quite a few years—ever since Pat found out that Mary, whom she considered a friend, was carrying on a secret love affair with my father, the man who evicted Super Drug when her husband, Gene, fell behind on his rent. Gene became so despondent that he went into the woods and shot himself to death. Pat has never forgiven my father. She still blames him for Gene's death. And she was furious with Mary for becoming romantically involved with him. She considered it the ultimate form of betrayal. As to why Pat chose last week to show up here and smash Mary's head in, I wouldn't know. She'd have to tell us that."

"There's nothing to tell," said Pat, who'd become very tight-lipped and angry. "I didn't do it. Any of it. And you've got some nerve suggesting I did. You don't care who you hurt, do you? Like father, like son."

I adjusted my sling a bit, trying to remember how many hours it had been since I'd taken my last pain pill. "That covers who may or may not have beaten Mary McKenna's brains in. It starts to get much murkier when it comes to who shot me shortly before dawn the day of her funeral. Shade, which is to say Clarence, whose knee I shattered with a tire iron, was on an operating table at Fulton Hospital, so he's in the clear. Sly had a definite motive for taking me out because I not only crippled his buddy, but decked *him* with a punch in the nose before I drove off and left the two them bleeding and helpless on the sidewalk in front of Mallory's like a couple of total losers. But while I was busy getting shot, Sly was busy having sweaty sex in his apartment in Willimantic with Destiny, who'd decided to dump Kevin for Sly at a party a few hours earlier at the Pardo brothers' house. When a trooper arrived at Sly's apartment soon after my shooting, Sly flatly refused to mop himself off, put on some clothes, and voluntarily submit to a paraffin test for gunpowder residue at Willimantic Police headquarters. They had to arrest him for drug possession, cuff him, and drag him in. Turned out he passed the test. He wasn't the shooter. He's just an asshole."

"I missed you so much while you were gone, baby," Destiny cooed at him.

"Not as much as I missed you, baby."

"Best sex *ever.*"

"*Ever.*"

"Shut up, shut up, SHUT UP!" Kevin screamed at them.

"As to cool, calm, collected Kevin here . . . Pete, do you have information on him?"

"I do," Pete said. "According to the Pardos, whose house is right around the corner from where you and Merilee have been staying, after Destiny ditched Kevin for Sly, Kevin got blind drunk on Southern Comfort and . . . You okay, Hoagy?"

"I am. Just a twinge."

"And he threw up and passed out on the living room floor. I don't know how reliable the Pardos are as witnesses, because they were plenty bombed themselves, but when Kevin submitted to a paraffin test, he passed it—not that I considered him a serious suspect. He was so wrecked it would have taken freakish luck for him to have shot you from ten feet away on that sidewalk in the dark."

"Agreed, Pete," I said. "I'm also at a loss for a motive. When he and Destiny broke into our apartment, I could have pressed charges against them. But I let it slide. I did Kevin a favor, even though he didn't deserve one."

"Fuck you," he responded.

"I told you to watch your mouth," Pete snapped. "There are ladies here."

My eyes settled on Mike Mallory. "Mike, you definitely had the opportunity to shoot me. You live walking distance away. Could have strolled over and waited for me to take Lulu out for her early walk. After all, I came down on you pretty hard for how far you've fallen since the last time I saw you. Before my father closed the mill you were a self-respecting saloon keeper. He left you high and dry when he shut it down. Not to mention all alone. The carcinogens from the mill took the lives of your wife and one of your daughters. Now you've resorted to pimping out Destiny in your back room, fencing stolen goods, loan sharking, and associating with known drug dealers. I made you feel really lousy about yourself, didn't I? Especially when I walked in on you pawing through the stuff that Kevin and Destiny stole from our apartment like a small-time hoodlum. Could be I pushed a button. Could be you decided to get even with my father by venting your rage against me. You passed the paraffin test, but you're no dummy. You could have hightailed it over to your saloon and thoroughly washed your hands before you were brought in."

"I didn't shoot you, Hoagy," Mike said. "God as my witness."

I turned to Pat Dennis. "That same motive applies to you, too, Pat. You had a chance to make me pay for the sins of my father. You were incredibly chilly toward me when Merilee and I showed up to stay in Rigby's apartment. You clearly resented me for being my father's son. Not to mention that I was a bratty kid who stole comic books from Super Drug, which Gene didn't dare complain about because he was afraid my father would double his rent."

"My poor Gene was so terrified of your father that he had to take blood pressure medication," she recalled, her voice trembling with rage.

"Your apartment is right across the driveway from Rigby's," I said. "You could have been awake when I took Lulu out for her predawn walk. A lot of older people are up early because of their aches and pains. You no doubt own a gun. I understand that everyone in town does. You followed us ever so quietly down the driveway and, as I stood there under the streetlight, you settled an old score," I said, before I turned to Pete. "No offense, but settling old scores could apply to you, too. My return to Oakmont brought back bitter memories of how much you resented me for tormenting you along with the other boys. Except that in my case, I was not only the town's rich kid but I also returned home as the author of a hugely successful novel who had a gorgeous movie star on his arm."

Pete said nothing. Just stared at me, stone-faced.

"You live a short walk away," I continued. "And, being a state trooper, I highly doubt you were asked to submit to a paraffin test. I also doubt that Pat

Dennis was. It would never have occurred to anyone that it was *she*, a hobbled, harmless old lady, who shot me. So maybe that's what my shooting was about. History rearing its ugly head. Deeply held resentments coming to the surface again. And when it comes to Pete Schlosski and Pat Dennis it makes even more sense to consider them suspects because there's the matter of Lulu barking in the predawn darkness."

"What about it?" Lieutenant Mitry asked, frowning.

"She didn't. Bark, that is. Didn't make so much as a peep while my assailant drew near enough to me to get a shot off. That means whoever shot me was someone whom she knew and had no reason to fear. She would have barked at Mike, I think. She would certainly have barked at Kevin, although I agree with Pete—I don't think Kevin was in any condition to shoot me." I turned to Pat Dennis. "If I were a betting man, which I'm not, you'd be my prime suspect. You were right there across the driveway, like I said. You hold my father responsible for your husband's suicide. What better way to get even with him than to take me out? Your blood was already aboil after you bashed Mary McKenna's skull in with her Mark Twain paperweight. They say it gets easier after you've already committed one murder. Does it?"

Pat didn't respond. Just sat there, glaring at me.

"After you shot me, you rushed—or I should say hobbled—home to call an ambulance and call Pete, who in turn called Maggie and woke her up to tell her what had just happened."

"I screamed," Maggie recalled, her eyes filling with tears.

"Pete was anxious to notify Merilee. Maggie, you had previously tracked down my phone number in New York to tell me about your mom's death. You gave him the number so he was able to notify Merilee."

"I completely fell apart," Merilee recalled, her voice quavering. "I could barely breathe."

"When the ambulance arrived, Pete grabbed a bath towel from our apartment and had to wrestle Lulu off of me. She was covered with my blood but she wouldn't let the EMTs near me, I'm told."

"She's grown very attached to you, darling," Merilee said.

"I carried her into Pat's apartment so that Pat could wash your blood off of her in the bathtub," Pete recalled in a quiet voice. "Rigby's place just has a stall shower. I dried her off while Pat found a can of Lulu's food in your kitchen and put it down for her in her own kitchen. That poor pup wouldn't stop whimpering. Pat finally calmed her down and kept her at her place until Miss Nash was able to make her way back out."

"That was awfully kind of you, Pat," Merilee said.

"She needed help," Pat said to her. "There are times when we all need help."

"And right now is one of them," I said. "Merilee, I'm afraid I'm not up to it. Will you do the honors?"

"Gladly, darling."

She stood up and strode toward the library's front door, every set of eyes in the place locked onto her mile-long legs and magnificently shaped behind. Even the women couldn't take their eyes off of her.

And out the door she went.

CHAPTER THIRTEEN

"I sure would like to know the fuck is going on," said Kevin.

"I *told* you to watch your mouth," Pete growled at him as Lieutenant Mitry resumed pacing back and forth behind the rows of chairs, his jaw muscles clenching and unclenching.

Merilee returned two minutes later walking Lulu on her leash and apologizing profusely to her. "I am *so* sorry we left you out there all by yourself, sweetness," she said as Lulu yipped and yapped at her, highly miffed. "You were all cold and lonesome out there, you poor thing. But now you're inside where there's a nice, roaring fire and you're with us. Are you happy now?"

Fat chance. Lulu wanted to tug her way into the librarians' lounge so she could raid Leon's dish.

"No, sweetness, the lounge is closed for the night and there's no food for you in there. Just Leon, who might scratch your big black nose."

Lulu stopped tugging, but not without a dissatisfied grunt.

"I swear, it's as if she understands every word you say," Maggie marveled.

"Only because she does," Merilee said.

"Mind you, we haven't tested her foreign language skills yet," I pointed out. "It's possible she only understands English. Lulu, would you like to say hello to everyone? How would that be?"

She tugged Merilee over toward Lieutenant Mitry, who was standing nearest to the door to the lounge, and let out a low whoop. He picked her up in his giant hand, gave her a pat, and put her back down. Then Lulu tugged Merilee around the rows of folding chairs and made her way to me, her tail thumping, and she rolled over onto her back for a belly rub.

"Hey, girl," I said, petting her.

"She's all yours, darling." Merilee handed me the leash.

I gripped it in my right hand and stood up.

"What's happening now?" Destiny asked Sly.

"Damned if I know," Sly said.

I started with the row that was closest to me. The first person whom Lulu arrived at was Shade, aka Clarence. As soon as she got a whiff of him, she immediately whimpered and cowered between my legs.

"Now why is she doing that?" Lieutenant Mitry wanted to know.

"Offhand, I'd say it's because she remembers the way he terrorized her when she was in her carrier inside of the Jag. But he paid a price for it, didn't he, Lulu?"

"And one of these days *you'll* pay a price," Shade promised me.

"You just keep telling yourself that, Clarence."

Next Lulu led me to Pete, whom she was delighted to see. Pete was delighted to see her, too. Scrunched her ears and told her what a good, brave girl she was. Then she moved on to Mike Mallory, whom she remembered from our visit to his saloon when we were taking her bedtime walk. She sniffed and snorted at Mike carefully, but had no reaction to him other than a neutral snuffle. Then she led me to Kevin, whom she sniffed at with extreme care, lingering for quite a length of time.

"What the hell's she doing?" Kevin asked me uneasily.

"Checking out your uncommonly rich brew of scents, everything from the crack that you free-base to the traces of dried vomit on your pants. You might want to think about bathing and changing your clothes a bit more often, Kevin. I can smell you myself, and I'm no scent hound."

When Lulu was finally done sniffing at him, she had no reaction whatsoever other than to gaze up at me expectantly.

And so we moved on to Sly and Destiny. She let out another whimper of fear as we neared Sly, who'd been there when she was being terrorized in the Jag by his pinhead partner, but her whimper was swiftly overtaken by a sneezing fit from Destiny's patchouli. She tugged on her leash to get away from them as fast as possible and led me over to Pat Dennis.

Pat smiled at her and petted her gently. "You remember me, don't you, Lulu? I gave you a bath and fed you and we watched soap operas together until your mommy got home."

Lulu responded by licking Pat's hand and making that little *argle-bargle* noise of hers.

"What a good girl you are. Such a good girl. Yes, you are."

And with that we'd circled our way back to the front desk, where Maggie smiled at her warmly and said, "Hi, sweetie!"

Lulu immediately bared her teeth and snarled at Maggie in a way I'd never heard come out of her throat before. And kept right on snarling, tugging harder on her leash.

Maggie's eyes widened in fright. "Hoagy, w-why is she doing that? I thought we were friends. She sat on my lap and played with me when you came over for dinner."

"She's doing it because she's a basset, Maggie. People are amused by bassets because of their long ears and short legs, but it so happens that they are the second-highest rated scent hounds in the entire world of dogdom, right behind bloodhounds. They were bred to hunt rabbits."

"Did you learn that from Lulu's breeder?" Lieutenant Mitry asked me.

"No, our Jaguar mechanic, actually." To Maggie I said, "She hasn't smelled you since that night we

331

visited you. She wasn't in my hospital room when you visited me after the funeral. Merilee had taken her to the pediatric cancer ward to help her with her hand puppet show. She's had no contact with you at all—not since you shot me."

The library fell into total silence.

Maggie looked at me in total shock. "You're accusing *me* of shooting you?"

"I'm not. Lulu is."

"Okay, but why does *she* think I shot you?"

"Since she can't speak for herself, allow me to translate. You've washed your hands numerous times since you missed murdering me by an inch, so there's no trace of gunpowder residue on your hand. You weren't paraffin tested at the time of the shooting because it was the morning of your beloved mother's funeral and it would have been unseemly. However, since it was chilly that morning in the predawn hours, I'm concluding that you were wearing that very same thick, hand-knit wool sweater you're wearing right now when you walked over from your house and waited for me to take Lulu out for her early walk. And I'm further concluding that you've neglected to dry clean or hand-wash your sweater, that it has retained the scent of gunpowder, and that Lulu's highly sensitive black nose picked it up immediately." I turned to Lieutenant Mitry and said, "Here's Mary McKenna's killer, Lieutenant. Her own daughter. She also attempted to murder me, her closest childhood friend and first sweetie."

"You have no proof of any of this!" Maggie protested angrily, which prompted Lulu to start snarling at her all over again.

"I have the best kind of proof there is, Maggie. Man's best friend, who doesn't know how to lie."

Maggie stared at me, her eyes beginning to shine. Then her breath caught and she let out a pained cry before tears started streaming down her cheeks. "You were my great love, Hoagy," she sobbed. "Since we were little kids. There was you and only you, and as soon as you left for Harvard you tossed me aside like I was garbage. Mom . . . Mom kept saying that you were destined for greatness, had a chance to get away and you took it. That I shouldn't resent you for it. But I did. And I ached inside. I've never stopped aching. We made love together in that lounge for two years. You told me you loved me. That you'd never love anyone else. And then you just totally disappeared from my life. Not one letter. Not one phone call. This is the first time I've seen you in *eleven* years, and who do you show up with? Only the most beautiful movie star in the whole world."

"Hold on, I have to stop you there," Merilee interjected. "You're forgetting Michelle Pfeiffer and Jacqueline Bisset, Catherine Deneuve, Diana Rigg, Julie Christie . . . I'm way, way down the list of filmdom's most—"

"Oh, shut up!" Maggie snapped, glaring at me through her tear-swollen eyes. "You abandoned me to a life in this hellhole with my drugged-out moron of a brother and my total bitch of a mother. All she ever talked about was *you*. Never, ever stopped talking about how wonderful you are. Not once did she ever appreciate me. She never thanked me for staying put here and getting my master's degree in library science so that I could keep this library alive and a vital part of the community, despite the fact that her own lover, your total asshole of a father, abandoned her for Vero Beach. I've had to pinch pennies ever since to keep this place afloat. Did she thank me? No! Did she thank me for taking care of her as the leukemia sapped the life from her? No! Instead, she accused me of being petty for resenting your success. And when Kevin stole her TV, she refused to help him get drug treatment unless he broke it off with Destiny. When

Kevin refused, because he actually believed that he and Destiny were in love, Mom kicked him out of the house and changed the locks on the doors. She could be so cold, so vicious."

"Mike Mallory told me much the same thing," I said as Mike sat there nodding his head.

"Honestly? It wasn't *one* thing that made me kill her," Maggie confessed. "It was *all* of those years of the way she treated me. Would you believe she never told me she loved me? Not once in my whole life. The night I killed her, I'd come to pick her up and drive her home. She was sitting here at this desk, gazing at the shrine she'd built to you, and started in again about how wonderful you are. I—I just plain lost it. It wasn't anything I'd planned to do. It just *happened*. I grabbed her paperweight, shouted, 'Shut up, you mean, rotten bitch!' and beat her brains in. Then I washed the paperweight, dried it thoroughly, and returned it to its usual spot as she slumped there dead, bleeding all over her desk. I took the money from her purse to make it look as if Kevin and Destiny were to blame. Then I pretended I'd just arrived and found her that way. Called Pete in a state of utter shock and horror. He rushed right over and took charge. It never occurred to him that *I* killed her. It never occurred to anyone. I was so loyal and self-sacrificing. The good daughter."

I gazed at Maggie, awestruck. "You've been so warm and welcoming toward me since we got here. My God, you just offered us your mom's engagement ring. And you and I had such a nice evening together at your house after Merilee went back to New York. So sweet and sentimental. You even made your mom's meat loaf and mashed potatoes for me."

"I was hating you with every fiber of my being that whole evening," she said viciously. "I'd settled my score with my mom, and now it was time to settle my score with you. I knew I'd never get another chance because I knew you'd never come back here again. After our dinner, Pete made sure you got home safely. You and Lulu enjoyed a good night's sleep."

"Actually, not that good. She snores. And thanks to that canned mackerel you introduced her to, her breath is also—"

"Oh, shut up! Puppies need an early morning walk when they're being housebroken. It's still dark at that hour this time of year. So I put on my warm sweater, just like you said, and grabbed the gun that Mom had bought to replace the one that Kevin had stolen."

"What make was it?" Lieutenant Mitry wanted to know.

"The same kind that she'd had in her dresser drawer for years—a Colt thirty-eight."

"Four-inch barrel?"

"I don't *know*, Lieutenant. It's not as if I got out a ruler and measured it." She turned back to me. "I waited on the corner for you in the bushes. And when the two of you were standing there under the streetlight I took two quick steps toward you, aimed, and shot you from about eight feet away. Then I ran like hell for home before Pat Dennis could see me, and pretended I'd been asleep when Pete called to tell me that you'd just been shot." Maggie looked at me in defiant silence for a moment. "I paid Mom back. And I paid you back. Or at least I tried."

"You came pretty damned close, too. Missed my carotid artery by an inch. I won't regain full use of my left arm for several months, if that's any consolation."

"It's not enough," she said, her voice heavy with hatred. "It's not nearly enough."

"Sorry to disappoint you."

Lieutenant Mitry cleared his throat. "Did you dispose of the gun or what?"

Maggie pulled open the middle drawer of the desk and removed the Colt, cradling it in the palm of her hand. "Or what," she said before she pointed it at me.

I could hear Merilee draw in her breath, because I was standing less than four feet away from Maggie. There was no way she was going to miss me from that distance. I realized that I was about to die. Yet after everything I'd been through those past two days, for some reason I wasn't afraid. There was no point. Acceptance was my only option.

Although Lulu was having none of that. She snarled at Maggie ferociously, straining at her leash. My protector.

"Oh God, darling . . ." whispered Merilee in horror. My love.

"Miss McKenna, you're in the presence of four armed state troopers," Lieutenant Mitry said, keeping his voice admiringly calm. "Let's not lose our head."

"I'm afraid that ship has already sailed, Lieutenant," I pointed out.

Pete Schlosski stood up, straight and tall, and said, "Lieutenant Mitry's right, Maggie. Stay calm."

"I'm perfectly calm, Pete. But I would like to ask you for a small favor."

"What is it?"

She turned her gun away from me and pointed it at the center of Pete's chest. "Since I have nothing to live for, I want you to shoot me in self-defense."

"There will be no officer-assisted suicide here tonight," Lieutenant Mitry declared in a clear, decisive voice. "Not on my watch. Not a chance."

"You heard the man, Maggie," Pete said. "Can't oblige you. Sorry."

"In that case I'll have to shoot you," she said matter-of-factly.

Pete stood there less than ten feet from her, breathing slowly in and out. "Okay, fine. Here, I'll make it easier for you." He started walking slowly toward her, one step at a time. "Go ahead and shoot me, Maggie. Shoot me. Go ahead."

"Don't make me do it, Pete!" she warned him as the gun wavered in her hand.

"I haven't drawn my weapon, Maggie, as you can see. It's still holstered. I've known you since we were kids. I refuse to shoot you. But if you want to shoot me, go right ahead."

"I *will* shoot you, Pete. You're *making* me shoot you. And when I do, one of the other troopers will shoot me."

"No, they will not," Lieutenant Mitry insisted. "I've already told you. There will be no officer-assisted suicide here tonight."

"Go ahead, Maggie," Pete said. He was no more than six feet from her now, his shoulders square, chin up. The Beater was not lacking for guts, let me tell you. I had a lot of admiration for him at that moment as he stood there facing her in the quaint old vanilla-scented library of my youth. He took another step closer to her. And another. "Go ahead."

And she did—although her hand was shaking so badly she missed the center of his chest and hit him in his meaty left bicep. Pete flinched but kept right on coming, grabbing the gun away from her.

Lieutenant Mitry rushed to him and relieved him of the gun. "Are you okay, Trooper?"

"It's just a flesh wound. No big deal." Although it was bleeding through his shirt and he was starting to look exceedingly pale.

I said, "You'd better sit down, Pete."

He sat down in my empty chair, exhaling slowly as Merilee dashed into the restroom and returned with a handful of paper towels, pressing them against the wound.

One of the other troopers radioed for help. "Officer down!" he barked. "Gunshot wound at the Oakmont library. We need an ambulance ASAP. Move it, move it!"

Everyone else in the library just sat there, wide-eyed and silent.

Pete was gritting his teeth in pain now. Lulu managed to climb up his leg and into his lap to comfort him. "Hey, Lulu . . . You're a good girl, aren't you? Yes, you are."

I grabbed a blanket from the sofa and wrapped it around his shoulders in case he was going into shock.

As for Maggie, she folded her arms on her desk, lowered her head to them, and wept.

"That was pretty brave, Pete," I said. "Bordering on awesome."

"It was," Merilee agreed, bending down to kiss him on the cheek.

"Whoa, I just got kissed by a movie star," he said. "Mary Ellen will never believe this."

I said, "Sorry I had to come down on you so hard just now. I threw a lot of nasty shit at you."

"That's okay, Hoagy. I understood. You were working a plan."

"Actually, I didn't have a plan. I was just making stuff up as I went along."

"Well, it worked," he said to me.

"So, listen, if they give you my old room at the hospital, I wrote some dirty limericks under the tray table. Check 'em out."

He let out a laugh, wincing. "I'll do that."

I looked at Maggie, who'd stopped weeping and was now just sitting there staring at me with total hatred again.

"Maggie . . . ?"

"What?" she demanded. "What do you want?"

"Just to say I'm sorry."

"Go to hell!"

One of the other troopers read Maggie her rights, cuffed her, and led her outside to deposit her in his Crown Vic.

Then I heard the siren as the ambulance drew near from Fulton. When it arrived, Pete insisted upon walking out to it and climbing in under his own power.

As they sped off to the hospital, I went over to Pat Dennis and apologized to her the same as I had to Pete. She wasn't quite as forgiving, but she did accept my apology in a cool voice.

Then I sat back down in my folding chair by the desk. I suddenly felt totally used up. I also needed a pain pill. Lulu climbed into my lap and licked my face. "You know what you are, Lulu? You're a genuine crime solver. How about that, girl?"

As an aside, I should mention I had no idea that night in Oakmont thirteen years ago that in the decade to come I would suffer crippling writer's block and snort my career and storybook marriage to Merilee up my nose. No idea that Merilee would kick me out of our beautiful prewar high-rise apartment on Central Park West with its eight windows overlooking the park, and that I would end up back in my crummy, unheated fifth-floor walk-up on West Ninety-third with Lulu, who'd insisted on staying with me, even though adopting her had been Merilee's dream, not mine. No idea that I'd spend the next decade scratching out a living as a ghostwriter of celebrity memoirs and finding myself mixed up in one murder after another with my short-legged sidekick by my side. Always, she would play a decisive role in solving the crime. But none as decisive as her role that night in the Oakmont library, which, as you now know, officially qualifies as Lulu's first case.

I did finally find my voice again and have recently completed a new novel that my editor is calling the best novel an American author has written in five years. Merilee and I fell back in love again, not that we ever truly fell out of love, and Lulu and I are back living large in that prewar high-rise apartment on Central Park West.

But I knew nothing about any of this that night in Oakmont.

Lieutenant Mitry came over to me, shook my hand with his huge one, and said, "I've got to take my hat off to you, Hoagy. You knew what you were doing when you proposed getting everyone into the library together this way."

"Thank you, Lieutenant. That means a lot coming from a man who's as serious as you are. All I can say is that whenever I'm in doubt, I always fall back on the immortal words of Soupy Sales: 'Be true to your teeth and they'll never be false to you.'"

The lieutenant furrowed his brow at me. "I'm . . . not sure I understand."

"And you never will," Merilee said with a huge smile on her face. "Isn't it wonderful?"

◆

In the morning Dr. Joe checked me over, found my wounds to be clean and healthy, and pronounced me fit to leave for New York City. As he handed me my file I thanked him for his excellent care.

Pete had already been treated and discharged so I didn't get a chance to say goodbye to him. But I did say goodbye to Nurse Judy and gave her a kiss on the cheek, which made her blush. Merilee said goodbye to her elderly heart patient and paid a last visit to the pediatric cancer ward. I could hear the roar of voices calling out "WE LOVE YOU, ROO-ROO!" from two floors away.

Our bags were packed and stowed in the Jag. Merilee had prepared sandwiches for us from the leftover roast chicken as well as a thermos of espresso. Our rent was paid in full on Rigby's apartment. The keys had been returned. We were good to go.

Merilee settled me in the passenger seat with Lulu in my lap inside of her carrier, my slinged arm resting atop it. Then she steered the Jag out of the hospital parking lot and we went tearing back to our life on Charlton Street just as fast as the Jag could get us there.